DELIVERING THE TRUTH

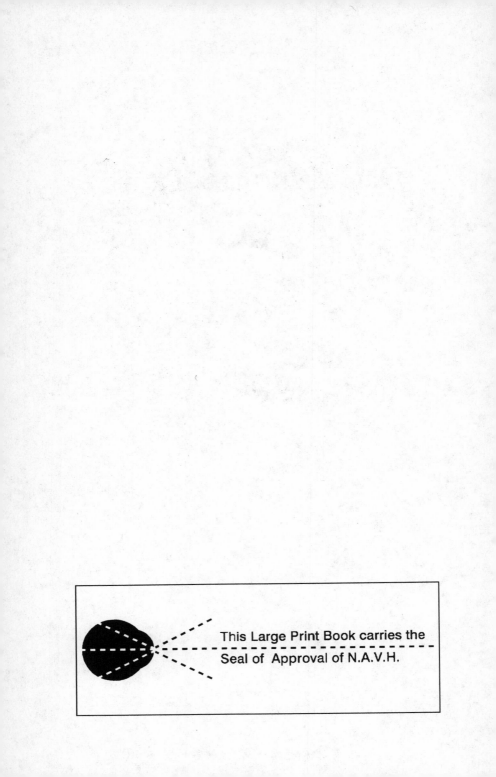

This Large Print Book carries the
Seal of Approval of N.A.V.H.

A QUAKER MIDWIFE MYSTERY

DELIVERING THE TRUTH

EDITH MAXWELL

THORNDIKE PRESS
A part of Gale, Cengage Learning

GALE
CENGAGE Learning·

Farmington Hills, Mich • San Francisco • New York • Waterville, Maine
Meriden, Conn • Mason, Ohio • Chicago

LIBRARY OF CONGRESS CATALOGING-IN-PUBLICATION DATA

Names: Maxwell, Edith, author.
Title: Delivering the truth : a Quaker midwife mystery / by Edith Maxwell.
Description: Large print edition. | Waterville, Maine : Thorndike Press, 2016. | Series: Thorndike Press large print mystery
Identifiers: LCCN 2016018041 | ISBN 9781410492777 (hardcover) | ISBN 141049277X (hardcover)
Subjects: LCSH: Large type books. | GSAFD: Mystery fiction.
Classification: LCC PS3613.A8985 D45 2016b | DDC 813/.6—dc23
LC record available at https://lccn.loc.gov/2016018041

Published in 2016 by arrangement with Midnight Ink, an imprint of Llewelyn Publications, Woodbury, MN 55125-2989 USA

Printed in Mexico
1 2 3 4 5 6 7 20 19 18 17 16

*For my best friend, my Scorpio sister,
my confidante, my fellow author,
Jennifer Yanco — who helped kindle
my interest in home birth and midwifery
over thirty years ago.*

AUTHOR'S NOTE

A historical novel involves much more research than one set in contemporary times. KB Inglee, who writes not only historical mysteries but stories about Quakers, helped with several crucial details. Sam Sherman, Barb Bristol Weismann, Margie Walker, and Robert Schledwitz each gave me valuable input with respect to the culture and practice of the late 1800s. In addition, the Amesbury Whittier Home Association, the Amesbury Carriage Museum, and the Amesbury Library historic archives were important resources, as was the Lowell National Historic Park with its working textile mill and informative Mill Girls exhibit. Amesbury reference librarian Margie Walker's book *Legendary Locals of Amesbury* also gave me ideas for real characters I slid into the story.

Quaker historian and author Chuck Fager contributed valuable comments on differences between Friends' practices then and now. Any remaining errors are my own.

The Agatha Award–winning historical mystery author Kathy Lynn Emerson (aka Kaitlin Dunnett) generously shared her bibliography of resources for how life was in 1888. She also read this manuscript and offered an enthusiastic endorsement before it was accepted for publication. The twenty-four hours I spent living the life at the Washburn-Norlands Living History Center in Livermore, Maine, opened my eyes about the work of cooking and home life in the second half of the nineteenth century — right down to the chamberpot — and what school was like in the period. Any errors of detail are entirely of my own doing.

This book cites portions of Friend and abolitionist John Greenleaf Whittier's poems "The Christmas of 1888," "Democracy," and "This Still Room." Whittier was on the building committee for the Friends Meetinghouse where my protagonist, Rose Carroll, and Whittier himself worshiped.

It has been a huge pleasure to stroll the streets of my town and imagine life almost a hundred and fifty years ago. The Bailey family lives in my house, built in 1880. I walk to worship every Sunday (or First Day, as Friends call it), as Friends have over the centuries, to the Meetinghouse portrayed in "This Still Room" and in this novel. Many of the original nineteenth-century buildings in Amesbury remain standing and in use, and the same noon whistle blows as did in 1888. I hope, as you read, that you feel that same sense of walking through history.

ONE

Minnie O'Toole screamed again, a long piercing wail. Her eyes bulged and her round face shone as red as hot coals. "I'm going to die," she whimpered when the pain subsided. "The babe and I are both going to die." She grabbed my hand and squeezed.

I wiped the pretty young woman's brow with a cool cloth. "Thee isn't going to die, Minnie. Look at me." I gazed into her eyes and willed her to listen. "Thee is a healthy nineteen and thy body is meant to give birth. Exactly like every woman anywhere in the world. I'm thy midwife and I'm here to help get this baby out. Now sit up a bit more." I leaned over, hooked my hands under her armpits, and raised her farther up on her pillows against the plain wooden headboard.

She had been in hard labor for hours and was becoming weak from the effort. I had trudged through the remnants of the Great

11

Blizzard to reach her. It had been scarcely three weeks since the storm buried us and the rest of New England in four feet of cold blowing snow, the worst storm we'd had in this year of 1888 or any year in prior memory.

But the girl's birth canal still wasn't fully open. I had finally sent word, asking Minnie's landlord to use his new telephone to call my doctor friend, David Dodge, with whom I sometimes consulted during difficult births. The midwife I'd apprenticed with, Orpha Perkins, was now too elderly to help.

I heard David enter Minnie's small flat. "I'm glad thee is here," I said to him as he walked into the bedroom. He set down a black bag, removed his coat, and rolled up his shirtsleeves. To Minnie I said, "We will be back directly. Try to rest between contractions." I led David back out into the hall.

"I'm always glad to see you, Rose Carroll." He smiled at me and winked, an unruly lock of his wavy dark hair falling onto his brow. "How's my favorite Quaker, with your *thee*s and your *thy*s?"

I blushed. David and I had been courting in recent months, but this was no time for that. "I am well. Now, her name is Minnie O'Toole. Her labor started yesterday morning, but the pains began coming a minute apart about four hours ago." I opened my pocket watch, which I'd pinned to my left bosom so I could easily check it. "Yes, it's now six in the morning. They became more intense at about two."

"And the opening?"

"Still has about a thumb's width to go. The baby's heartbeat is fine, although the mother is tiring. She's neither too young nor too old, so it isn't her age slowing the labor. Perhaps a fear of supporting the babe holds her back. She has no husband and won't tell me who the father is."

David raised dark eyebrows over deep blue eyes.

I ignored his expression. I'm a midwife. As part of my calling, and because I'm a member of the Society of Friends, I serve rich and poor alike, and I don't refuse to care for women who land in circumstances outside what society expects.

Another scream resounded from the next room. "That cursed man," she wailed.

I hurried back, followed by David. Women often revealed much during their birthing travails. Perhaps we'd learn the identity of the baby's father.

"Minnie, this is David Dodge. He's a doctor at Anna Jaques Hospital in Newburyport. He's going to help us get the baby out."

Minnie let the scream go and nodded, panting. Her fine white nightgown was soaked with sweat. I'd noticed she wore expensive clothing and fancy shoes, despite living in a tiny flat at the back of a family's house.

"I'm glad to have a doctor, but when will these pains be over?" She sounded desperate.

David greeted her. "Let's check you again. I'm going to feel the baby, Miss O'Toole." He palpated the baby through her gown, checked the position of the rump and the head. "The head seems engaged and the baby is vertex, so that's good."

I already knew the baby was in the proper position with the back of its head at the front of Minnie's pelvis, but also knew David had to verify it for himself. I knelt and slid my hand up her passageway. I used my knuckles to feel the opening to the womb, then drew my hand back out.

"Thee is ready." I smiled at her over the mound of her belly. "With the next pain, you must hold thy breath and bear down. Does thee understand? It will help to hold fast to the bedstead."

She nodded and grasped the iron frame

behind her head with both hands. It took only eight pushes and a few more screams for the baby's head to ease its way out. I cleared the nose and mouth. "Thee is doing wonderfully. With the next pain, bear down hard, please."

A moment later, Minnie pushed again. But the baby's body didn't follow, and its face began to redden. I glanced at David. He frowned and knelt next to me.

"Push again, Minnie," he urged, but the baby still didn't birth. "Pull your knees right up by your ears, hold them with your hands. Now."

Minnie obliged, but grunted as she did so.

"Shoulder?" I asked David. I prayed not. I'd observed a birth during my training where the baby's shoulder became caught on the pelvic bones and when it was finally born, it had a dead brain. In my eight years of practice, I had gratefully seen only the one case.

"Perhaps. We'll try the screw maneuver. Have you done it? Your hands and arms are smaller than mine."

"I haven't, but I saw Orpha perform it, explaining to me as she did so." I closed my eyes for a brief moment, holding Minnie and her baby in the Light of God, after the manner of Friends. And myself, for attempt-

15

ing this urgent procedure. I had to act fast and correctly. I took a deep breath and opened my eyes.

"Go in and turn the shoulders," David said in a low urgent tone. "If you must break a shoulder bone, do it. Bones heal; brains don't. I'll catch the birth." In a normal voice he said, "Miss O'Toole, refrain from pushing for a moment."

"What is happening?" Minnie cried. "Is there something wrong with my baby? Why hasn't he come out yet?"

I slid my right hand in through the warm wet opening past the head, producing a deep moan from Minnie. Sure enough, one shoulder was in the canal but one seemed to be stuck. I grasped the tiny bones and turned. I felt movement. I slid my arm out. The baby came with it in a gush of fluid and landed in David's large hands. My relief made me a touch weak.

He held the tiny boy up so Minnie could see. "Here he is." The baby took a breath and let out a hearty cry. David smiled. "Perfect," he whispered to me. "No need to break a bone?"

I shook my head. I pushed my glasses back up the bridge of my nose with my clean hand. I took another deep inhalation and let it out. This was the business of midwifery. Women giving birth go down into death and bring forth life. Usually. It was my job to help it be so.

David and I cleaned the baby. I tied off and then snipped the cord. He was pinking up nicely and breathing well. I wrapped him in a blanket and handed him to Minnie. She wiped tears from her cheeks with her free hand. She stroked his face.

"Thee will have another pain soon when the afterbirth comes out," I said. "What will thee name him?"

"I don't know yet." She grimaced. "What's happening now?"

"Your body is expelling the afterbirth. It's normal. Hand the doctor the baby and then bear down."

David cradled the warm bundle while Minnie pushed out the placenta into a bowl I held waiting. I examined it.

"It's all there," I said. A woman could bleed and even die if a portion of the placenta was retained in her womb.

David handed the baby back to Minnie. "Congratulations, Miss O'Toole. You have a healthy baby boy. Thanks to an expert midwife."

Minnie nodded, her eyes only for her new son.

"I'll be off," David said to me. "I have

rounds at the hospital on Thursdays."

"Thank thee for assisting." I smiled at him.

"You did it all yourself." He bade Minnie farewell and left.

After I cleaned her and then washed up, I spent more than an hour making sure she was able to nurse the infant and instructing her on her own care.

"Will thee have help?" I'd noticed a stack of neatly folded diapers on the dresser and several new infant dresses atop a soft yellow baby blanket edged with satin binding, all of a quality that matched Minnie's fine nightdress. The father must be an attentive one, whoever he was.

"My sister is coming soon." Minnie couldn't take her eyes off her baby. She stroked his dark hair and cooed to him.

"Good. I'll visit thee again tomorrow."

She thanked me. "That pouch on the dresser is your payment." She pointed to an embroidered bag.

Where had she found the money? I put that thought to the back as I extracted two dollars from the pouch and gathered my things. After I left, I walked slowly along High Street carrying my birthing satchel. Spring in Massachusetts was late arriving this year, despite it being already Fourth

Month, or what non-Quakers called April. Tightly wrapped flower buds guarded themselves against another snowstorm. The Fifth Day dawn lit up only a fuzz of green on the trees, and piles of snow remained on the north side of buildings.

Shovelers had valiantly tried to clear the paths in our town after the blizzard. When I was summoned to a birth the day after the storm, I'd had to strap on my snowshoes to make it only three blocks away. I'd been lucky the baby boy had made an uncomplicated entrance into our world. David could never have navigated the few miles northwest across the bridge over the wide Merrimack River from the bustling shipping town of Newburyport to assist the delivery on that day. I could conceivably call on John Douglass, a doctor who attended births in town, for assistance, but he wasn't as kindly toward midwives as I would have liked.

I yawned at the long night behind me. I'd be able to nap for only an hour or two before my clients began arriving for antenatal visits. As I walked, I mused on how David was becoming much more than a friend over recent months. I was feeling quite sweet on this slender doctor only a few years older than I, with his clear skin, sparkling eyes, and gentle manner. I had invited him to join my late sister's family and me for dinner last week, and he'd seem to quite enjoy the company of the lively but motherless family.

I still missed Harriet a year after her sudden death. She'd been my guide, my dearest friend, and my model of how to be a good mother, although I myself was making no progress whatsoever on that front. I was an excellent assistant to mothers, but I was neither married nor in possession of offspring of my own. And at twenty-six, I was getting a bit past the so-called marriageable age.

Two

I pulled aside the parlor curtain in the
Bailey house where I made my home as the
clock chimed twelve times, followed closely
by the blast of the noon whistle several
blocks away in the town center. In front of
the house, the finest carriage I had ever seen
pulled up. The polished wood on its shafts
shone in the midday sunlight and the large
spoked wheels were as graceful as dancers.

Lillian Parry stepped out, assisted by a
driver in a dark uniform. Lillian's long cloak
didn't fully disguise her seven months of
pregnancy. This would be her last visit to
my office in the parlor. From now on I'd be
visiting her in the couple's large home on
Hillside Street. She lifted her skirts to climb
the stairs. Hurrying to the door, I welcomed
her in and extended my hand, helping her
up the last two steps. She wiped the snow
off her boots on the mat and we moved into
the parlor, where I shut the door to the hall

21

and pulled the curtain over the glass upper portion of the door.

"William was complaining again." She stood with both hands resting on her lower back, elbows out, as pregnant women do. "He still thinks I should be seen by Dr. Douglass instead of you."

"John Douglass delivers a good many babies in town. He has a fine reputation."

"I told him I want a woman and that's that. I don't want some man touching my . . ." She shuddered as she trailed off.

"I understand." Many women were more at ease exposing their private parts to another woman than to a man. "I'm pleased to attend thee, Lillian. Now please make thyself comfortable on the chaise." It had taken some time for this upper-class woman to get used to my not addressing her as Mrs. Parry. But because of my reputation as the best midwife in the town, she acceded to my Quaker ways.

She sank down onto the day bed, pulling her gloves off and then removing her stylish hat. Her equally stylish frizzled bangs set off an upswept hairdo ending in ringlets. Her dress, in a lovely lavender-sprigged lawn, featured tiny pleats now stretched tight across her full bosom with the waist pulled high above her belly.

With the chaise's raised back, it doubled as an examining table. "My feet hurt mightily these days, Rose. And this boy kicks at me all night long." Dark patches under her eyes confirmed she was short on sleep.

I smiled. Of course she and William Parry wanted a boy for their first baby together, but I also knew we had no means of determining if a boy or a girl would greet her at birth.

"That's good. It means it's a strong, healthy baby. How has thee been eating? Plentiful meat and vegetables, I hope?" As I spoke, I knelt to loosen her shoes so I could examine her ankles. They were swollen but not too badly.

"I don't have much of an appetite. I pick at my food. How long after the birth can I start going out again? It's miserable eating alone." Her nasal tone sounded more like a petulant child's than a first-time mother's.

I glanced up. "Your husband must be busy running the Parry Carriage Factory. Your transport is as lovely as a piece of art."

"Oh, that. He's giving me a nicer, more spacious model after the baby comes." She sniffed. "He says he's busy with work, but I know better. I —" She bit her lip and said nothing more.

I stood. I held her wrist and counted the

beats of her pulse while watching the mantel clock that had been my grandmother's, with its bucolic meadow landscape painted on the glass in front of the pendulum.

"I need to check the baby now, Lillian."

She nodded as I knelt again. I lifted her skirts and exposed the skin over her womb, which looked like she housed a large ball inside. She was one of those women who gained their pregnancy weight solely in the belly. I pressed the flared Pinard horn on her stomach and laid my ear against the narrow end of the tube, listening to the baby's heart this time, counting the beats. I then used a firm touch of my hands to locate the baby's head and its bottom.

As I felt the babe, I said, "Does thee mean to say William isn't busy with his work? Surely such a renowned factory provides much business for him to attend to."

"He's out with that strumpet. I know he is."

I kept my silence. I brought out my tape and measured from her pubic bone up to the top of the womb. I jotted the number down in my book, adding the date and the baby's heart rate before lowering her skirts.

Lillian looked away, out the window, and then back at me. Tears filled her eyes. "My sister saw him enter that O'Toole woman's abode as she returned from a visit to South Hampton. He has no reason to see that woman. My sister was quite outraged, and a bit scornful, too. I was humiliated beyond belief. What'll I do, Rose?"

Oh, dear. Minnie O'Toole. "Perhaps it was company business. Has thee asked thy husband?" I patted her hand.

"Oh, I couldn't. He wouldn't tell me the truth, anyway." Her voice wobbled.

"Was he in agreement about conceiving a child with you?"

She nodded. She wiped her eyes and cleared her throat. "Yes. We were married last April and we wanted to start our family right off. He's nearly two decades older, and he has a son of twenty, Thomas, from his late wife. Not much younger than I am. We don't exactly get along. Thomas resents me and I . . . well, he's hard to like." She shook her head. "But I've made my bed and I must lie in it. There's no going back now."

"Well, thee has a lively child inside. It hasn't yet settled into the birth canal. I want thee to eat as much as thee is able of good wholesome foods. Beef, chicken, and well-cooked pork. Fresh milk and cheese. Try to have some squash and an apple every day. Some spinach or other green vegetable if thee can find it. And drink weak tea."

"What about wine?" This privileged woman's whiny tone was back.

"A drop once in a while won't hurt the baby now. It is big enough."

"Good," Lillian said with a toss of her head. "Are we finished?"

"We are. I'll visit thee at home in one month's time. Attend to thy baby's movements. If they cease for more than a few hours, send for me at once. After my next visit, I'll see thee more often." I extended my hand and helped her stand.

While she fastened her hat on her light hair, Lillian said, "Please forget what I said. I am happy with my husband. I am sure he is, indeed, merely busy with the carriage business." She lifted her chin as she pulled on her gloves.

We said our good-byes. I showed her out and made sure she descended the stairs safely. Her driver helped her into the carriage, where she sat alongside a slender, light-haired young man, and they drove off down the hill. Perhaps I should also hang out a shingle advertising my services as a pastor. With some clients, more of my work was in listening and counseling than in making sure a pregnancy ran smoothly.

My eldest niece lifted her skirts and stepped

over a pile of manure at the edge of High Street, then dropped them quickly before anyone could glimpse her ankles as we walked at the end of the day. Faith Bailey dipped her head in her plain bonnet as we passed James Nilan climbing into a carriage, his clerical collar a pristine white against his black cloak.

I glanced at her. "Why did thee bow to that priest?"

I knew my sister had instructed Faith to keep her head up when she encountered any adult, whether the priest of Saint Joseph's or President Cleveland. "As members of the Society of Friends," I'd heard her tell Faith many times, "we believe in equality under God." That was why my brother-in-law — Faith's father, Frederick — didn't doff his simple hat when he met an Amesbury selectman on the street and why Friends didn't use titles to address each other, not even children to adults. Both Frederick's family and my own father's were Friends, although my mother had come to the faith only after meeting my father.

"Mother is gone, Rose. Annie Beaumont, my best friend at the mill, respects her priest. I don't want to tempt fate by not showing him courtesy."

I shrugged. Faith was still young, only

seventeen. What harm could it do? Yet, I felt a pang to see her discard Harriet's teachings so lightly, and then a renewed pang of missing my sister.

We passed the closing shops on Market Street. A bitter wind rushed up from the Powow River despite it being past the spring equinox. The thrum of the textile mills' waterwheels filled my ears. I pulled my shawl closer around my neck as we trudged up Carriage Hill.

"I hope I can see Zeb when he finishes his shift. He works longer hours than I," Faith said.

"And I know thee pines to see him as he leaves work." I smiled at my niece with her rosy cheeks and then looked down at the roadway again. I was pining a bit to see David again soon, myself.

Faith hurried ahead of me. A moment later, she stumbled. An arm stretched out to break her fall before I could reach her.

"In such a hurry to see my brother, Faith?"

Faith straightened and smiled at her tall rescuer. "I thank thee, Isaiah. I admit to an eagerness that overruled caution. I turned my ankle a bit on the cobblestone."

"Greetings, Isaiah." I surveyed the road outside the Parry Carriage Factory gates.

Workers trickled out from the ironwork opening. We must have missed the earlier surge. "Is Zebulon working late?"

"He wasn't scheduled to work longer than his twelve hours." Isaiah frowned. "But we're on different shifts. Mine starts now and continues until dawn."

"I'm lucky to work only ten-hour shifts," Faith said. "Twelve would ruin me. Even so, I feel a tiredness that barely goes away by the end of First Day. My feet hurt constantly and my ears ring after a day monitoring four looms in a room so noisy from the hundred machines I can't even talk to the girl next to me."

But she was the eldest, and strong. Frederick, a teacher at the Academy, couldn't take on the burden of five children alone, no matter how much he wanted Faith to continue her education.

"Did thee see my Annie this day?" Isaiah asked Faith.

"Only on our break. It must be hard for you to find time for each other, working opposite shifts."

He smiled ruefully. "Indeed. 'Tis only on First Day we can visit. And then only after she's been to her church and I've been to mine."

"At least her family finally agreed to let

her see thee," Faith said. "She told me they weren't so happy about thy courting her at first."

"I seem to have won them over. Even Catholics can learn to like a charming Quaker." His smile was self-deprecating in a truly charming way.

A man in a ragged cap pushed by us on his way out, bumping into Faith. Isaiah steadied Faith with a hand again.

"Ephraim Pickard!" Isaiah called. "Has thee changed thy work to the day shift?"

The man turned, glowering. "They've given me the boot. I was on warning. And now how will I feed the family, what barely gets enough as it is?" The collar of his woolen coat shone from years of wear, and a neatly sewn patch at the shoulder was beginning to fray.

"Why did they release thee?" Isaiah asked.

"That son of Mr. Parry's said I was late once too often." He shook his head hard. "And he didn't like me reading on my lunch break. How's a man supposed to get ahead?" He clomped away with an uneven gait, a tattered book in one hand.

"More's the pity." Isaiah watched Ephraim go. "Thomas Parry isn't much of a manager. No one cares for him, and he has the worst manner of dealing with the men I have ever seen in a supervisor. I'd best go in so I don't risk being late myself." He smiled. "I'm sure Zebulon will appear in a moment."

Faith and I bade Isaiah farewell as he strode toward the two-story wooden factory. We waited, inhaling the sharp smell of impending rain. Faith paced outside the tall fence. She squinted at the large clock on the building's face.

When the new electric streetlights twinkled to life down the hill, I said, "We need to return home."

"I must have missed Zeb." Faith hung her head. "I suppose I tarried too long putting supper on the stove."

The damp wind chilled as we began to descend Carriage Hill. I whirled when I spied a moving shape in the gloaming. I peered back at the side of the carriage factory. A flowing figure crept by the fence, walking with a limp, I thought. The shape dissolved into the falling darkness. I shuddered and shook my head before I continued on my way.

THREE

I sat at home by the stove in the sitting room later that evening. Faith knitted while my brother-in-law Frederick read and Luke, the oldest boy at thirteen, did ciphers for school. I had been trying to catch up with my recordkeeping of whose baby was due next and who owed me a payment, but mostly I was helping Luke when he had an arithmetic question, since I had an aptitude for mathematics. The ten-year-old twins, Matthew and Mark, and eight-year-old Betsy slept upstairs.

"Rose, what about this one?" Luke extended his notebook. "I can't figure it." He pointed to his penciled calculation.

I took the book and peered at it under the gas lamp. The new system of electric lights in town hadn't yet extended to this modest abode. A moody, difficult man, Frederick and his five children lived in a tidy home just uphill from the Hamilton Mill, where

Faith had taken over her mother's job after Harriet's death a year earlier. The mill owner, Cyrus Hamilton, had ordered three identical houses built to house several workers and their families. Normally it would have been let out to a male employee. However, my brother-in-law had given special tutoring to Cyrus Hamilton's difficult son and Cyrus apparently felt he owed Frederick some kind of debt. When the first occupants left town, Cyrus offered Frederick and Harriet the middle house of the three, now only eight years old.

After Harriet's death, Frederick had asked if I'd like to join their household and take possession of the parlor that fronted on the lane. Despite how I felt about his moods, which sometimes resulted in a shouting match between him and his eldest children or looks of scorn delivered to his younger ones, I'd agreed. I was grateful to now have both an office in which to see clients and a bed in a real home.

My own parents lived in distant Lawrence, but I had come to Amesbury to apprentice with Orpha and to be close to my dear sister. Orpha had delivered all my sister's children, and I'd met her at Betsy's birth shortly after I finished my schooling in Lawrence. I was so drawn to Orpha's profession, to her care and skill, to her understanding of both the human body and the mind, and to the miraculous process of childbirth, that I'd asked to study with her. To my great good fortune, she'd agreed. I moved to Amesbury the next week. I'd known of the New England Female Medical College, a training school for midwives, but Orpha's teaching had been so detailed and complete that I never felt the need for further studies.

For seven years I'd rented a room in Virginia Perkell's, an Amesbury boarding house for ladies, and visited my pregnant women in their homes. Now I helped Faith with the considerable chore of fixing meals and doing housework when I wasn't seeing clients or out ushering a baby into the world.

When a shrill whistle went off outside and then bells began clanging in town, I set down Luke's notebook.

"It's the fire bell. I can smell the smoke." Frederick was already on his feet, his heavy eyebrows lurking close to his eyes. He pushed up the sash and sniffed.

I could smell the fire, too. Luke darted upstairs. A moment later he was back.

"It's on Carriage Hill. The flames are shooting into the sky!"

34

"I hope it's not the Parry factory. Isaiah is at work." Faith brought her hand to her mouth.

The four of us rushed up the stairs, then tiptoed into the front bedroom Luke shared with the sleeping twins. We clustered around the windows and opened one to the cold air. Sure enough, flames teased ever higher into the black sky and the smell of smoke snapped at my nose. I couldn't tell which of the dozen carriage factories was burning. Amesbury was famous nationwide for its graceful, and well-built carriages, and the town was home to more than a dozen establishments that produced them.

The two young men who lived up the road rushed by below, buckets in hand.

"I must join them," Frederick said, turning for the stairs.

"Father, I'm going, too." Luke, not yet fully grown and still a string bean, pulled at Frederick's sleeve.

"Thee? Thee is too young, Luke." Frederick tossed his son's hand off. "Amesbury has a fire department and many dedicated volunteers. We will extinguish the fire."

The crushed look on Luke's face made me want to weep. Harriet had buffered her husband's moods for her children, but now they bore the brunt of his occasional flares

35

into anger or contempt, which had worsened since my sister's death.

To the sound of Frederick clattering down the stairs and the never-ending whistle piercing the night, I linked one arm through Faith's and stretched the other around Luke's shoulders. Faith leaned into me as a windswept rain dampened our clothing. I closed my eyes, holding Isaiah Weed in the Light.

FOUR

I added wood to the cook stove in the kitchen the next morning at first light, put water on for samp — the corn porridge little Betsy loved — and the washing, then ground coffee and measured it into the blue enameled pot. I hadn't slept well, as the awful whistle had screeched until nearly dawn. Zeb had stopped over last night on his way to help fight the conflagration. He'd been determined, despite his own anguish about his brother, to reassure Faith that he himself wasn't in the factory, and it had helped to set both Faith's and my mind at ease about his safety.

When Frederick opened the back door, I glanced up. He trudged in, carrying the smell of smoke and tragedy. I watched as he sank into a chair at the table and unlaced his shoes without speaking. When he tossed his hat on the table, the soot streaking his hands and face stopped at a sharp line above a thick forehead that jutted out above his eyebrows. He padded to the sink and pumped water, then scrubbed until his skin was clean. He finally met my gaze.

"Isaiah Weed is gone. Along with a dozen other men. Trapped inside the Parry factory."

I gasped and brought my hand to my mouth.

"Let us pray they didn't suffer too much." Frederick let out a deep, mournful sigh. "All the major carriage factories burned, plus other places of business. The post office and telegraph office. Many homes. All gone." He shook his head, gazing with light eyes out the window in the direction of Carriage Hill.

"Poor Isaiah. And Zeb, and his parents. What a sad, sad day." My throat thickened and my eyes threatened to overflow.

Frederick nodded, taking a seat again. Faith appeared at the doorway, securing her hair with both hands raised behind her head. She stopped with wide eyes. "Oh, Father. I see terrible news in thy face."

"Sit down, my daughter." He patted the chair next to him. After she sat, he went on in a low tone. "Isaiah is dead, I'm afraid."

She lay her head on her arms for a moment, then sat up with a tear-streaked face.

"I must go to Zeb. And then to Annie."

"There will be time for that," he said. "Sit here and have thy breakfast first, Faith." He laid his thick hand atop hers.

I was grateful he acted kindly toward her. I could not predict when his mercurial temperament would strike, but at least for now he was tender. I doled out a serving of samp for both of them and set the dishes on the table.

"How can I eat cornmeal porridge, or anything, with so many in pain?" Her brown eyes — so much like her mother's, so much like my own — pleaded with me.

"Faith, dear." I smiled gently at her. "If there is one thing I have learned in my practice, it's that I can't help others if I don't take care with my own well-being. Thee must eat and drink if thee is to be strong for thy friends." Despite my advice, I often violated it myself when my schedule grew too busy.

She nodded but wrinkled her nose.

"Does anyone know how the fire started?" I asked Frederick.

He shook his head. "There was much talk, of course. A careless worker. A spark on old wood. Perhaps we'll never discover the cause. With the recent disagreements between Amesbury and Salisbury about who would annex whom, our fire-fighting equipment has grown out of date and isn't in good repair. The wind caused the blaze to jump from the factories to the post office and thence to the telegraph office, so they couldn't send word by any fast method. By the time help arrived from Haverhill, Salisbury, and Newburyport, it was almost too late."

"What a pity," I said. Haverhill was ten miles distant to the west, but Newburyport lay directly across the river to the southeast, and Salisbury, of course, was just to Amesbury's east.

Frederick rubbed his forehead. "Only the blessed rain prevented further damage."

"How will I live?" wailed Annie.

I embraced her shaking shoulders. God bestowed such hardship upon us. Faith and I sat with Annie in the three-room tenement apartment down on the Flats where she lived with her mother, two brothers, and her mother's parents — all French-Canadian and all textile mill workers except her dotty Grandmere. Because it was Good Friday, Hamilton Mill was closed. Thankfully it had been spared from the fire, as had the other textile mills on the Powow.

Faith stroked Annie's hair. "Thee will live.

Life goes on, no matter how painful." She tucked an errant red curl back under the green ribbon holding it.

Annie paused her sobbing and gazed first at me and then at Faith. "I'm sorry. Of course you both know this better than anyone. You lost your mother, and you, Rose, your sister, so recently."

Faith patted Annie's hand. "Thee will come to Isaiah's Memorial Meeting for Worship tomorrow?" Faith asked.

Annie nodded, her eyes filling again.

Faith smiled at her. "Thee and thy pretty ribbons. I wish I could wear some."

Faith must be trying to take Annie's mind off the death for a moment. I hoped it would work.

Annie smiled back, but it was only a shadow of her usual bright expression. "You should. I'll lend you some." At my raised eyebrows, Annie said, "Oh, that's right. You're not supposed to."

"Yes, I have told thee before. Friends are to wear plain dress." Faith sighed, sweeping her hand over her very plain dark green dress. "I'll simply enjoy thy ribbons on thee, the ones Isaiah always delighted in."

I knew Faith loved bright colors as much as Annie. I had, as well, when I was seventeen. Now I had grown accustomed to my plain dresses in dark colors and my simple bonnet. I was too absorbed in my work to pay colorful items much mind, anyway.

Annie pulled the ribbon from her hair and handed it to Faith. "Take this. Curl it up in your pocket. Wear it to bed. Do with it what you'd like, even if it's only gazing upon it. Anyway, I shouldn't be wearing bright colors myself while I mourn. It would be disrespectful to Isaiah." Another tear slipped from her eye and trickled down her cheek, finally dripping onto her lace collar.

"Thank thee, Annie." Faith took the ribbon and slipped it into her pocket.

"I must get home," I said and squeezed Annie's hand. "Be well, friend."

"I'll stay for a while," Faith said.

I made my way slowly back up Water Street toward Market Square.

"Rosetta!" a woman's voice called out.

Only one person in the world called me that. Smiling, I turned to see my friend Bertie Winslow hailing me. The wiry little woman, postmistress of the town, rode toward me waving from atop her horse. As usual, strands of her curly blond hair escaped out from under her hat, which was, as usual, set at a rakish angle.

"Bertie, how is thee?" I asked when she

got close enough. "Surely thee wasn't still at work last evening?"

"No, I was home. What a time, eh? Whoa up, Grover." She pulled on the reins of the compact black horse.

Only Bertie would name a horse Grover. I always smiled to hear her refer to a large animal by the name of our country's president. It was delightfully subversive. And only Bertie had the nerve to ride astride instead of sidesaddle. She slid a leg clad in a long bloomer over Grover's back and hopped off the animal, her skirt falling back down over her pantaloons. The bloomers, made from a cloth that matched the skirt, always showed when she rode. Bertie didn't care what people thought.

She was in her thirties, unmarried, and unconcerned about it. She and I had grown friendly after I had delivered her sister's child several years earlier and Bertie had been there helping out. I enjoyed her always sunny and unconventional spirit. And since single working women were few in our town, we had that in common, too. Although she wasn't exactly single.

She hooked her arm through mine and we strode toward the square, Grover clopping behind. Bertie always strode.

"Was there anything to salvage from the

post office?" I asked.

"Nothing. Even the boxes were melted down. We'll have to start from scratch."

"What a pity."

"I consider it a fresh start. Or would if men hadn't died in the fire," she said.

"Such a tragedy. Where is thee bound for?" I asked when we arrived at the busy intersection.

"Have to meet with the postmaster in Salisbury to talk about reestablishing services, where the government wants us to rebuild, that sort of thing." She squeezed my arm before mounting Grover. "Let's go have fun one of these days, shall we?" she called back as she clattered off.

"We shall," I called after her.

In the square, wet ash coated awnings and smelled of sadness. The storm had blown through leaving a sunny, breezy day at odds with the town's mood. Residents and businesspeople talked outside in small clumps with much shaking of heads and faces red with anger at the town's failure to extinguish the fire. I overheard an older man refer to it as the Great Fire. Following close on the Great Blizzard. What was the world coming to?

A cluster of several men standing outside Sawyer's Mercantile included Stephen

Hamilton, the student Frederick had taught and tried to help. Now in his twenties, he wore a coat of fine cloth and carried a Bible in his gloved hand, but his hat sat askew and mud covered his fancy boots. He shook the book in their faces.

"Now settle down, Hamilton. Everything is God's will. Even accidents," an older man said.

Stephen wagged his head and pointed a trembling finger. His eyes burned with anger.

"Why don't you go home and try to calm down?" the man asked.

Stephen stalked away, muttering. As I passed, the other man said, "That boy is touched in the head. He rarely speaks."

"He's no longer a boy," the older man replied. "His father should make him work. He needs a good honest job."

I watched Stephen go. I sighed as I made my way up High Street.

"Rose!"

I turned to see Zeb hurrying toward me. "Zeb." I held out my hand to the tall, wiry young man.

He grasped it in both of his. His usually delighted expression was replaced by haunted eyes and a wide mouth turned down in grief.

"I'm so sorry about dear Isaiah," I murmured. "How is thee? And thy parents?"

"We can barely believe it. Rose, if only we could roll the clock back to yesterday." He blinked suddenly full eyes.

"If only." I laid my other hand atop his.

"They're saying it might not have been an accident."

A cold knot grabbed my stomach. "Does thee mean someone set the fire with intent?"

He nodded, his face a study in *troubled.*

"Who would do such a thing? And why?"

He only shrugged. He disengaged his hands and shoved them in his pockets, looking up toward Powow Hill. I wished him well and watched him walk away with bent shoulders. As I continued toward home, I mused on who would have purposely set such a fire. Who would want to destroy much of the town's livelihood, and human lives, as well?

I caught sight of John Whittier strolling toward the square. I seemed to be encountering all my favorite people on this morning of grief. His prominent nose, erect carriage, and the deliberate gait of his long, lean legs made the well-known abolitionist and poet unmistakable about town. He must have recently returned to his home on Friend Street from his cousin's at Oak

46

Knoll in Danvers, where he spent his winters of late.

"Rose Carroll, how is thee this morning?" His visage was somber above a snowy-white chin beard that left his mouth fully exposed. But he harbored the twinkle in his eye I was accustomed to.

"It's a sorrowful day, John Whittier. We've lost Isaiah Weed in the fire, and so many others."

He nodded slowly. "Has thee heard talk of arson?"

My face must have given away my surprise at what he said. Two people talking of arson in as many minutes, nearly.

He continued, "I see thee has. My friend Kevin Donovan was speaking to me not twenty minutes ago of the idea. Thee knows there is that of God in each person."

"I cannot fathom who might be led to destroy so many lives, so much property."

"If the story of arson is true, we must seek to understand how the manifestation of God in the arsonist could allow him to act in such a destructive way. I admit it is difficult to reconcile this contradiction, but persons ignoring the divine within and willfully hurting others occurs all too often in our earthly sphere."

"True. First we must understand who set

the fire, and why." I smiled at John to cushion my response. I hoped he wouldn't find me harsh. I was known for being a little too forthright and I saw no reason to temper my attitude with this famous but personable Friend. I had been a member of the Religious Society of Friends my entire life, and had known John Greenleaf Whittier since my sister's marriage to Frederick nearly twenty years ago.

"I am sure we shall, as way opens."

I nodded. The Quaker concept of waiting for guidance, or for further events to show the way, was a tricky one for me. Patience was not one of my virtues.

I bade John farewell. There was much to consider. I was surprised he called Kevin Donovan "friend." I'd had a run-in with the burly policeman in the past when I'd asked him to take to task a husband I knew was beating his wife, even while she was with child. He'd responded in his Irish accent about how the law said the business of a man and his wife should remain behind the closed doors of matrimony. I didn't agree. And because of his opinions on the right of a man to abuse his wife, I hoped he was a competent detective when it came to other crimes. If the fire was set by an arsonist, Kevin needed to find this criminal before he or she acted again. That shadowy shape I had seen as I left Parry's the evening before. Could it have been the arsonist?

John Whittier could seek to understand that of God in the killer *after* such a person was safely locked up.

FIVE

After Faith returned home, I spent the rest of the day working alongside her. I had no ladies scheduled for visits, no births pending until the next week. We did the washing, running the wet clothes through the wringer we were fortunate enough to own, and hung them on the line out back. We scrubbed down the kitchen, put together a lamb stew, and baked dozens of gingersnaps and sugar cookies for the service. The twins and Betsy helped on the last, especially when it came time to clean the remnants of sweet batter from the bowl.

As we worked I mourned for Isaiah. And I thought of all the families now without homes. All the men, mostly, now without jobs. The parents without children and children without parents. Those grievously injured by the flames. Zeb's remark about the fire being set stuck in my brain like the incessant grumble of a mill wheel.

My thoughts turned to Ephraim, forced out of his job before the fire. Perhaps he had wanted to destroy the factory that deprived him of his livelihood. But also burning up the men inside — that was a horrific thought.

When we were finished baking, Faith let out a sigh of exhaustion. "I'm going to collapse and read in the sitting room. Or perhaps just collapse." She paused with her hand on the door jamb.

"Thee has earned a rest, niece."

I, too, felt tired to the bone, but I had other plans. I packed a basket with a bowl of stew, a loaf of bread, and a small paper of cookies.

"Faith, I'm going to pay a visit on the Pickard family. I'll be back for supper," I called in to her.

"Thee is a kind woman," she called back.

Kind, perhaps. Curious, certainly.

Ephraim Pickard and his family lived on Friend Street beyond the Meetinghouse in a building housing four families. I had assisted his wife with the latest addition to their family some months earlier. Ephraim now sat on the stoop in the sunlight, a book open on his knees. He glanced up when he saw me, then stood, closing the book. His coat fell open, showing a dark smudge on the front of his white shirt.

"Miss Carroll, isn't it?"

"Yes. I brought thy family a meal, Ephraim." I extended the basket but pulled it back when he kept his hands at his sides.

"We don't need charity." He frowned.

The door opened behind him and two girls about Betsy's age ran out, leaving the door open. One bumped into Ephraim. "Sorry, Papa!" She ran off with a laugh.

"Please consider it a gift from a friend instead of charity."

He nodded slowly and accepted the basket, setting it on the stoop.

"Has thee heard talk about the fire, Ephraim?"

" 'Tis the only talk in town." He shoved his hands in his pockets and looked away. "It must have been a lazy welder or sparks escaping from the warming stove."

"I have heard it was set with intent."

"Arson." He snapped his head toward me. I nodded.

"Who would do such a thing?" he asked.

"Who knows? Perhaps someone with a grudge against the management." The smudge on his shirt looked much like soot.

Scowling, Ephraim stepped toward me. "What do you imply?" he shouted, his fists clenched.

I backed up a step and cleared my throat. Harriet had often reminded me I needed to temper my natural forthrightness with tact. I might have overstepped the bounds.

Ephraim's daughters ran giggling around the corner of the house. He scooped up one in his arms, still frowning at me. As the girl squealed, a woman with a fat-cheeked baby on one hip appeared in the doorway behind him. The lines in her face measured years of toil and childbearing. She laid a reddened hand on Ephraim's shoulder and squeezed.

"Calm yourself, husband. Greetings, Rose."

I greeted her. "The baby looks well."

"Yes, he is, thank you."

Ephraim took a deep breath. "Miss Carroll has kindly brought us a gift of food." He picked up the basket and handed it to his wife.

"We gladly accept and thank you," she said.

"There are some sweeties for the children, too," I said, keeping my voice friendly.

A quiet smile spread across her face. "You're very kind. They have few treats." When the baby began to fuss she stepped back into the house and closed the door.

I took my leave. As I glanced back,

Ephraim glared at me over his daughter's dark curls.

I sat knitting that evening. I'd been working on a patterned sweater for Betsy for months. I liked to have a project to bring along to births, where I often sat and waited with a laboring woman for some hours before the baby's emergence became imminent. My special pair of steel needles clicked through the woolen yarn dyed a lovely muted shade of lavender, Betsy's favorite color, since children were indulged in wearing somewhat brighter shades than adult Friends if they wished. My mother, always creative, had made me a present of the needles, and she had painted tiny flowers and vines twining through my initials in fine detail on the slender, pointed needles.

But I kept making mistakes on this project. My attention would wander and I'd not realize it until I found myself with a sleeve twice as long as it needed to be, or I'd have forgotten to change back to the other color, a cream shade. So many times I'd had to unravel a section and begin again. And now winter was over, it likely wouldn't fit the growing girl in the next cold season.

Faith, reading Louisa May Alcott's *Jo's Boys,* occupied the rocker next to me in the sitting room. Frederick perused the *Ames-bury and Salisbury Villager* from his arm-chair. The younger children slept upstairs, after many somber bedtime questions about death, heaven, and whether Isaiah now sat near God with their mother. I thought of David, and how nice it would be if he were here sitting next to me, perhaps reading or making simple conversation.

"Is there any news about who set the fire, Frederick?" I asked. I looked up from my yarn.

He shook his head, glancing over both the paper and his reading glasses perched on his nose. "Nothing. It's quite soon, though. There is a long article mentioning each family who lost someone."

"How is dear Zeb, Faith?" I asked. "He would usually be here of a Sixth Day evening, wouldn't he?"

She sighed. "Yes. He needed to stay with his parents, of course. His heart is very heavy."

"As are all of ours." I patted her hand.

"And thy visit to the Pickard family today, how did that go?" she asked.

"His wife was most grateful for the meal I brought, but Ephraim himself seemed out of sorts. As is understandable, being let go from his position at the Parry factory." I kept the detail of the smoky smudge on his shirt to myself.

"And now there's no factory for anyone to work in," Faith said.

"It's difficult for me to imagine who would want to wreak such destruction on our town." Frederick folded the paper and set it on the table next to him. He clasped his hands behind his large head and stretched his feet out toward the fire. "How will the police find the culprit?"

"It's truly a puzzle," I said. "I suppose another factory owner might have wanted to get rid of the competition that was Parry's and didn't intend that the fire spread to nearly all the other factories."

"We should at least be glad we have an honest police department in Amesbury," Frederick said. "I've read of great corruption in the larger metropolises, especially New York City."

"I hope it's honest. The detective, Kevin Donovan, holds some views about husbands and wives I don't agree with."

"Oh? What are those views?" Frederick asked.

"I observed bruises on one of my clients. She confessed to me her husband was striking her, even as she was heavy with child. I took the case to Kevin and he said the law had no jurisdiction in the affairs of a married couple."

"He's likely correct," Frederick said. "And he is obliged to hold up the law of the land."

"But that doesn't make a man beating his wife right!" Faith looked up from her book.

"Of course not, my dear," Frederick said and then sighed. "But thee knows many in this land don't follow equality between men and women and nonviolence in the home. I don't suppose this client was a Friend? The husband could be eldered in the matter and let to know his behavior is not sanctioned by Friends."

"No, I believe they attend the Episcopalian church downtown, more's the pity." I took off my spectacles and rubbed my eyes with one hand. "I'd venture a guess my dear mother is already working on this issue of men acting unkindly toward their wives."

"My mother-in-law, always lobbying for women's rights." Frederick frowned at Faith. "Watch that thee doesn't take a lesson from thy grandmother."

"Father, I admire what she does," Faith protested. "I do plan to join her. Well, when I find the time."

Her young face already showed lines of overwork and fatigue. Assuming both her mother's job and much of her housework was taking its toll. I helped as much as I was able, although it usually wasn't enough. I knew Harriet would have insisted that Faith stay in school. She would be sorrowed that Faith had felt pressure to leave and take the job. Pressure mostly coming from her father. I'd quarreled with Frederick before about the need to hire household help, but he always refused. And now was not the time to continue that discussion.

"I'm ready for my bed." I stuck my knitting into my midwifery satchel where it rested on the floor. I rose and headed for the parlor, which was my bedroom as well as my office. "Sleep well, Baileys."

I prayed my own dreams would be free of shadowy figures, smoke, and the image of a woman's bruised body.

I scrubbed up in the basin the next morning, smiling at the squeaky coo of the newborn girl behind me. Her father had fetched me in the wee hours of the morning to attend his wife's birth. I turned, drying my hands on my apron. Genevieve LaChance had birthed her fourth child slightly early but easily, with a minimum of blood, and her first daughter had cried at first breath. Now the baby suckled at the breast as her tired mother stroked a strand of black hair off her own brow, and then did the same to the child.

"Thee has done well," I said. "Remember to drink plentifully and offer her the breast often so thee makes enough milk. The more she sucks, the more thee will produce."

Genevieve looked up and nodded. Then she frowned. "She came so early, I haven't quite saved up enough from my piece work for your fee. And Jean, well, he barely makes enough at the factory to pay our rent and feed our sons and ourselves." Her French-Canadian accent was still strong. "He's not happy about another one coming along so soon." She pursed her lips.

"Thee isn't to worry with that. Thee will pay me when thee is able. Or perhaps I'll bring thee piece work of my own and we will settle that way."

"You Friends are a generous sort," Genevieve said. "Or should I call you a Quaker?"

"As thee wishes. It's the same." I smiled at her, patted the baby's head, and took my leave. Many babies decided to make their appearance near daybreak. I didn't know why. Perhaps they craved those first moments of quiet alone with the exclusive attention of their mothers, moments unlikely to be repeated very often for the rest of their lives, especially in a poor immigrant family

59

like Genevieve's. Baby number four was surely not the last for these Catholics, despite the husband's displeasure. I hoped he would refrain from raising a hand to this gentle, hardworking woman.

I walked near the railroad tracks that ran along the river, enjoying the fresh breeze. I gazed at several dozen white-shrouded shapes, taller than a man, strapped carefully to flatcars. The shapes were finished carriages that had already been loaded aboard the train. Each was wrapped in white canvas to keep it pristine on its journey. It was great good fortune an entire Ghost Train had been spared from the fire. I didn't know who had imagined the name Ghost Train, but it was an apt one.

As I traversed Chestnut Street, I passed the wreckage of the fire. A wisp of smoke curled into the air from a massive pile of timbers and dark, twisted metal. Even the stones at the back of the cemetery had been split and crushed by the burning factories. Such a grievous loss.

I headed for Minnie O'Toole's apartment on Fruit Street to check on the baby's well-being and make sure Minnie herself was coping with her new motherhood. I climbed the stairs and let myself in.

"Minnie?" I called from the dark hallway.

I set my bag down. "It's Rose." I heard no reply and didn't see the sister anywhere, so I opened the bedroom door and peeked in.

Minnie lay nestled in bed with her son, both of them asleep. I walked to the side of the bed. The baby breathed comfortably. Good. I felt Minnie's forehead. It was of a normal warmth. Also good, as it meant she harbored no fever. Her eyes fluttered open.

She greeted me. "He's a hungry little man, he is. He tires me out all night and then sleeps all day. So I reckon I just sleep when he does." She smiled at the baby.

"That's a wise choice for now. Is thy sister still here?"

Minnie frowned. "She went out for a bit. She don't get along with my brother, who just stopped in."

A man in a tightly buttoned sack suit walked into the room. He held a bowler hat and had the same round cheeks as did Minnie.

"I'm heading to my job, then, sis. The hopper is full of coal and I left you some bread and sausage in the kitchen."

"Thank you, Jotham. This here is the midwife, Rose Carroll."

"Nice to meet you, miss." He touched his forehead.

"I'm pleased to meet thee. It was good of

thee to bring provisions for Minnie."

He folded his arms. "When's that fool sister of ours coming back?" he asked Minnie with a scowl.

I raised my eyebrows at his sudden change in demeanor.

"Sometime soon, I hope," Minnie said. "She's helping me out and don't you forget it. I don't understand why you can't get along with her."

"Well, and you won't understand, neither, because I'm not explaining it again. And I suppose you still don't want me bringing my nephew's daddy to account? I can think of a couple of ways to do it."

"No." Minnie's tone was firm. "Brother, that is my business and not yours."

"Even though he's brought shame upon our family?" His nostrils widened like he'd smelled a rotting fruit. "And humiliated you?"

Minnie sighed. "Jotham, leave it be, will you?"

He seemed to shake off his mood. "I'll be off, then." He looked at me and then at the baby. "I thank you for helping get my little nephew out into the world," he said in a softer voice as he moved to the bedside. He leaned over the baby and touched his cheek. "We'll be playing ball before you know it, laddie." He set his hat on his head and walked out.

"The two of you share a resemblance," I said to Minnie. "What's his name again?"

"Jotham." She bit the side of her lower lip. "He means well. And I wish he and my sister were more friendly."

"No one chooses their blood relatives." Every family had its intrigues, its members who feuded either silently or with great noise. And a brother and sister who didn't get along wasn't my business.

"Ida accused him of stealing from her." She wrinkled her nose. "Nobody ought to steal, related or not. I don't know if he did, though. And he's always been good to me."

"I'm glad," I said. "Now, how is thee feeling? Has thee been up? Is thee passing water?"

She nodded. "I'm a bit sore down there. But I'm hungry, like always. And I have a wicked thirst, too."

I told her that was normal with a suckling babe. "Thee must drink frequently. Even some ale will help the milk flow. Can I get thee something now?"

"A drop of ale would be fine. It's in the kitchen there."

I located it and brought her a tankard half full. "I'll be going, then. Send word if thee

63

has any problems. And Minnie?"

She looked up. "Yes?"

"Thee can make the father be account-able. I can help thee."

She shook her head, hard. "I'm fine. Thank you. But I am taken care of."

I let myself out, looking forward to an hour or two of rest before Isaiah's memorial service this afternoon. As I rounded onto Market Street, a well-appointed carriage passed me. I glanced back down the street a minute later to see William Parry disappear through Minnie's door. I didn't know for certain why the owner of one of Amesbury's most successful carriage factories would be paying his respects, but I could guess, especially given Lillian Parry's suspicions. And if he was the father of Minnie's baby, he certainly wasn't making any secret of it.

Six

I trudged through Market Square. Perhaps I should pick up staples for the household. I paused outside Sawyer's Mercantile and swayed a little with fatigue. As I covered an unavoidable yawn with my hand, I caught sight of a thin woman hurrying up Friend Street away from me. It looked much like Nell Gilbert, whom I had delivered of a daughter the year before.

"Nell," I called out. She stopped short but didn't turn around. I opened my mouth to hail her again, then shut it when a man stepped out of the doorway of Skeel's Fish Market. It was none other than Jotham O'Toole. I watched them converse, tall Nell gazing down on him a little, but they were too far away for me to hear, even if I hadn't been standing at the edge of the noisiest, busiest area of town. He laid his hand on her arm and she shook her head with great vehemence. I hadn't realized Nell and

Jotham knew each other, but Amesbury was a well-populated place with nearly ten thousand inhabitants. I was sure there was much I didn't know.

A large cart filled with squealing lambs clattered by in front of me. When it had passed, Jotham no longer stood with Nell. She seemed rooted in place, so I made my way toward her.

"Oh, Nell." I waved as I called. I stepped around two men smoking cheroots. Keeping my eyes on Nell, I nearly stepped in a pile of vegetable refuse.

She turned toward me and waited.

"How is thee?" I asked when I reached her. "And baby Lizzy?"

She gazed at me with dark eyes. "She's fine." Her voice was flat, and her eyes, while on me, seemed to be out of focus, as if she saw something else than my face.

"That's good. Has thee been well, too?" I asked.

"I'm fine." Her arms fell straight at her sides, her left hand clutching a canvas bag hanging as limp as her arm.

"Thee is out doing the marketing," I said.

She finally seemed to see me. "Yes. The marketing. I'd better be getting on with it."

"I think I'll pick up some fish while I'm here." I gestured toward the fishmonger's door. "Say, was that Jotham O'Toole thee was speaking with? I delivered his sister of a baby this week."

Her eyes became unfocused again. "I don't know him." She turned and walked up Friend Street as if a machine governed her movements.

I watched her go with concern. Something was ailing her, I thought as I entered the fish shop, the bell on the door jangling, the smell of brine pricking my nose. I resolved to pay Nell a visit early in the week. For now, I'd bring home a nice cod for supper and then try to rest before heading to the sad event at the Meetinghouse.

The end of Isaiah's Memorial Meeting drew near as the bell at Saint Joseph's tolled three o'clock. The worship room at the Meeting-house overflowed with Friends, townspeople, and Isaiah's family and friends. Even William Parry, owner of the factory, was there, clearing his throat constantly and checking his pocket watch with great regularity.

When I'd entered with Frederick and the children an hour before, I glanced at John Whittier, already seated with straight back in his customary seat on the facing bench, watching people stream in. Little Betsy's hand was in mine and I saw him wink at her. She looked up at me, delighted, and then waved at him before he closed his eyes. To the outside world he presented a serious, almost stern demeanor. From what I had seen, he loved young people and wasn't above a wink at them.

As Clerk of Meeting he had broken the initial silence with a welcome and introduction to worship after the manner of Friends, inviting those present to celebrate the life of Isaiah, whose spirit had been released to God. He asked attenders to leave a few moments of silence between each message. I sensed several non-Quakers' unease with the stillness. For me it provided a lifelong calming comfort.

Book in hand, the disturbed son of the mill owner, Stephen Hamilton, arrived late and squeezed into a back-row pew. I didn't know he was a friend of Isaiah's, but it was a public service, after all. He jittered in his seat and never seemed to settle into the quiet place that is Friends' worship. John Whittier opened his eyes and trained them on Stephen in a moment of unspoken admonishment.

During the service Annie bravely stood and shared a memory of Isaiah's warmth and humor as they had walked along the

Powow one afternoon only a week earlier. After she sat, Faith held her hand while Annie wept softly into her kerchief. Seated across the rectangle of pews with his parents and younger siblings, Zeb waited until nearly the end of Meeting to talk about his brother. When he was finished, he sank back onto the bench and bent over with face in hands, shoulders heaving.

Afterward, mourners flowed out onto the grassy area in front of the Meetinghouse. The weather was mild for the season, with sunshine melting snow and encouraging new leaves to open. A gentle breeze ruffled the attenders' hair. I was glad to take a deep breath of such fresh air after our long winter.

Several older ladies and I laid out refreshments on a trestle table. The gathering continued on a somber note, with townspeople and friends of Isaiah's offering their condolences to his parents. A knot of young men gathered around Zeb and told stories about escapades with the brothers when they were younger, bringing a much-needed smile to Zeb's face. Stephen Hamilton stood alone on the periphery of the gathering, his eyes darting here and there.

Kevin Donovan approached the food table and helped himself to a gingersnap. The ruddy-faced detective wore a dark suit instead of his police uniform. Perhaps he was a friend of the family. I could tell him about the person I had spied near the factory.

"Good morning, Miss Carroll."

"It's a sad day, Kevin Donovan." I took a breath. "How is the fire investigation going? Has thee found a cause for it?"

He looked sharply toward me. "What business is that of yours?"

"I live in this town." I folded my arms. "A young man from this Meeting died in the awful conflagration, along with other workers. And I heard talk yesterday of someone deliberately setting the fire."

"We still seek answers," he said in a terse voice.

"I have some information thee might want to hear," I said in a low voice, gesturing to move away from others. "Before the fire began I was near Parry's factory. And I saw a shape outside the fence creeping in stealth, possibly limping. He held an object."

"He?" The detective leaned toward me across the table.

I was startled. "The person might have been wearing a cape or a cloak. In truth, as it was darkening, I didn't see so clearly. It's possible it was a woman."

"And what was the object?"

"It was flat and thick. About the size of a book. I couldn't see more."

"Thank you, Miss Carroll. I assume you would have come forth with this information even if you hadn't seen me here?"

"Of course." I wondered why I hadn't, then remembered how full the time had been since that evening, not yet two full days.

"If you remember, think of any other detail, or see anything suspicious, please let me know." He smiled. "Alert citizens can be a great help in these kinds of cases."

I nodded before he turned away, his head moving to scan the assemblage. Perhaps he was not here as a mourner, after all. And he seemed friendlier than in my past encounters with him.

I surveyed the table and combined two half-full plates of sweets into one. The punch was running scant, so I made my way around the back of the Meetinghouse where we had left an additional jug in the shade of the roof overhang. My feet rustled dry leaves from last autumn. I had hefted the heavy container when Stephen Hamilton rushed around the far corner. When he spied me he halted.

"Stephen," I called. "We're happy thee could join us."

He strode in my direction. "You Quakers should be quaking at the wrath of the Lord." Scowling, he shook his Bible in the air.

I held up my hand, relieved he stopped three feet distant and surprised he was speaking. "Our God is a loving one and is in each person. Now, would thee carry this weighty jug for me?" I held out the container.

He blinked several times. The scowl disappeared, replaced by raised eyebrows and a small smile. "You want my help?"

I nodded. "If thee pleases."

He nodded, then handed me the book and pulled the glove off his right hand. He hefted the jug with a hand marred by small red scars on the back. I tried to see what had caused the scarring but couldn't see clearly. It was likely smallpox, although these marks appeared more raised than indented. I followed him to the front where he set down the container and took back his book.

"May I help you with anything else, Miss?"

He seemed a different person from the wild ranter of a few moments earlier. Perhaps, as the man in town had suggested, Stephen did need a job, or at least an avenue to help others.

"Does thee know aught about who set the fire?" I thought it wouldn't hurt to ask.

He shook his head and strolled away, swinging the Bible.

SEVEN

The women and I were nearly done clearing up the food after the memorial meeting's social time. Many of the visitors had left and it was mostly Friends who remained in conversation with the Weed family. I looked up to see William Parry shaking Isaiah's father's hand. William shook his head sorrowfully and walked toward the street.

"William Parry?" I called. I hurried toward him.

He stopped and turned. He was an imposing man, tall, with a well-fed midsection and rich-looking clothing. His waistcoat fit snugly and his white collar stood up perfectly starched. A chinstrap beard framed his face under his high rounded hat.

"Rose Carroll." I extended my hand.

He raised his eyebrows, but took my hand and shook it briefly.

"I thank thee for coming," I said. "What a

terrible accident, thy factory burning down."

He frowned. "It's terrible, that is certain, but the police are telling me they think it might have been set. Not an accident at all. I can't think what dastardly soul would have lit a place afire that had men working within."

"It's a sad time for all the families."

"Mr. Clarke has decided to rebuild his factory. I shall rebuild, as well. I have resolved to do so." He clasped his hands in front of him and raised his chin.

"That's wonderful news. What a benefit for the town, for all of us." Indeed it was. So many relied on the business the carriage industry fostered. From the workers themselves, to the mercantile selling goods to the workers, to the seamstresses who finished off the insides of the finer vehicles, to the railroad that carried the white-cloaked new carriages away on the Ghost Trains — the entire populace was the beneficiary of a thriving industry.

He put his hand to his hat as if to doff it before leaving.

"But I have another matter to bring up with thee," I said, looking him directly in the eye, even though he was a good half foot taller than my five feet eight.

He blinked as if annoyed, but stayed put.

"I attend thy wife. In her pregnancy," I added when confusion crossed his face. Surely he should know this, but apparently he didn't. I went on. "It's important for her health and that of the baby that she feel happy and at ease in the last weeks before the birth. She mentioned how occupied thee has been of late with thy business." Or with Minnie O'Toole. Much as I'd like to ask him about that, now wasn't the time. I wanted to keep the conversation about Lillian.

"I have. And now with the fire —" He pursed his lips and tapped his leg with one hand.

"I hope, though, thee can find time to dine with her regularly." I knew I was overstepping my bounds but I wasn't afraid of this wealthy, powerful man. He had no hold on me.

He looked at me as if he hadn't quite seen me before now. "I will conduct my family business as I see fit, Miss . . . Miss . . ."

"Rose Carroll. Of course. I'm only thinking of thy wife's health. That and thy baby's."

"Good day." This time he did tip his hat, ever so slightly, before striding away to his carriage and the driver who stood waiting.

76

I watched the carriage roll down Green-leaf Street. Perhaps he was on his way to visit Minnie and her baby again.

Faith and I were washing the dishes in the wide black soapstone sink after supper that evening. It was such a blessing in this house less than a decade old to have a pump right at the sink instead of needing to carry water in from the pump outside every time we needed some. What modern time-saving device would they invent next? Betsy came running into the kitchen.

"It's that handsome man thee is sweet on. He's here. The doctor!" She nearly jumped up and down with excitement.

I dried my hands. My heart suddenly thudding and with cheeks also suddenly flushed, I followed her down the hall to the front door, where Frederick stood speaking with David Dodge. David wore, as usual, a modest coat and carried a simple derby in his hands, even though I knew his family's finances could afford him much fancier attire. His face lit up like a spring sunrise when he saw me.

"Rose, I wondered if you'd be willing to go for a buggy ride with me on this fine evening."

"David, how nice to see thee. I was just
—"

Faith spoke up behind me. "I'll finish it.
Thee should go for a ride." She poked me
in the back and whispered, "Go."

I turned and thanked her, then fetched
my bonnet and cloak. Twenty minutes later
I rode with David in his single-horse buggy
along the wide Merrimack River. The air
continued mild and I needed no more than
my cloak for warmth. The buggy was new
and provided a comfortable ride, and its
roof provided shelter from both sun and
rain.

"I scarcely feel the bumps in the road." I
gazed to my right at David as I stroked the
fine leather of the seat we shared.

"Bailey's buggies are the finest to be had."
David made a clucking sound in his mouth
and did something with the reins he held in
both hands. His handsome roan mare began
to trot. "Isn't Ned Bailey some kind of
cousin of yours?"

"He's a distant cousin of my brother-in-
law." I sighed. Ned had tried to court me in
the past, but I wasn't interested. "He's of
the family branch who fell away from
Friends."

At a wide spot near Lowell's Boat Shop,
David pulled over. The full moon shone on

the water like a silver pathway.

"It's beautiful," I said. "I feel like I could walk right across."

"Yes." He stared at the horse, who gave a snort and tossed its head.

I glanced at him. "What's the matter? Thee seems pensive."

He wrapped the reins around the whip holder and removed his gloves. He stretched his arm across the back of the seat and turned those deep blue eyes toward me. "Rose, I mentioned to my mother I was keeping company with you. Now she wants to meet you. And Mother is, well, she's a force of nature."

I returned my eyes to the moonlight. "I see." Meet his mother? Were we so serious? I'd known him as a colleague for a year. Our relationship had gradually become one of courting, and we had been spending quite a bit of time together in the last several months. My heart fluttered when I thought of him. But what if his mother didn't like me?

"What do you think? Is my Rosie feeling courageous?"

I cringed a little. "Rosie? No one has called me that since I was a child."

"May I call you that?" His voice turned low and husky. "I care very much for you,

Rose Carroll."

His arm was warm along my shoulders. In a flash my irritation with the nickname vanished. I knew it came out of his affection. Right now all I wanted to do was sink into his arm, but I was afraid if I turned toward him I'd lose myself, give myself over to these feelings I hadn't let myself experience since the first time I fell in love. I had been a teenager smitten with a boy who had violated me and then abandoned me as soon as he realized the depths of my emotion for him. His actions had hurt me, and I'd kept my heart carefully guarded since. Until now. David had won me over with his smiling eyes, his gentle manner both with me and the ill patients he treated, even with the simple clothing he wore despite his family's riches. He lived much like a Friend, I sometimes thought with an inner smile.

"And I for thee, David Dodge." My voice shook.

He reached over with his right hand and turned my head toward him. The feel of his skin on mine was the spark that lit the tinder. Could I trust him with my feelings? He had always acted the gentleman. A warm wave rolled out of my control through my body. I looked into his eyes with the moonlight revealing their startling blue. And laughed when one of them winked.

"Thee is a delight, Mr. Dodge. For that wink alone I must kiss thee." I leaned in and carefully planted a kiss on his cheek. I savored the slight rasp of stubble and inhaled his clean scent of soap and some kind of tonic mixed with the hint of a healthy man's sweat. I sat back.

"What? That's all I get?" He laughed, too, lowering his hand to take mine.

"For now." I felt a somber mood take over. "I confess I'm a bit worried about meeting this mother of thine."

He grimaced. "Yes. She's asked me to bring you to tea tomorrow afternoon. Can I fetch you at four o'clock?"

"Of course. What's her given name, by the way?"

"Clarinda. Clarinda Chase Dodge. My father is Herbert Currier Dodge."

I gulped at the family names well-known for industry and wealth as well as art. "I suppose I should wear my good frock, such as it is. Does she know I'm a Quaker?"

"Not quite yet. I thought you might be the best person to tell her."

I nodded. "I'm capable of that. I have been explaining the odd ways of Friends for twenty some years, ever since I became aware of our differences from the rest of the world. Will thy father be at tea, too?" David had told me his father ran a successful shoe business in Newburyport.

"He will, and he'll adore you, and you him, although I must tell you Mother rides roughshod over us all. But you, Rosie, give me strength to be my own person. That's one reason I adore you so. You speak your mind. You're independent and a successful businesswoman."

I tried to wave the compliments aside.

"No, truly," he said, squeezing my hand. "I admire your fortitude in following your calling. Many women are neither so strong nor so determined."

"Our society makes it difficult for my sex. We're not allowed to own property in our own names. We can't vote, except for school committee members. Why, even officers of the law allow a husband to abuse a wife with impunity." I told him about my earlier disagreement with Kevin Donovan.

"I have seen such maltreated wives in my practice. One last week came into the hospital sorely beaten, but claimed she'd merely fallen down the stairs. I think she was afraid if she told the truth, the news would get back to her husband and she'd be beaten worse when she returned home. Such treatment should be a crime."

"I've seen this, too, and I agree with thee."

"Any wife of mine would be treated with tenderness and respect." His voice grew husky again, and he stroked my hand with his thumb, a simple gesture that sent a thrill through me. "Always."

A cloud passed over the moon, darkening the river and bringing the fingers of a cold breeze with it. I pulled my shawl more tightly about me as I mused about what my life would be like if I married outside my faith. Amesbury Friends tended to be more tolerant of individuality than other Meetings, probably influenced by John Whittier's expansive view of life. I didn't foresee a problem, should a union with David come to pass, from the elders in the Meeting. I imagined David's mother could present a much larger obstacle.

I sniffed smoke and peered past David to the left toward town.

"I fear another fire," I said. "They must catch the arsonist who burned down Carriage Hill."

"I'm certain your Detective Donovan and the others are working on it even tonight." He put both arms around me and drew me into his embrace.

It was a comfort, but it didn't change the

fact that an arsonist walked our streets and could strike again.

EIGHT

As I prepared the porridge the next morning, my mind wandered thinking about the fire, about Minnie, about Lillian, and about the tea with David's mother, of course. I wasn't paying close attention as I struck a match to light the stove, and a spark flew onto my hand. I flicked it onto the stove but my hand stung from the burn.

After the family had eaten, Matthew protesting bitterly about having to eat samp instead of the oat porridge he preferred, Faith and I left the house an hour early for Meeting but we headed in the opposite direction. She tucked her arm through mine as we walked toward Carriage Hill. I wanted to see the ruins of the fire again. Perhaps if I stood in the same place as before, I might remember more about the figure I had seen and I could report it to Kevin Donovan.

"Faith, does thee know Stephen Hamilton?"

She nodded, rolling her eyes. "He's a bit crazy."

"It might do him good to have employment. Why doesn't his father hire him at the mill?"

"I don't know. Stephen did work for some time," Faith said, "on Zeb's shift at Parry's. Thomas Parry let him go, though. Hamilton spent every lunch period reading that Bible and exhorting the rest to mend their ways. Zeb was glad to see him gone."

We arrived at the gates to the Parry manufactory. The wrought iron still stood, but the property was now a wasteland of dark shapes. A tortured metal rod stuck up out of a pile of charred timber and the skeleton of a bent wheel lay in a heap of burned parts.

"I hope Isaiah didn't suffer." Faith's voice quavered.

"We must trust he didn't." I squeezed her hand and thought of a way to distract her. "I heard good news yesterday, did I tell thee? Robert Clarke has decided to rebuild his carriage factory immediately, and William Parry told me he will, as well." I stroked her arm as I glanced to the right, to where I had seen the figure. But in the cool daylight and with the building no longer standing, it didn't even appear to be the same location.

"Oh, good!" She clapped her hands. "So my Zeb can continue his work, along with so many other men in town."

"It's indeed good news." We headed back down the hill toward the Meetinghouse.

A carriage carrying a family clattered by us. The women and girls sported lovely Easter bonnets in springlike colors. The Society of Friends recognized the sacredness of Easter but didn't celebrate with a change in clothing or any special ritual.

"I wish I could have a pretty bonnet trimmed in pink and purple," Faith said. She drew Annie's green ribbon from her pocket. "But I'll have to settle for this."

We arrived at Meeting on time and made our way into the worship room. I spied Kofi sitting in worship across the light-filled room, a former slave John Whittier and other Friends had harbored beneath this very floor some thirty years earlier as part of the Underground Railroad. After Emancipation, John sponsored him as a handyman until the literate and intelligent Kofi found his way to employment at the town clerk's office.

I struggled, as often happened, to tame my thoughts as I sat. The rustling of skirts and adjusting of coats soon quieted until all

I heard was the echo of a hundred Friends silently seeking God. I knew I needed to quiet my mind so I could listen for the Light instead of to my own brain. Instead the silence amplified my turmoil.

Agitated, I stared at my hands as I examined who might have set the fire. Truly, I had seen neither trousers nor skirts on the figure in the shadows. Could a woman with a grudge against William Parry have lit the match? If so, I couldn't imagine who. Maybe it was crazy Stephen Hamilton who did the deed. Although I had not heard of him being violent before, who knew what thoughts arose in his disturbed mind? I hoped angry Ephraim Pickard wasn't the culprit, with those spirited children and hard-working wife, yet the soot on his shirt could have come from the factory fire.

Suddenly I knew who the firebug was. I had to tell Detective Donovan. I risked approbation by leaving Meeting early, but censure was worth it. I rose and made my way to the door. John Whittier opened his eyes and frowned at me but I continued, wincing as I broke the silence by catching my boot toe on the leg of a bench and nearly tripping.

When I closed the outer door behind me, I took a deep breath. I sniffed. It wasn't the smoke of coal and wood with which every resident in town cooked and heated. The smell brought to mind autumn and crisp apples, but this was springtime. Puzzled, I set off for the street. As I passed the front corner of the building, I bumped into Stephen Hamilton. I looked at him with alarm.

"What is thee —" I began.

He spun, running to the back of the Meetinghouse, where he must have been coming from. But why? He kept close to the building. I picked up my skirts and followed at a trot, thankful for once that I walked so much in my occupation and was fit because of it. He disappeared around the back of the building. When I turned the corner, I halted.

Fire flared up from a pile of burning leaves. It licked at the back wall of the building. Stephen stood watching it with an intense stare, rubbing his hands.

I rushed to the pile. I stamped at it, but it had already begun to eat at the wood above.

"Fire!" I yelled. "Help me, Stephen."

He cackled as the flames crept higher.

I grabbed the Bible from his hand and threw it hard at the high window above us, but it bounced off. It fell on the flames and began to burn. Stephen didn't move.

Desperate, I leaned down and grabbed a

stone. This time I aimed at the bottom pane and used all my strength. It shattered the pane.

"Fire! Get out!" I screamed. "Fire! Bring buckets!"

I heard a shriek from within.

Stephen turned toward me. "I saw how you looked at me, asking me about the fire." He waved his hands, which were covered with phosphorus burns from the matches he must have been lighting every chance he got. This was what I had realized during worship.

Coughing now from the smoke, I threw my cloak onto the burning leaves but the fire was too great to smother. "Thee set the factory aflame." I beat at the burning wall with my hands. I wouldn't let my beloved Meetinghouse fall victim to Stephen's warped mind.

"Not I, although I wish I had." He threw his head back and laughed again. "Thomas Parry looked at me the same way. I hate him."

Suddenly we were surrounded by Friends. Stephen tried to slip away in the confusion, but Zeb and another young man wrestled him to the ground. Others filled buckets full of water from the pond down the slope and threw them on the wall. Frederick, John

Whittier, and another elder spread coats on top of the burning leaves, finally extinguishing the flames. Someone hailed a passing police officer, who cuffed Stephen's hands behind his back. I explained what Stephen had said. The officer said Detective Donovan would find me and marched the still-grinning arsonist away.

I sank to the ground, fearing my shaky legs would no longer hold me. John Whittier bent over to speak with me, supporting himself with his hands on his knees.

"Rose, what made thee discover poor Stephen and the fire?"

"I saw the marks on his hands yesterday. When I lit the stove this morning, a bit of phosphorus split off and singed my own hand. But it wasn't until my thoughts ranged far from the Light this morning that I realized those marks were a sign of a careless person lighting match after match."

"By breaking the silence thee saved us all and our Meetinghouse." John patted my arm.

For this I was grateful. And prayed I wouldn't have occasion to meet an arsonist ever again.

NINE

At a sound that afternoon, as I sat fretting about the impending tea even as I looked forward to seeing David again so soon, I peeked out the front window to see Kevin Donovan rapping on the front door, then waiting with his police hat in his hands. One of the twins ran to the door. I listened.

"I'm Detective Donovan. I'd like to speak with Rose Carroll, the midwife, young man."

I walked into the hallway to hear Matthew say, "Yes, sir!" The boy saluted with a grin. "Come with me, sir." He turned and marched into the house, swinging straight arms and nearly crashing into me.

Matthew looked up with a start. "Auntie Rose, a policeman to see thee."

"Kevin Donovan, what a surprise," I said. "Come in, please."

Matthew stood staring, a delighted smile still on his face.

"Thank thee, Matthew," I said, matching his smile.

"And I thank you for answering the door, young man." Kevin ruffled Matthew's hair. Kevin was in full uniform today, his blue serge fastened up with silver buttons and his detective badge a shiny silver on his chest.

"Is thee really a detective?" Matthew's eyes were wide.

"That I am. Are you wanting to be with the police yourself when you grow bigger?"

Matthew nodded.

"I'm glad to hear it." Kevin placed his hat on Matthew's dark curly hair. "I can't say as we've ever had an officer from your faith. But there's always a first time. Study hard, and stay out of trouble. And come see me in about ten years' time."

This was a side of the detective I'd not seen before. Despite his views on domestic relations, he clearly had a soft spot for children.

Matthew stood up as tall as he could. "Yes, Mr. Detective, sir." He put a hand up to feel the hat, now listing over his right eyebrow. He pressed his lips together but a smile escaped anyway.

I laughed. "Would thee like some tea?" I asked Kevin.

"Thank you, no."

"Then please sit down." I gestured to a chair in my parlor office.

He glanced at Matthew as he sat. "You can wear the hat while I visit with your auntie."

"Mattie, run along, now." I smiled but closed the door firmly, leaving my nephew in the hall. "What's the cause of your visit? I trust thee has Stephen Hamilton firmly behind bars?" I sat facing him.

"We do. That was quick thinking and acting on your part, Miss Carroll." He folded his hands in his lap but kept worrying one clean trim thumbnail with the other. His full reddish-brown mustache curved right down to his jawline, hiding his upper lip.

"Call me Rose. I only did what any able-bodied person would do."

"We've arrested Hamilton for arson on your meetinghouse." He frowned. "And he'll do time for it, mark my words. He's a real firebug, that one. We've nabbed him setting small fires before."

"And thee has charged him with the Parry factory fire, as well, of course?" Surely they had.

"Well, there's the problem. He claims he didn't do it."

"He said as much to me, too. Surely

people like him lie about their crimes all the time." I leaned forward, my hands clasped in my lap.

"It's just that he was in McFarley's Pub at the time the fire was getting started, Miss Carroll — I mean, Miss Rose. He'd been there for several hours and stayed until the alarm was raised. A dozen men attest to it."

I sat back in my chair as if I'd been pushed there. "With his crazy ideas and burn marks all over his hands? But a dozen men wouldn't lie, I suppose."

"Especially not for a disturbed person like young Hamilton."

"If not him, then who else could have set the fire? Who would want that factory, and all the others, incinerated?"

"It's my job to find out." He tapped his hand against his leg. "And with Hamilton out of the picture, my job just became much harder."

"I don't envy thee this profession."

"That is the cause of my visit." He cleared his throat. "I wondered if you might keep your ears and eyes out. You most certainly travel in circles I have no place in. Your midwifery affairs and your Quakers and all."

"I'd say that is true. I don't suppose thee would ever attend a birth in progress or sit in a group of silent Friends for an hour or more."

"No, no." He smiled. "And you seem like an intelligent woman and a courageous one. Can you keep a listen out for me, Miss Rose?"

"Thee doesn't have to call me Miss."

"Old habits." He shrugged. "I can't call you simply Rose. It isn't right."

"As thee wishes. I'm not sure how much help I can be, though. I'm a midwife. I'm not trained in the art of detecting. I'm not sure I'd know a clue if I saw one."

"Leave the clues and such to me."

I thought of something. "Does thee use the lines on people's fingertips to convict them? I read about it in Twain's memoir."

"What, *Life on the Mississippi*?" He snorted. "That's more likely fiction, Miss Carroll. Although I have heard rumblings about how it might have basis in fact. We're still waiting for the science on it to be presented."

"I see."

"But much of detecting is simply watching people, listening to them. That you can do."

Which was what he had done at the reception after Isaiah Weed's service, after all. He had been watching and listening. "I agree, then," I said. "I'll try to help the investigation. I admit to hearing quite a lot in my practice that might not otherwise be said. Should I learn something pertaining to the destruction of Carriage Hill, I'll tell thee if I can."

"If you can?"

"Kevin, I'm at times like a counselor of sorts to my laboring mothers. If I learn something said in confidentiality, I feel I must keep it to myself."

When he began to object, I held up a hand. "I've said I'll help thee with the search and I will." I looked out at the street for a moment, then back at Kevin. "Should the people of our town fear another fire? Are we in danger?" I frowned.

"We could be. It all depends on why the fire was set in the first place. It's almost too bad the arsonist isn't Stephen Hamilton. The town would now be safe. But this is my job, and I've brought in plenty of criminals in the past. I'll find this one, too." He stood. "So I'd best be off and back to the job. I thank you for agreeing to assist. Don't do anything that puts you at risk, of course. But if you happen to hear anything, see anything — that's what I'd like to be knowing."

I stood, too, and followed him to the

parlor door.

In the front hallway, Matthew sat on the floor reading. Mark sat beside him, his hands on raised knees, looking like a copy of his twin, except a towheaded one. He wore the police hat tilted back on his head. When they saw the adults, they both jumped up.

"I want to be police, too," Mark said. He extended the hat to Kevin with a hopeful smile.

"I'm glad of it, young man. What's your name, now?"

"Mark, sir."

"I'm studying, Mr. Detective." Matthew held up his schoolbook, *McGuffey's Third Reader,* with eyes wide. "Just like thee said to do. I memorized my work for tomorrow. Want to hear?"

Kevin nodded in all seriousness.

"It's called 'The Blacksmith.' " Matthew set his feet straight with each other and clasped his hands behind his back. He screwed his face into concentration, gazing beyond Kevin at the glass doorknob. " 'Clink, clink, clinkerty clink.' " His head bobbed the rhythm of the poem. " 'We begin to hammer at morning's blink, and hammer away 'til the busy day, like us, aweary, to rest shall sink.' " Matthew looked

98

at Kevin, mouth open to go on.

The detective held up a hand. "That's perfect, laddy. Keep it up, now. Both of ye."

I showed Kevin to the outer door. "I thank thee for the attention to the boys. They are much impressed."

He waved off my thanks, trotting down the front steps and walking with a purposeful stride along the path back toward Market Square and the business of the town.

I turned back to the boys. "Taking a job with the police department isn't quite in line with Friends' holding with peace, boys." I folded my arms in mock chastisement.

"But Auntie Rose . . ." Matthew entreated.

"And don't the police need some peaceful officers?" Mark asked with a knit brow.

Amused, I ruffled his light hair. "I dare say they do."

David handed me up into his buggy at the appointed hour.

"I thank thee." I sat and gathered my best cloak around me with nervous hands. As I had watched Kevin disappear around the corner onto High Street an hour earlier, I'd remembered about the smudge on Ephraim Pickard's shirt. I should have told Kevin about my visit to Ephraim, but I had been so disarmed by his request for help that I had completely forgotten to relate Ephraim's behavior and the condition of his shirt.

David went around and sat in the driver's seat. He smiled at me, handing over a plaid lap blanket. "You look beautiful, Rose."

"Thee is most kind," I said with a voice that quavered. I cleared my throat to try to master my anxiety. I knew I wasn't any great beauty, but had been reasonably satisfied with my examination in the mirror a few moments earlier. Faith had helped me arrange my dark hair, even adding a curl to the side of my brow, although I thought my eyeglasses somewhat spoiled the look. My deep red best dress was plain but was fairly recently sewn, so at least it was tailored in something like the current fashion, with the new covered buttons and slimmer profile. Mother had tatted the lace collar only last year and I had made sure it was freshly laundered and starched this afternoon. I was glad I'd only worn my everyday cloak to Meeting this morning, as it was now singed and imbued with smoke from Stephen's fire. It was my nerves that weren't satisfied.

"I hope I'll be able to eat something. I'm nervous about meeting thy mother."

"She won't eat you alive, I promise." He

clucked to the horse, who set off down the road.

I silently repeated the names he'd told me. Chase and Currier were as well-known and prosperous families as the Dodges. What was I getting myself into? A voice inside told me I didn't deserve these people. Or David's affection, for that matter. I tried to silently answer myself that indeed, I did deserve goodness and love. It was an ongoing battle.

"How was your day, Rosie?" David glanced at me as we traveled up the Elm Street hill. "Was it as lovely as you?"

"Oh, no." I uttered a laugh without any humor behind it. "It was quite momentous, as it turned out. I discovered young Stephen Hamilton setting fire to the Meetinghouse during worship. I sent up a cry of alarm — I had to break a window to do it — and Friends managed to both capture him and put out the fire."

David took in a sharp breath. "You could have been hurt!"

"But I wasn't. It was just that I realized during Meeting the scars I had seen on Stephen's hands were from match sparks. I went out and found him with a pile of leaves aflame that had spread to the back wall." I shuddered. "He simply stood there and laughed. He's an ill man, David."

"I should say. So he must have been the firebug who set Carriage Hill on fire, as well. I hope he's in police custody now. Perhaps more rightly he should be in the prison asylum."

I nodded. "He's in jail, all right. But that's the thing. Kevin Donovan, the detective on the case, stopped by this afternoon. He said Stephen has a clear alibi for the hours prior to when the fire started. Many men saw him at McFarley's Pub. He's certainly under arrest for trying to burn down the Meetinghouse, though."

"The real arsonist is still at large, then." David frowned.

"It's a fearful thought. Do arsonists strike twice?"

"I'm not sure. I suppose some do, and some don't. It would depend on the motive. If the carriage factory fire was started to settle a grudge, that might be the end of it."

"We can only hope." I gazed at the water as we clattered over the new Essex-Merrimack Drawbridge leading to Deer Island, which sat just two miles from the center of Amesbury, and then over the chain-supported suspension bridge to the busy shipping port of Newburyport. A white-headed eagle streaked feet first into the river and came up with a wriggling fish in its talons. A few strong beats of its wide wings brought it to a tree overhanging the water. A chilly breeze came off the Merrimack and I was glad for my woolen cloak and the blanket.

"But why did Donovan come to the house to tell you about Stephen Hamilton?" David asked.

"I suppose because it was I who stopped Stephen in his evil task. But then he asked me to keep a watch out for him and report anything I might learn around town."

"He wants you to become a detective?" David frowned again as the mare took us up the hill to High Street.

"No, silly." I laughed. "But I do go places he can't and hear things he would not. As does thee. A detective would never hear a laboring mother cry out about a man who beat her or a pregnant woman confess her husband was seeing what she called a strumpet."

"I hope you will be careful. Very careful."

"Of course. I'll just be going about my life. And if I glean any information, I'll inform the detective. Don't worry thy head."

We continued to talk as we drove the additional two miles to David's house. He made me laugh with a tale of *The Henrietta,* a humorous play he'd seen about the she-nanigans of Wall Street, and I told him about Matthew and Mark's aspirations to become police officers.

"I'll have to give them some gentle elder-ing about treating all equally. They ad-dressed Kevin as Detective and Sir over and over." I smiled. "But they're young yet."

"Here we are," he said as we finally turned onto Olive Street and pulled up at the first house, which sat on the corner with High. A large home with elegant proportions perched there, with lights in every down-stairs window despite the early hour. Even the plantings emerging from snowbanks ap-peared well tended and graceful.

Acting as assistant detective was child's play compared to the ordeal I anticipated.

I perched on the needlework seat of the chair Clarinda Dodge had assigned me to. It was beautiful, with glowing cherry wood shaped into curving lines. A low table in the middle of the cluster of chairs and settees held a silver tea service as well as plates of tiny sandwiches and sweets that a uniformed colored maid had delivered. I tried to hold my cup and saucer steady in my lap. The cup, decorated with sprigs of roses, was of a china so fine I could see light through it.

"So David tells us you work as a midwife, Miss Carroll. How quaint. Women still use midwives, do they?" Clarinda smiled ever so slightly. Her silver hair was drawn into an impeccable knot on top of her head and she wore a gown in a matching color. She poised her slender figure with erect posture.

"They do, and I am one. Helping mothers to have healthy pregnancies and assisting babies to enter the world safely is my calling, and it serves a great need in the community." I smiled back with somewhat more feeling. "And please call me Rose."

"She's as good as a doctor with deliveries, Mother." David sat next to his mother on a settee upholstered in a burgundy damask that nearly matched my dress. "I've seen her in action. Why, just the other day —"

"I don't think the details of giving birth is an appropriate topic of conversation, dear." Clarinda's mouth twisted as if her tea were laced with sour lemon.

"Thee has a lovely home," I said, hoping to lighten the conversation. It was true. While the style was more ornate than one would find in the home of any Friend, the rich reds and deep greens of the cushions and the draperies were harmonious and all the pieces of furniture were of the same gleaming cherry as my perch, except the black grand piano that sat in the far corner of the spacious room near tall windows.

"Thank you. Your speech sounds quite old-fashioned." Clarinda cocked her head. "And your dress is quite plain, as well. Lovely, but unadorned."

I winced inwardly and then sat up straight. "Yes, I am a member of the Society of Friends, and —"

"Ah, the peaceable religion," a deep voice boomed. A man strode into the room, stopping in front of me. "Sorry I'm late. I'm Herbert Dodge, David's father. And you must be the lovely Rose." He bowed slightly and winked at me, with identical eyes to David's and the same dark hair, except Herbert's was shot through with gray.

Winks must run in the family. "I'm pleased to meet thee, Herbert." I held out my hand and he shook it heartily, then sat in the chair next to me.

"Don't you know, dear?" Herbert said to Clarinda. "Quakers believe all are equal under God, and long ago decided to use the familiar form of speech for family and presidents alike. But now, of course, the formal has become the familiar in our language, so we say 'you' when we address another person and Quakers say 'thee.' It is old-fashioned." He accepted a cup of tea from Clarinda and popped two sandwiches into his mouth. "I happen to like it."

"That's a correct description," I said. "And our way of speech now distinguishes Friends as different. But we're accustomed to it and so it continues."

"I find the study of language fascinating," Herbert said. "But you use 'you' when you address more than one person, isn't it true?"

I smiled. "Yes. It's odd, but that's how we speak."

"And I like the fact you called me by my first name. I approve, young lady." He set his cup and saucer down with a clatter and rubbed his hands together.

Clarinda blinked several times and pressed her lips together. I had carefully avoided addressing her by name because I had the feeling she would only want me to call her Mrs. Dodge. Now I wanted desperately to steer the conversation away from me.

"How fares the shoe business?" I asked Herbert. "David tells me thy factory is quite large."

"Oh, it's faring splendidly. We have near one hundred employees. Everyone needs shoes and always will."

"Mr. Dodge was disappointed David did not wish to follow him into the business." Clarinda lifted her chin. "But I approved of his becoming a doctor."

"Now, Mother, you don't need to start that conversation all over again. Rose doesn't want to hear about our petty family quarrels, do you?" David gave me a wry smile.

"Son," Clarinda turned to face him, "I heard from my cousin that her niece Violet Currier is coming to visit from New York. I shall be eager for you to call on her. Or perhaps we shall have a dinner and invite her. Yes, that would be more appropriate."

David rolled his eyes but kept his silence. I'd have to ask him on our way home what Clarinda implied about this Violet, and about his reaction.

"Have the authorities apprehended the arsonist in your town, Rose?" Herbert leaned toward me, his large hands splayed on his knees.

"No, not that I know of." How much should I say?

"Rosie herself caught one trying to burn down her church just this morning, Father," David said, eyes twinkling even as Clarinda gasped.

"You don't say!" Herbert fixed his full attention on me.

"It's true," I said. "But unfortunately the police have learned he wasn't the man who set the Parry Carriage Factory aflame."

"So you wrestled this fellow down yourself? I admire such spunk," Herbert said.

"Surely you didn't engage in physicality with the arsonist," Clarinda said, the edges of her mouth drawing down.

I laughed. "Oh, no, I didn't fling myself upon him. Several Friends managed to wrestle the man to the ground and others worked to extinguish the fire. I was grateful more damage wasn't done."

"I believe the poet Whittier is one of you?" Clarinda rose and fetched a slim book from a table near the door. "I am quite fond of his work."

"He's an elder of our Meeting, yes," I said. "And threw his own coat upon the fire today."

She brought the book back to the settee and leafed through it. "Here we are. I particularly enjoy his work titled 'Democracy.' " She began to read.

O fairest born of love and light,
Yet bending brow and eye severe
On all that harms the holy sight,
Or wounds the pure and perfect ear!

She closed the book. "Does he ever recite poetry in your services?"

"Not usually, but he does once in a while. We normally sit in silence, waiting upon God's Light."

Clarinda blinked several times again. "In silence? No sermon, no hymns?"

"No. We all minister to each other, and our only lesson, our only hymn, is that which we hear directly from God. But I could arrange for thee to meet John Whittier if thee wishes."

Clarinda's eyes widened as her mouth dropped open. David smiled at me with a little nod.

"You've no idea what your offer means to her, Rose." Herbert nodded in approval. "She does go on about Mr. John Greenleaf Whittier."

I set my cup and saucer on the table. At least I'd done something right.

TEN

"Violet Currier. Thy mother seemed quite enthusiastic about your seeing her," I said as we clattered back across the Chain Bridge an hour later. The setting sun had dyed the Merrimack a pink that matched the clouds above. I glanced over at David.

"She thinks I should marry Violet — that it would be a suitable match." He pursed his lips. "I haven't even seen the girl since she was a child."

I kept my silence. Perhaps Clarinda Dodge would find a way to get what she wanted.

He glanced toward me, frowning. "Violet was a twit then and no doubt is a twit now. I have no more interest in her than in dining with a stone. She'd be about that interesting, too."

"Perhaps you should see her. I'm sure she's more fitting for your class than I." I stared straight ahead.

"Nonsense. That's only Mother's fanciful

thinking. I doubt Violet would like me in the slightest." He patted my hand. "Anyway, I don't care to and that's that. Now you, my dear, certainly scored a point by offering to introduce Mother to Mr. Whittier. Do you think you can actually pull that off?"

"Of course." I inhaled deeply, glad of the change in topic. "He's a kindly gentleman, although quite busy with his writing and all the callers who want a piece of his time. I'll visit him tomorrow and raise the subject." I wanted to get John Whittier's opinion on the Amesbury arsonist, too.

"I know Mother and you will get along famously before too long." David smiled as he shook the reins and encouraged the horse to trot. "And I'm going to do my level best to make sure that happens."

My heart relaxed a little. He was confident I could win his mother's favor and wanted to help it happen. I wasn't sure it would be so easy, but I hoped so. Any woman who raised such a tender, intelligent man for a son had to have a place in her where the two of us could meet in harmony.

I sniffed the air and smelled smoke. My heart pounded. "Does thee think another fire has been set, David?" I scanned the hills above the center of town to my left as we emerged at the top of Portsmouth Road.

He laughed and pointed at each house we passed. "Rosie, it's suppertime and a chilly day. Do you see smoke coming out of every chimney or am I imagining it?"

"I suppose thee is right. But I have fear now of the arsonist striking again. I don't wish for any more families to have to grieve for a lost son, brother, or father. Or even worse, children and mothers. Who knows where the criminal will strike next?"

"You're correct, of course." David steered the mare up Elm Street, his expression now somber.

When we crested Carriage Hill, the devastation from the fire was everywhere. At least tendrils of smoke no longer twisted up from the piles of wreckage as they had yesterday. I saw Robert Clarke in front of his property conferring with two men, likely planning their rebuilding even on First Day. He was a man to be admired, to not be defeated by this calamity, and to stand as an example to the other factory owners.

We pulled up at last in front of the Bailey house, the middle one of the three Hamilton had built within a year of each other. I thought of them as the triplets, since the plans must have been identical. In each, three small windows ran across the top. At the left of each house a window was set diagonal to the front wall. At the right the front stairs led to a covered porch open on two sides. On which porch at my home a man now paced, turning his hat in his hands.

"Oh, dear. It looks as if I'll be off to a birth." I only vaguely recognized the man, but that didn't signify anything. By now everyone in town knew they could call on me to assist a laboring woman.

"It certainly appears that way." David halted the buggy and hurried around to my side to help me down. "Thank you for indulging me, Rose, in meeting my parents. It meant a great deal to me." His eyes were full of feeling and he kept my hand in his even as I stood on the ground.

"I was truly glad to meet thy family, David."

"It wasn't as bad as you feared, I hope?"

"Not at all." Although I'd certainly enjoyed the company of Herbert more than Clarinda. "Now I must go, though. I'll speak with thee soon." I squeezed his hand and then extricated mine.

"Not as soon as I'd like. I'll wait and convey both of you to the home if you'd like."

"Oh, would thee? That would be a great assistance." I turned to the house. The man ran down the stairs toward me.

"It's me wife." His face was full of anguish. "She's screaming something terrible."

ELEVEN

I yawned as I turned onto Friend Street at nine the next morning. Last evening's birth had been well along by the time I arrived with the worried husband via David's buggy, the three of us squashed together on the one seat.

The mother, Patience Henderson, had delivered a small but healthy son, despite her screams. Before I left, the father, Hiram, who had a steady job with the railroad, had paid me the full two dollars with a huge smile. They named the child Timothy. I'd seen pneumonia take their firstborn infant son a year earlier, whom they'd also called Timothy; that was why I recognized the father. I saw this in my practice frequently, a family calling a succession of babies by the same name until one lived to wear it.

I hadn't achieved quite a full night's sleep, however, not arriving back home until midnight. The household had been up at the usual early hour to get the children off to school and Faith and Frederick off to work. I helped out with breakfast and with lunch pails, but I did hope to rest for a bit when I returned from my planned visit to see John Whittier.

I rapped the knocker on the front door of the simple clapboard frame home. While I had shared worship with John more times than I could remember, I had never visited him at home. His housekeeper opened the door and was apparently accustomed to acting as his gatekeeper. She questioned me about my reasons for seeing him. But when I started to explain, John himself peered over her shoulder and beckoned me in.

"Mrs. Cate, this is Friend Rose Carroll. I have time for her, of course I do."

I found it curious this famous lifelong Friend used a title to address his own housekeeper. Perhaps he felt she would have accepted it no other way. But I didn't ask him about it. As I moved through the hall, I passed a longcase clock and was delighted by the sight of a peaceful meadow, like the one on my own clock, painted across the top where the days of the month were marked, held up by maps of the halves of the world. A quizzical rosy-cheeked man-in-the-moon peeked out behind the flat globe on the left. He must move across the heavens during the month, one day at a time.

I followed John into his study, which was warm from the heat of a small stove. The pipe connecting it to the wall glowed nearly red. He sank into his rocker, looking every one of his eighty-one years. On one wall of the study was a chaise much like the one in my own office. A small desk against the wall bore an inkwell, a pen, a rocking blotter, and a folio of blank paper. A black top hat rested next to the paper. The great poet's writing space was simple and humble, as was its owner.

"Thank thee for seeing me, John." I perched on a small chair. "And for understanding why I needed to leave Meeting for Worship yesterday."

"I am glad thee uncovered the arsonist in our midst," he said.

"There lies a problem. Thee told me of thy friendship with Kevin Donovan."

"Yes, the able detective." He tented his fingers.

"He paid me a visit yesterday and said our Stephen Hamilton isn't the Carriage Hill arsonist because he has a secure alibi for the hours preceding the fire."

John raised his eyebrows. "This is indeed news. I had not heard of it."

"Kevin told me Stephen was at the pub with plenty of men to vouch for him."

"I wager the detective then begged for thy help in the matter." He smiled.

"How did thee know?" I cocked my head. "Did he tell thee?"

"No, Rose." He laughed. "But thee is a courageous and intelligent woman. And thee has the gift of seeing."

"That is correct — about his asking for my help, I mean." I didn't know what the "gift of seeing" meant, but I was more concerned to get on with my investigation of the arson than to ask John at this time. "I agreed, of course. And now I ask for thine."

"I shall be happy to assist. I must advise thee of something, however. I am afraid I have grown overly popular with both ladies and gentlemen who appreciate my work. At times I receive callers with whom I am not disposed to speak." He gestured toward the hat on his table. "I keep my eye out through the glass in this door that faces the street, and if way opens, I make my exit unseen." I followed his gaze to a door off the hall that led to the back of the house.

I laughed. "If this comes to pass, I'll walk out with thee."

"And thee will be most welcome. Now, how may I help?" he asked.

"If I might use thee as a sounding board of sorts, I'd be grateful. I don't wish to bother the Bailey family with ideas they could find frightful, especially the children. Thee knows this town and her inhabitants better than I. Perhaps together we can arrive at some hypothesis for the able detective to work on."

"Please." He spread his hands. "Present what information thee has so we might think of some solutions."

"I will. But first I need to ask thee a favor of a different sort. I had occasion to meet a Clarinda Dodge of Newburyport yesterday. She's quite an admirer of thy writings. Her son, David, a physician at the hospital, and I are becoming, well, sweet on each other. And I too boldly offered to introduce Clarinda to thee. Would that be possible?" I raised my eyebrows and straightened my spine, hoping I hadn't transgressed.

John threw back his head and laughed, his beard quivering with his enjoyment. "Thee is a bit nervous about this request, I see. If it will further thy sweetness, as thee puts it, with the physician, I am happy to oblige. Bring this Clarinda Dodge to call whenever thee wishes."

"I'm grateful, Friend." That should help put me in Clarinda's good graces. And anything that helped me become closer to David was what I wanted.

"But thee need not be worried about speaking to me, no matter how well-known I am. We are equals in God's eyes."

I smiled, but I couldn't help feeling I wanted to honor both his fame and the wisdom that came with his advanced age. "Now, about the setter of fires," I said. "I believe we must mainly consider who would profit from destroying the Parry factory. Perhaps William Parry's competitors?"

"But Parry is neither the most successful nor produces the best workmanship." John stroked his beard, which was the same snowy white as what remained of his hair. "I would say Clarke, or perhaps your distant kin Bailey, would be the ones to envy. Mind you, Parry does make some vehicles pleasing to the eye. But I have heard the quality does not merit the price."

"That's interesting. Here is another piece of the puzzle. I assisted a young single lady named Minnie O'Toole with the birth of a son the day before the carriage fire. Despite having no visible means of support, she paid my fee in full and said . . ."

I paused. I might be about to reveal too much of a confidence. The clock in the hall dinged the half hour.

"Go on," John urged.

"Well, she said she does not need to hold the father accountable."

"I see."

"Later that same day I examined William Parry's wife, who is heavy with their first child. This is in confidence, but I feel I must tell thee. She complained her husband has been spending all his free time either at work or with a strumpet, as she put it. And then two days ago I observed William Parry entering Minnie's home, and I surmised he might be her baby's father."

John nodded, rocking with a somber expression.

"After Isaiah's service, I had occasion to speak with William. I told him his wife misses his company, especially at meals. I tried to phrase the concern in terms of her health during her last months of pregnancy, but he pushed my thought away and said he could run his family without my help."

"Not all in our town behave by the morals we would wish them to adhere to, Rose. They are also children of God, though, and hold God's light within them."

I felt myself growing impatient. "Yes, of course. But what I wondered was if somehow this affair of William's could be responsible for the fire. By some connection I've not yet made in my mind."

"That is possible."

"Or maybe his wife arranged for the factory to be torched so he might spend more time with her instead of with the business," I said. "She would certainly have the funds to pay a criminal to do her bidding, although I am not sure whether she would act so desperately or with such vindictiveness."

"Aye, but then she would have destroyed the source of those same funds. We might need to let these thoughts season a while."

Season. Another Quaker habit that wasn't easy for me: waiting, letting a situation rest and evolve. John gave a sharp glance out the glass inset of the door. I heard steps on the front porch and the door knocker thudded twice. He stood and donned a cloak that hung on a peg. "Will thee walk with me a spell?" Opening the door to the back garden, he placed his hat on his head, his eyes twinkling, and picked up a silver-tipped cane.

"I'd be happy to, Friend." I grabbed my own wrap and saw Mrs. Cate heading to answer the front door as I preceded John out into the garden with its perennial herbs sticking their heads through the remaining snow on our left, and along a path through garden beds on both sides.

"I could have Mrs. Cate act as stern guard, but I am more comfortable letting her tell the truth to visitors, that I am not at home," John said. He paused in front of a tree, one of four in a row. "These pear trees make the very finest compote." He stroked a bud not yet in flower. "The variety is called Bartlett of Boston."

"The shape of that one looks like an apple tree," I said, pointing at a taller tree toward the back of the garden.

"Indeed it is. A Blue Pearmain. The fruit has a bluish bloom over dark purple skin and they glow like plums against the foliage. Was thee also raised up on a farm?"

I nodded. "I was, in distant Lawrence." We strolled through the gate, along the street in back of the house, then past St. Joseph's Catholic Church on School Street before turning onto Sparhawk.

"Like my cane?" he asked, twirling it.

When I nodded, he continued. "It is made of walnut saved from the fire that burned down Pennsylvania Hall." He shook his head. "That beautiful edifice was only three days old when the pro-slavery folks burned it, simply because Garrison and I were writing our abolitionist newsletter within. And holding meetings, too, of course. They would have liked to have burned us down along with the presses for the *Pennsylvania Freeman.*" He sighed. "But that was going on fifty years ago now."

"It's a lovely cane, John." The dark wood gleamed with the warmth of years of use. "I'm glad thee wasn't caught in the fire."

He laughed. "Look. Has my name engraved in the silver. I suppose they thought I might lose it." He then asked after the Bailey children's health and mentioned a poem he was working on.

"I have been rolling this passage around in my mind," he said, holding his index finger in the air. "What thinks thee of this? 'A summer-miracle in our winter clime, God gave a perfect day.' "

"I like it. Does thee mean for it to —"

"Miss Carroll! Mr. Whittier!" A voice hailed us from the opposite side of the street. A thin man hurried across. He removed his hat and held it in his left hand while he pumped John's hand with extra vigor. The man's smile was full of nervous energy, as were his movements. His sandy hair stuck out in all directions from his head, like it was electrified.

"Ned Bailey, how is thee?" I smiled but wished my brother-in-law's relative hadn't appeared to pierce the friendly bubble of my visit with John Whittier. Ned was of the family branch who had laid down their membership in the Religious Society of Friends, which didn't concern me. I simply didn't care for his company.

"Most excellent." Ned's open-mouthed smile revealed missing teeth, with those remaining stained by nicotine.

"Greetings, Ned." John smiled a little, his tall calm carriage a study in contrast to our visitor's enthusiastic agitation.

"Why, I'll bet you two were working up some new poem together, am I right?"

Despite that being nearly true, I protested. "John Whittier writes beautiful meaningful verse entirely on his own, and I deliver beautiful healthy babies, not alone at all."

"Certainly, certainly." Ned replaced his hat. "Now Rose, you know I long to take you away from all that. I've had my cap set for you for a great while now."

I cringed inwardly. I was aware of his feelings, which I had never reciprocated in the slightest. I tried to be kind but he was very persistent.

"And why would thee wish to take a talented midwife away from her much-needed services?" John's voice boomed deeper than usual. He fixed unsmiling eyes on Ned.

"Well, sir. I mean to make her my wife, you see. And after that happy event, of course, she wouldn't want to be out working in public. Wouldn't need to, what with the income from the Bailey carriages. Best in the country, they say." He preened, oblivious to both John's somber reaction and my barely concealed grimace. "Rose here would be taking care of me and of our babies."

An image passed through my brain of a me with no profession, forced by circumstance to marry a man I did not care for, ending up an unhappy wife and the mother of five whining children. I blessed Orpha again for taking me in at my request, teaching and training me, and sending me out to catch babies, first at her side and then alone. If I ended up wife and mother, it was to be my own choice and with a man of my choosing, as well.

John drew out his pocket watch and glanced at it rather pointedly. He glanced up again. "Ned, it was good to see thee again. If thee will excuse us, we have some business to conduct." John extended his elbow to me.

I tucked my hand through his proffered arm and we turned away.

"I'll visit you at home soon, Rose! Then we'll have a night on the town," Ned called after us.

I pretended not to hear.

John cleared his throat. "Now, I was thinking to begin my new poem with, 'Through thin cloud-films a pallid ghost looked down, the waning moon half-faced.' "

A shiver ran through me at the image of a pallid ghost, and I huddled in my cloak.

TWELVE

After John and I finished our walk and parted ways, I decided to stop into the police station before I went home. I needed to tell Kevin Donovan what I'd forgotten to relay about Ephraim Pickard, as well as the results of my conversation with our Meeting's most esteemed elder.

On my way, I passed by the construction for the new Armory, workers sawing and hammering with great commotion. I sneezed when the breeze blew a fine sawdust my way. I glanced up at the stately Opera House. Its red brick lined in red mortar held a dignified air, and the slate roof came down to meet fancy tile work with designs depicting the dramatic arts. I hadn't attended a single play there and secretly longed to, but I imagined the price of tickets was a bit beyond my budget, although I had never actually checked.

Reaching the station, I pulled open the

heavy door and entered. A tall officer not much older than I sat at the desk. I had delivered his wife of a daughter the year before. The same wife, Nell, who had acted oddly downtown only a couple of days ago. Why had she spoken with Jotham in public and then denied knowing him? Could the two be having their own illicit dalliance?

"Guy Gilbert, isn't it?" I smiled.

He stood and began to bluster. He threw his chest out so far the buttons seemed at risk of popping off despite his thin build. "That would be Officer Gilbert to you, Miss —" He took a good look at me and caught himself. "Miss Carroll! How good to see you." He extended a hand. "I apologize. We often have unmannerly folks comin' in, and . . . oh, never mind."

I shook his hand. "How are those girls of yours, Guy, thy wife and thy daughter?" I clasped my hands in front of me.

He beamed and his dark eyes shone. "Oh, little Lizzy is quite well, Miss Carroll. She's starting to walk a bit and she says 'Dada' to me. She's so smart. Imagine that, her first word being my name." He bounced on his heels, his hands behind his back.

"That's splendid. But I saw Nell downtown recently and she didn't seem to be herself. Has she been ill?" Would he tell me

130

what was wrong with her?

A shadow passed over his face. "Nell's not what I'd call well, exactly. But she loves our Lizzy." He brightened. "Lizzy says 'Mama' too." He gazed into his own memories.

"What seems to be the problem with Nell?"

Gazing at me with dark shadows under his eyes, he said, "I don't know. She's indeed not herself." He stared at the desk as if into an abyss.

"I'll pay her a visit soon."

"I'd appreciate that, Miss Carroll." He glanced up but still seemed lost in his thoughts.

I cleared my throat. "Is Kevin Donovan in? I have a few pieces of information for him regarding the Carriage Hill fire."

"Oh! I'll fetch him. Won't you sit down?" He gestured at the waiting bench and then disappeared through a door behind the desk.

Kevin approached me as I stood examining a large framed photograph. Twenty men in matching dark uniforms stood in two rows, shoulders back, expressions stern, identical rounded helmets perched atop their heads. Their hands hung slack at their sides and polished buttons marched up the middle of their jackets. Who had told them

131

all to point their toes slightly outward? Perhaps they thought it a suitable pose for a photograph. Kevin Donovan stood at one end of the group and at the other posed a taller man who I thought was the captain. I peered more closely. Guy Gilbert formed part of the back row.

"How do you like my photographic image? I'd say I'm the best looking in the entire department."

I glanced at Kevin as he came to stand beside me. He shoved his hands in his pockets and regarded me with a single eyebrow raised into the vast expanse of his shiny forehead. His hair, of a rusty color indicating he'd been a carrot top as a child, had receded halfway back to the crown of his round ball of a head. He was clean shaven except for the mustache.

"Exceedingly handsome," I said, not even trying to sound sincere, then faced him. "Does thee have a moment free? I'd like to share several bits of information."

"Right this way, Miss Carroll." He gestured toward the interior door with a little bow.

A moment later I sat opposite him on a chair that complained mightily when I descended upon it. Kevin's broad oak desk was scarred and dented. Scrawled-on scraps of paper, an ash receptacle, and pens in various stages of assembly littered its top. He lowered himself into his own seat behind the desk with a sigh and patted a midsection that proved he rarely missed a meal.

"So, do you have an answer for me?" He rubbed his hands together. "Did you find our firebug?"

"Thee might temper thy anticipation. I did forget to share one piece of information yesterday afternoon, however, that I feel obliged to tell thee." I proceeded to relate my visit with Ephraim Pickard at his home. "His shirt showed a definite smudge of soot. But, of course, it could have come from his own cooking fire." I frowned, unsure how much to speculate in front of him.

"What? You know something else." He leaned forward. His tongue darted out to smooth the closest section of mustache, then he wiped his knuckle over that section as if to dry it.

"Faith Bailey, Isaiah Weed, rest his soul, and I spoke with Ephraim as he was leaving the factory. Almost early evening, it was. I remember because the electric lights came on not too much later. Ephraim said he was fired from his job on the afternoon of the fire."

"Fired? For what cause?"

"He said it was because he was late once too often, and because he'd been reading on his lunch break. He said it was William Parry's son Thomas who let him go. And it was directly after that when I saw the person in the twilight of which I told thee."

Kevin's mouth looked like he'd tasted spoiled milk. "Thomas Parry isn't well regarded in town. What is it with the self-made, rich owners around here? They work hard themselves but then indulge their sons until they become worthless spoiled brats of men."

"If thee refers to Stephen Hamilton, I do believe he suffers from a mental disorder, not simply the indulgence of his father."

"I suppose." Kevin glanced out the window and then returned to look at me. "What else, Rose Carroll? How can we solve this mystery?"

"I discussed some ideas with John Whittier." When I saw Kevin begin to object, I held up a hand. "He's a wise elder and he knows this town better than both thee and me put together. I wondered who would profit from destroying the Parry factory. William Parry's competitors might well want to see him put out of business."

"That had occurred to me, too." Kevin laced his fingers behind his head and leaned back in his chair. "It'd be Babcock, Clarke, Bailey, even Osgood. They all do better than Parry."

"And something else." I hesitated. I might be about to violate Minnie's confidence. Perhaps I wouldn't if I spoke in a vague manner. "I attended the birth of a young woman the day before the fire. She had a baby boy, and while she was able to pay my fee, she wouldn't name the father."

Kevin narrowed his eyes.

"I also care for William Parry's wife, who will bear their first child in eight weeks. She complained her husband has not been at home much. And I observed William Parry entering that young woman's home."

"Aha," Kevin said. "I've heard rumors of Parry's mistress. What's this harlot's name?"

"I can't reveal that, Kevin. And she's not a harlot, only a young woman who was taken advantage of."

He frowned at me and rapped his fingers on the desk.

"I told thee yesterday I needed to keep certain confidences. But what if this affair of William's was somehow responsible for the fire?" I asked.

"How?" he scoffed.

"I don't know. I simply feel there might be a connection."

135

"Feeling doesn't enter into police work, Miss Carroll. You know, maybe his wife hired someone to burn down the factory so he might spend more time with her instead of with the business, although that doesn't make much sense, since it would cut off the money that supports her. But maybe it truly has nothing to do with a mistress."

"I suppose," I said. "The baby's father could be someone else entirely."

"So we have competing factory owners, an unhappy wife, or a fired worker." Kevin slapped the table and sat up straight. "I doubt it's the wife, and I was already working on the competitors, but I thank you for the lead on Ephraim Pickard." He got to his feet.

I followed suit, suppressing both a yawn and my frustration that the detective dismissed my ideas. He ushered me into the hall and back into the lobby. At the desk, Guy stood in a hurry, smoothing down his uniform jacket.

"I'll be in touch," Kevin said. "Thank you, Miss Carroll, for the tip."

"Thee is welcome." I glanced at Guy. "Good-bye, Guy. Tell thy wife I will stop by and check on Lizzy," I said. "I like to visit my babies and mothers some months after the birth to see about their well-being."

Guy cocked his head, his eyes dragging down at the edges and a sigh escaped, as if a visit might not make much difference to Nell's situation. "I'll tell her, miss."

Kevin pushed open the outer door. I made my way down the stairs, then turned. "Let us pray this arsonist won't strike again."

"Prayers might not be quite what we need right now," Kevin said. "I plan to apply some good old-fashioned detective work instead. Although I suppose a prayer can't hurt, either."

"Roberta," I called out. I hadn't walked yet a block before I saw Bertie turning onto Aubin Street.

She glanced behind her with a scowl that turned to a broad smile when she caught sight of me. She set her hands on her hips and waited for me to approach.

"Thee looked well displeased at being hailed by thy given name." I raised an eyebrow.

"You know nobody but you gets to say that name to me. I've worked long and hard to be called Bertie, and by gum, I won't let anybody change it."

"One day thee must tell me the reason thee so hates being called Roberta." I knew she'd had some quarrel with her mother long ago and they were estranged, despite her mother living just across the river in West Newbury. Perhaps the quarrel had played a part, since surely it was her mother who'd bestowed on her the now-despised name.

"Maybe. Maybe not. Where have you been, and where are you off to?" she inquired.

"I've just been to see the police with a few ideas I had concerning the fire." I told her about the shadowy figure I'd seen right before it started.

"I'd love to help find this cursed arsonist who burned down my place of employment," she said. "It's headache after headache trying to plan, trying to answer the concerns of the town's selectmen, trying to get the mail delivered again, I'll tell you."

"Thee has been successful on that front. I received a letter already this morning from my mother. If thee hears any gossip around town regarding the arsonist, please tell me," I said. "Or better yet, tell the detective."

"I will." She sighed. "We've had to cancel the afternoon delivery for now and people are not happy about it."

I yawned, this time not concealing it.

"I'm so boring, am I?" She poked me with her elbow.

"Of course not," I protested. "But last night I was at a birth until late and I have clients coming in two short hours."

"Get yourself home for a rest, then. I'm heading for my own abode, in fact. Sophie just returned from New York." The color rose in her cheeks and her eyes sparkled.

I had heard a client refer to Bertie and Sophie as having a Boston Marriage, since the two unmarried ladies lived together without a man. Some used the term simply to describe women sharing a household. Others spoke it in a disparaging tone, indicating the relationship might be a romantic one they disapproved of. I knew Bertie and Sophie, in their own eyes, were as married as any man or woman, and it didn't bother me one whit. When love was present, who were we to judge if God had let it be so? I was simply glad I had a good friend. And Sophie traveled so much for her work as a lawyer that Bertie and I often were able to grab time together to go for a swim in Lake Gardner or attend a meeting of the Literary Society.

I said good-bye as I turned away, hoping I would not encounter a fire in progress on my route.

I reclined on the chaise in my parlor half an

hour later. I needed sleep before my first client arrived. Sunlight streamed through the front windows making motes dance in the air. I closed my eyes but rest wouldn't come for all the thoughts dancing in my brain.

Ephraim and his anger at being let go from a job he sorely needed. Lillian, with her knowledge that her husband was stepping out on her, or worse. Minnie, who seemed secure in being supported by her baby's father. William, likely the baby's sire but also an afflicted factory owner. Not to mention all the grieving families and friends in town, including our own Zeb and the sweet Annie. And now I worried, as well, about Nell Gilbert. I feared she was experiencing the unexpected sadness some mothers feel after giving birth. I'd pay her and the baby a visit later in the day.

I wished Kevin Donovan hadn't asked for my help with the case. It was keeping my mind overly busy. I opened my eyes and let out a breath. Sleep was clearly not coming. So perhaps, since I had agreed, I could attempt to organize my thoughts. I moved to my desk and took pen to paper, inscribing all my thoughts in an orderly fashion. I drew lines for columns and rows and hoped to fill in motive and opportunity for setting a fire that had wrecked lives and businesses. But beyond Ephraim, Lillian, and perhaps a competitor to William Parry, I didn't arrive at much. To even write down Lillian's name made me feel sick.

My stomach complained of emptiness, so I left my desk and stoked the fire in the kitchen. I heated a bit of soup and broke a chunk of bread off the loaf. I stood to eat, too restless to relax at the table. From the window at the back of the house I could see the small upholstery factory that faced onto Powow Street. I watched the comings and goings at the business, where they created cloth and leather seats for some of the carriages and sleighs made in town. That had been made in town before the fire, at any rate. A man pushed a cart full of hides onto the premises and stood talking outside with the factory owner.

The man looked familiar, with his round cheeks, ample belly, and bowler hat. I snapped my fingers. It was Minnie's brother Jotham. I put down my dinner, grabbed a shawl from a hook, and walked down the back stairs to the low picket fence separating our garden from the factory yard.

"Oh, Jotham," I called. I waved my hand. "Hello, there."

He glanced in my direction and frowned,

but turned away from the owner and walked toward me. "That's me. Who are you again?" He removed his hat and glared.

I smiled, hoping to ease the conversation. "I'm Rose Carroll, the midwife. I attended thy sister's birth last week. We met —"

"That's right," he said. "Birth of a bastard nephew." A smile crept over his face. "I'll allow as how he's a cute one, though."

"And at least he's healthy, and Minnie survived the labor." I continued, "Not all women do live through childbirth. Thee has much to be thankful for."

"I suppose." He wrinkled his nose. "What's that funny way you speak?"

"I belong to the Religious Society of Friends. I'm a Quaker and we call it plain speech."

"Well, it sounds odd to me."

I nodded. "Has thee seen Minnie and the baby today?"

"No. My cursed older sister is there lording it over the household. We don't see eye to eye."

"I'm sorry to hear that. I will stop by tomorrow and pay Minnie another visit." I gestured at the factory. "Thee works with leather, then?"

"No. I only deliver it. I deliver anything. Work is hard to come by, and now what

142

with the fire —" He knit his brows and shook his head slowly. "I don't know where I'll be getting my next meal."

Another man out of work because of the fire. At least he wasn't at risk of starving anytime soon, not with that belly.

"I saw thee talking in town with one of my clients, Nell Gilbert. How does she seem to thee?"

"No, miss. You're mistaken. I don't know no Nell." He turned away.

So they both lied about knowing each other, unless it was a chance meeting. It hadn't looked like one, though. They'd been speaking directly for several minutes, not the behavior of a stranger inquiring of directions from another, which of course neither would need, being local residents. I turned away, too, wondering why Jotham put me in mind of an actor instead of a sincere person.

THIRTEEN

Baby Lizzy was a round and cheerful child of a suitable size for thirteen months. I dandled her on my lap in the late afternoon, her chubby hands grabbing for my glasses as I tried to speak with her mother. Nell, Guy, and the baby lived with Guy's parents in a modest house on Summer Street.

"What is Lizzy eating these days?" I asked.

A thin and pale Nell shrugged. Her dark hair wasn't properly done up and she reacted little, even when I placed the baby on her lap. Her hands still rested limply on her legs. She hadn't changed since I'd seen her on the street.

Nell's mother-in-law Josephine swooped in and set Lizzy on the floor. She shot me a look of caution I well deserved. The baby could have fallen off her mother's lap.

"Lizzy's eating porridge, bread, eggs, a bit of applesauce," she told me. "She's a hungry girl." She left the room again, and I watched that Lizzy didn't crawl near the hot stove.

"I'd like you to take this tonic," I said to Nell, handing her a script. "It's strong in iron." I knew she needed more than that. I had seen this type of postpartum melancholia before. Some mothers simply outgrew it, but I'd heard one horrific tale from my teacher, Orpha Perkins, about a mother who had methodically suffocated each of her five children, including her tiny newborn, saying God had told her to do so. She was sentenced to live in the insane asylum for the rest of her natural days.

Nell clutched the script and stared at it but didn't speak. I scooped Lizzy up and carried her in to be with her grandmother, since she clearly wasn't safe alone with Nell.

"Nell is not in a good way," I said.

"That she is certainly not. I'm afraid she'll do harm to Lizzy." Josephine watched Lizzy crawl to the window and pull herself up to standing.

"I gave her a prescription for a tonic. Is she eating and drinking?"

"Very little. But I watch the baby constantly."

I thanked Josephine and bade her farewell. After retrieving my satchel from the room where Nell sat, I walked slowly away from the modest house. The sun had warmed enough that a great deal of the remaining snow on the ground was now transformed into rivulets of water running along the edge of the road. The late afternoon light burnished the budding trees with tints of gold. My feelings weren't so lovely. Nell Gilbert was most certainly ill with melancholia.

I thought it might be time to pay Orpha a visit. She always provided me with good counsel and I hadn't seen her in some weeks. She'd lived eighty-two years already, and I couldn't trust she would always be there to visit, at least in the flesh. Orpha now lived with her granddaughter, a dressmaker, and her husband and children over on Orchard Street, only a few blocks distant, so I headed in that direction. Within minutes I sat in the parlor with a cup of hot tea in my hands and a plate of shortbread cookies on the table between us.

"I am right pleased to see you, Rose." Orpha beamed from her rocking chair. She rocked back and forth with a slow rhythm, her feet on the needle-worked cushion that topped a small stool. A Bible sat on a round table to her right. Her kinky grizzled hair was tied back in a bun. She had once confessed to me, knowing of Friends' views on equality, that a slave was part of her ancestry. It didn't concern me, and her facial features didn't reveal it. I knew some in town would have refused her services if they were aware she harbored even a drop of African blood, no matter that slavery had been abolished decades earlier or that many in the Commonwealth of Massachusetts had welcomed escaped slaves.

"I have missed thy company and thy counsel, Orpha." I sipped my tea.

"I miss working with you too, dear. And how is the work lately? No losses of mother or child, I hope?"

"Not a one this year, for which I am grateful, although I had a difficult shoulder dystocia only last week." I told of her calling for David's help and then not needing it. When I mentioned David's name I blushed, and of course she noticed.

"You are sweet on this doctor. I thought you were looking well. Now I see why."

"I am quite fond of him." I smiled. "But I do worry. He took me to meet his parents yesterday. I survived it, but his mother is a true society woman and I'm afraid she disapproves of his spending time with me." I twisted my hands in my lap.

"If you love him . . . do you?"

I nodded slowly. This full, warm sensation whenever I thought of him, my respect for him, my genuinely liking him — it couldn't be anything else.

"And he you?"

"I believe so."

"Then the two of you will find a way. You know that, Rose, in your heart." She cleared her throat. "Now, about that birth. Would it be the illegitimate infant I heard word of?" Orpha's glance was sharp despite her eyes' watery appearance.

"Indeed. Minnie O'Toole is the name of the unmarried mother. It's not that part which bothers me, and she and the babe are both healthy." I told my teacher of my suspicions about William Parry being the father. "And he's also about to be a father again. His wife is seven months along."

Orpha nodded. She leaned forward and took a shortbread. "The Parry factory was the first to burn." She took a bite and rocked some more. "What a curious confluence of events in our town. Sad, true, but curious."

I agreed. "Minnie's brother Jotham seems sore aggrieved about the bastard baby, as he put it."

"I don't know this man. Jotham is an unusual name." She pursed her lips. "It's biblical in origin. Jotham was a king of Judah who ruled long because he followed the Lord steadfastly."

"This one doesn't look much like a king. He also said he's likely to lose work," I went on. "He delivers supplies to the industries that support the carriage factories. But something about the way he talked seemed passing strange to me. As if he wasn't sincere."

Orpha laughed, loud and long. It always surprised me how this frail old woman maintained a hearty guffaw in her.

"My dear Rose, do you expect only sincerity from the human race?" She wiped a tear from the edge of her eye. "Good heavens above, that will be the day." She snorted and laughed a little longer.

"No!" I protested, but I smiled with her. "Oh, never mind. I have another matter I wanted to discuss." I described Nell's melancholia and her inattention to her daughter. "She is truly in a bad way. I gave her an iron tonic, but I know she needs more than that."

"I have seen this more times than I wished. Have you tried Saint John's wort?"

"No. Of course, that has an antidepressive effect." I should have thought of it myself.

"Yes. I recommend combining it with chamomile, and then add in portions of peppermint, licorice, and star anise for soothing."

"I'll bring her some at the next opportunity. Now, tell me how thee is getting along." It had been over a year since Orpha had made the decision to cease attending births or even doing prenatal examinations. I had supported her in her choice. She had grown increasingly wobbly, with her thin legs and hips made stiff from osteoarthritis. The strain of staying up all night accompanying a laboring woman was too much to ask — yet I sorely missed her. She had been generous in making sure her current client list turned to me for their care instead of to another midwife in town, or even the doctor.

"I am well. I have my books." She motioned to a well-stocked bookcase behind her and the Bible on the table next to her chair. "And my great-grandchildren keep me young."

With that, two little girls ran into the room, the smaller cradling a doll and the older holding a piece of paper.

"Great-granny, look!" The taller girl, aged about six, pushed the paper into Orpha's lap. "I wrote a screepipshun for the new mommy. She needs a tonic. Don't you agree?"

The younger girl held her doll forward. "She just had a baby yesterday and she's looking right poorly. Isn't she?"

Orpha took the doll and gave her a careful examination. She handed her back to the girl and told her big sister, "I agree a prescription for a tonic is exactly right for a new mama. Very nice work, dear. Both of you, say hello to Miss Rose, now."

Each of them curtsied, said their hellos as quickly as possible, and ran out, the doll now relegated to being dragged by one foot.

"Training my replacements, I see?" I finished my tea and set the cup and saucer on the table.

"Why not? Unless you're planning to have your own daughter take over the business?" She cocked her head.

"My . . . what? Thee knows full well I'm not yet even married." With that, David's gentle face popped unbidden into my mind.

Orpha's voice grew gentle. "And is it not about time you made that happen, Rose Carroll?" She gazed into my eyes. "You cannot let a painful experience in your distant past govern your future, you know. That would be giving it more power than it deserves."

FOURTEEN

When I arrived home, Faith was stirring a pot and Annie worked with dough, her apron front showing smudges of flour. I greeted them and sank into a chair at the table. I took in the warmth and the aromas. I was grateful for the respite from a day of no sleep, an overactive brain, the memory of a depressive Nell Gilbert, and Orpha's reminding me of my past.

"You have been busy," I said. "It smells like heaven in here."

"Doesn't it though?" Annie pushed her hair back from her face with her wrist, leaving a streak of white on her forehead.

"Beef-potato soup," Faith said with a smile. "With lard biscuits. Annie's Grand-mere's recipe."

"And treacle cake." Annie pointed to a rectangular pan full of the moist molasses cake cooling on the table, then pressed an inverted drinking glass onto the dough. She shook out the fat round patty she'd cut with the glass onto a nearly full pan, and popped the biscuits into the oven.

"It's good to see thee, Annie," I said. "How is thee and thy heart?"

Annie gathered up the remaining scraps of dough. She pressed them into a small loaf pan and added it to the oven before turning to me, wiping her hands on the apron.

"I keep thinking I see Isaiah around town. I catch sight of a lanky man, walking with energy as he did, and I'm about to hail him by name." She joined me at the table, her voice trembling. "Then the man turns and I see it isn't my Isaiah. Of course. It never will be."

"No, it won't." I laid my hand on hers.

She wiped her eyes. "But Faith and I, we're planning our futures, isn't that so, Faith?"

Faith looked at us and nodded, her eyes bright.

Annie went on. "We're both going to get ourselves out of the mill. She's going to be a writer. And I want to study with you, Rose. I want to be a midwife, too."

I laughed and clapped my hands. "These are fine plans. I approve. When do we start?"

"We haven't quite finished the plan," Faith

said. "We're saving our money, though. I give half of my earnings to Father to help with the household. But the other half I take directly to the Powow National Bank and put it into my account."

"I do the same." Annie nodded. "Because, if we become apprentices, we won't be earning as much for a while." She cocked her head at me. "I guess I should have asked first if I may become your apprentice."

"I'll consider it, Annie."

"Oh, good!" Faith exclaimed. "See, Annie? I told thee she would say yes."

"In truth my practice becomes busier and busier," I went on. "And thee has a lovely manner with people. That's important. Thee might want to start studying a bit. I can lend thee a text to begin with."

Annie examined her hands. She twisted the apron between them.

"What's wrong?" I asked.

She glanced up with eyes full of shadows. "I don't know how to read, Rose. I can't read your text, or any other. My parents took me out of school in St. Hyacinthe when I was seven to move here, and I was just learning to read French. When we arrived here I had to help in the house and then I began to work. I never completed my schooling."

"I'll teach thee, my friend." Faith gave her a quick fierce hug. "Thee must learn. We will start with Betsy's *McGuffey's First Reader* from last year. Thee'll be reading *Little Women* soon enough."

"All right." Annie mustered a smile. "I do wish to learn. But will I need to wear eyeglasses after I learn?" She gazed at mine, which were in their habitual position halfway down my nose.

I laughed. "No, my nearsightedness has nothing to do with my love of reading, dear Annie. My father wears spectacles, too. Otherwise all I can see is a few feet beyond my outstretched arm, and I like to look far into the distance when I get the chance."

"But Mother didn't need eyeglasses," Faith said with a frown.

"True. In our family it's only thy grandfather and me. Now, thee, Faith?" I smiled at her, with her rosy cheeks and clear eyes. "Who will thee apprentice to? John Whittier, perhaps?"

"I don't know as yet. I'm not aspiring to write poetry." She frowned. "Perhaps the *Amesbury and Salisbury Villager* would let me write a news story now and again, or publish a serial." A dreamy look came into her eyes. "But I really want to write like Alcott. I want to write stories, novels that everyone will want to read. I wish she hadn't passed on last year. I wish I could meet her."

Luke burst into the room. "I'm hungry." He grabbed an apple from the wide wooden bowl in the pantry and took an enormous bite out of it.

"When is thee not hungry, beanpole?" Faith said. "We'll have supper in fifteen minutes. Run and wash up, and tell the rest to do the same."

Faith's more carefree life as a teenage girl had been snatched from her with my sister's passing, but she was doing an admirable job of mothering her younger siblings and being a responsible worker while still managing to enjoy her own life as much as possible. And, of course, there were plenty of girls of seventeen who were already married and mothers of babes in arms. The ambition of both Annie and Faith to be more than that pleased me, as I knew it would have Harriet. Being a mill worker hadn't been her career of choice, but I knew she'd been saving what money she could so she might follow her dream of being a horticulturist. Poor Harriet had left me that small nest egg wrapped in a handkerchief. I was saving it for an emergency, since I had already followed my own dream.

Luke ran into the house as we all sat eating our porridge the next morning. He'd been out getting Frederick's horse ready for the two of them to ride to the Academy. One of the blessings of Frederick's position was that his older children could attend classes free of the cost of tuition, so these days Luke rode to school behind Frederick on the family horse. As Faith had done before my sister's passing.

Betsy picked at her breakfast, more interested in playing with her little straw doll than eating. Matthew and Mark bickered quietly about the rules to a new game they had made up.

Luke stood in the doorway. His face was pale, his eyebrows drawn together.

"Come in, Luke, and shut the door," Frederick said. "Thee is letting the cold in. Now, what's this face?"

Luke shut the door. "Terrible news! I heard some men across the fence in the factory yard," he choked out. "Thomas Parry was killed."

Faith brought her hand to her mouth. Frederick's square face turned stern. I narrowed my eyes. Everything seemed to revolve around the Parry family this week.

"That is tragic news. Did they say how or when?" I asked.

"Sometime in the night. He was stabbed." His mouth turned down. "To death."

Faith held out an arm. "Come here, Luke. This is indeed terrible news."

Luke hurried to his sister's side and let himself be embraced. The children were all still so affected by Harriet's demise that any new death was a reminder of their own loss. I wished Frederick had been the one to comfort Luke, but that was not his habit.

"What does stabbed mean?" Betsy asked, kicking her chair with her feet.

Mark opened his mouth to answer.

I held up a hand to Mark. "It means he was hurt, Betsy." I said.

"But to death means he died," Mark said. "Like Mother." His eyes filled.

"And like Isaiah." Matthew laid his head on his arms, the sound of his weeping filling all our hearts. Mark put his arms around his twin and Betsy watched them with wide eyes, her hands stroking her doll.

"Our town has seen too much violence this week," I said. "Let us take a moment, all of us, to hold Thomas Parry's soul in the Light, and that of anyone who cannot find a peaceful way in which to live."

Frederick pursed his lips. Perhaps I should have waited for him to call for a moment of grace, but in my experience I would have waited a goodly long time, and the children needed the comfort of silence now. He finally joined the rest of the family members as they closed their eyes and fell silent, Matthew's sobs quieting, Betsy's feet stilling. I joined them, but my mind was not so still. Thomas Parry dead. William's son murdered. Who would kill him? It had to be connected with the arson of the factory. I prayed it wasn't a revengeful act by Ephraim Pickard.

After Frederick cleared his throat, his signal that the time of prayer was complete, I stood. "Now, there's still school in your day," I said to the children. "Let's get you ready, shall we?" I bustled the three youngest into the next room to don their coats and make sure their shoes were properly laced up.

When the children were ready, I led the way back into the kitchen. Faith was preparing the lunch pails, speaking in a soft voice to Luke, who helped her. Frederick must have gone out to bring the horse around, a gelding Betsy had named Star. I pulled on my cloak and clattered down the back steps. Frederick stood at the fence holding Star's reins and talking with a man from the factory. When I joined them, Frederick shook his head.

"Not much more information than Luke told us, Rose."

The man tipped his hat and greeted me.

"Who did thee hear it from, the news of Thomas Parry's death?" I asked him. I stroked Star's soft nose.

"Well, miss," the man said, "it was my sister who works up to Haverhill. She was on her way to catch the Ellis trolley when she met the Parrys' kitchen girl going out for fresh milk at dawn. That household is all a flurry. My sister came back right quick to tell us about it."

"We thank thee," Frederick said. He turned back to the house and I followed. "We must be off to school, Luke and I. This is a sad and serious turn in events, though." He shook his head.

"I'll see thee tonight. I might venture to the Parry home to make sure Lillian isn't too distraught." And to see what else I could learn about this serious turn of events, I added to myself.

I arrived at the stately Parry home on Hillside Street. The large house, almost a mansion, which had been built only a few years before, featured all the latest styles in the homes of the financially comfortable: the hexagonal corner room with its own pointed hat of a roof, elaborate shingling, various slants to the other portions of roof, large rooms, and the covered porch that wrapped around three sides of the home ending in a portico.

Kevin Donovan rushed down the stairs of the wide veranda. He halted when he saw me walking up the path from the street.

"Miss Carroll, what are you doing here?" He folded his arms across his chest.

"I heard the news. It's so very sad. Has thee learned who killed poor Thomas?"

"Now, I know I asked you to keep your eyes and ears out about the case of arson, but I can't be talking about a murder case with you. I repeat, what are you doing here?"

"I'm Lillian Parry's midwife. I came to make sure she isn't suffering from distress." I looked him straight in the eye.

He snorted. "If I didn't know better, I'd say it was more a case of her doing a happy jig now Thomas is gone. For all I know she stabbed the young man herself, just to be rid of him. It's no secret they hated each other. And many others in town didn't like him, either."

"She did once mention Thomas didn't

care much for her. Did thee speak with William, too?" I asked.

"His grief is relentless, poor man. Who wouldn't drown in sorrow, losing his only son? I regretted having to question him at such a time, but a case of murder demands it."

I nodded. "Indeed."

"Aye. Well, I'm off to speak with that Eph—" He cleared his throat. "With a possible suspect."

"Does thee mean Ephraim Pickard? Oh, no. I'm sure he wouldn't kill a soul."

Kevin sighed. "You were the one who told me about him, and that Thomas Parry fired him. That he had soot on his shirt. Maybe the fire wasn't enough, because Thomas survived it. Maybe Ephraim did him in. What do you think of that idea?"

I shook my head and pulled my cloak closer about me. "I don't believe it. Does thee have evidence? Does thee have the knife, the murder weapon?"

"How do you know about that?" His tone grew even more exasperated.

"I don't." I shrugged. "Thee said he was stabbed. I assumed it was with a knife. Was it something else?"

"Miss Carroll. Rose! Leave off these conjectures. Get in and see your patient. I'll do the police work around here. Do you understand?" He pointed to the front door with his arm extended.

I understood that all of a sudden he didn't want my help, after all. "Thee needn't be so harsh with me. Good luck in thy investigation." I walked up the stairs.

Kevin climbed into the police wagon waiting at the edge of the wide street. He glanced at me and shook his finger before signaling the waiting officer to drive off. I waved at him, then tapped the heavy door rapper shaped like a carriage wheel. If I uncovered a piece of information, that would only help him in his job, wouldn't it? I wasn't sure why I was so driven to discover the truth, but I knew that drive was part of who I was and always had been.

The house maid pulled the door open. Her white cap sat askew and her apron sat a little off kilter, as well. I had met her on my initial visit to Lillian.

"Oh, Miss Carroll. It's a dreadful day. Just dreadful." She ushered me into the elegant foyer and shut the entry door behind me. Both the door to the parlor on my left and the door to the library on my right were closed. I removed my cloak and bonnet and handed them to her.

"I came as soon as I heard the news. How

is Lillian taking it? And William?"

"Mr. Parry is beside himself. He treasured that boy so. He's locked himself in the library there. He let the policeman come in, but that's all. He won't even take a cup of coffee or his breakfast. The missus is upstairs in her bed, still."

She made as if to show me up, but I stopped her. "I know the way. Thee has other tasks this morning, I'm certain." I had made one home visit early in the pregnancy, so I'd know where the birth chamber would be and to ascertain it would be suitable. Hardly an issue with a rich family like this one, but it was part of my practice, and I carried it out for every client.

She thanked me and hurried off to the back of the house. I climbed the gentle curving stairs stretching the width of two arm spans. The dark wood of the railing gleamed from polish and contrasted with the lighter wood of the balusters. A tall arched window marked the landing, but the cloudy day let in little light. I continued up to the second floor and turned left into the hallway toward Lillian's rooms at the end. I tapped lightly on her door.

"Lillian, it's Rose Carroll. May I come in?" I heard nothing but turned the knob anyway. I poked my head into the room.

164

The tall drapes were still drawn and a gas light shone above the bed. Lillian sat up amid a half dozen pillows and cushions reading a letter with a small smile of satisfaction on her face. Her hair looked remarkably well arranged for one still abed. A breakfast tray sat on the small table next to her.

"Lillian?" I said again.

She glanced up and whisked the letter under the puffy coverlet. Her expression transformed into one of pain.

"Oh, Rose, I'm so glad you came." She patted the bed next to her. "You heard our tragic news? Poor dear Thomas has met an early demise."

I sat next to her. "Thee must be grieving for thy stepson."

She nodded gravely, although her eyes were dry. "And for William. It has hit him hard, I'm afraid. That policeman, a Donovary —"

"Donovan. Kevin Donovan. He's the detective looking into the arson, too."

"Yes, yes." She waved a hand. "He came at first light to tell us. William received him and then came wailing up the stairs to tell me. Wailing, I tell you. A grown man."

"Thomas was his firstborn, and his son," I said. "Anyone would so mourn, as I'm sure thee is for thy stepson. How is thee feeling physically? Has thee noticed any change in the baby's activity?"

"No. Why should there be?" She shrugged, as if a member of her household hadn't just died by violent means.

"I'm glad. Sometimes a stressful event can cause the body to react. I'd like to do a quick examination, only to be sure you both are well. May I?"

"If you'd like."

I drew out the Pinard horn and checked the baby's heartbeat. It was strong and regular. I palpated the baby and got a little kick into my hand for my efforts. No change in position from last week. I monitored Lillian's pulse for half a minute and listened to her heart, as well.

"You both seem perfectly healthy. And thee doesn't seem to need a calming tonic, of which I'm glad."

"Would you look in on William before you go?" Lillian asked. "If he'll let you? He's the one who might need a tonic."

"There's no reason not to go down and speak with him, thyself, Lillian. Doesn't thee want to?"

"I will, by and by. I have also sent for Robert Clarke. They're close friends, and perhaps Robert can comfort my husband. But will you, please, see if you can calm William a bit?"

"I shall. Please accept my sympathies for losing Thomas."

Lillian tossed her head ever so slightly. "It's really William you should be saying that to, Rose. In truth, Thomas didn't like me and I didn't like him. His death doesn't change that."

I nodded as I rose. I thought as much. I bade her good-bye and made my way slowly down the staircase. As I did, a tall, slender young man burst through the door from the outside and rushed up the stairs toward me, a shock of light hair falling in his eyes. When he saw me, he slowed. He brought his hand to his brow and gave me a mock salute with a single raised eyebrow. I was about to greet him when he clattered on past me. I watched him go, realizing he must be the man Lillian had gotten into the carriage with after her visit to my office. A relative, most likely, possibly a younger brother.

At the library door I knocked.

"Don't want any," William's voice barked.

"William Parry, it's me, Rose Carroll. The midwife."

"Wife's upstairs," he said in a gravelly voice.

"Yes, I just saw her. May I come in? She

asked me to check on thee."

Silence. I waited. "Please?"

At last the knob turned. He opened the door and stood before me. His face had lost the flushed look of a man who indulges in rich foods and fine liquors without benefit of fresh air and exercise. Now his skin was pale and his eyes devoid of light.

I held out my hand. "I want to express all my sympathy for the loss of thy son, William. I was truly sorry to hear the news." When he kept his own hands at his side, I dropped mine.

"Lillian is concerned for thy health," I went on. "I can bring thee a sedating tonic."

He sank into a large leather armchair, rubbing his brow with one hand. He gazed up at me. "I don't want to be sedated. I want to feel the same stabbing pain my boy felt. And I want to feel the rage when it replaces the millstone of sorrow that's within me. When they catch this person, I'm going to rip him apart with these hands." He held his hands up in front of him, turning them from side to side.

"I lost my own sister last year, mother to five children. I know that millstone well."

He looked into my eyes. "But this was my boy, Miss Carroll. He was my baby, then my little boy, and then my son, the man. I know he was a prickly type, but he didn't deserve to die. Not before me. And to be brutally murdered." His voice wobbled and he swallowed hard. "Please go." He sank his face into his hands and mumbled something I didn't catch.

"I will. Once again, please accept my sympathies. I hold you all in the Light."

I donned my outerwear and let myself out. As I walked away, a fine carriage pulled up and Robert Clarke stepped out. Perhaps he could comfort his friend. So much death in our town in so few days.

FIFTEEN

I walked slowly toward home, barely seeing my path. I had Genevieve's postpartum call to make and two clients to see this afternoon. But for now, my brain was full of possibilities about who could have stabbed Thomas Parry in the dark hours of the night, and my gait kept pace with the fullness of my thoughts. Kevin had joked Lillian might have killed her stepson. I thought that highly unlikely for several reasons, primary being that she was a typical upper-class young woman with no muscles in her arms to speak of. She never needed to work a busy loom, lift a hod of coal, or wrestle a calf out of its mother. She didn't knead bread or scrub laundry. That said, what if she so detested Thomas that she hired someone else to do him in? She'd been reading some kind of missive when I'd first entered the room, and had been smiling, not full of grief. I supposed that didn't necessarily make her a murderer or even a conspirator, especially when she was the first to admit she was not sad about Thomas's passing.

Ephraim was a logical choice for a suspect, but I didn't want him to be a killer. I prayed he was not. Maybe William had an enemy who chose to strike at him by killing his son. The same carriage business competitor who started the fire could have also killed Thomas, if that theory were correct. But Kevin had rightly pointed out Parry's factory wasn't the one to envy of the top three or four. That honor would belong to the Clarke factory, or perhaps Ned Bailey's establishment. I wished I'd asked Kevin where the murder had happened and who had discovered the body.

I longed to discuss all this with David and wondered where he was today, what he was doing. I smiled to myself, picturing him examining patients, smiling at them, reassuring them, explaining both their ailments and their treatments. He had a bedside manner much to be emulated. But in place of being able to talk through the murder with David, I suddenly realized where I might be able to learn more. In a town this size, I was sure that information was already running through all the gossip channels. I changed course slightly and headed down Main Street to Market Square and Sawyer's Mercantile. The busy general store was always an active source of news. Whether the details were accurate or not was a different matter.

Two minutes later I glanced in all directions and lifted my skirts slightly to cross the busy, muddy, manure-laden intersection where Main, Elm, Market, and High Streets meet. I entered the store, which sold all manner of goods. Thread. Awls. Cheese. Great coats. Sacks of flour. Toys. Ale.

Bolts of fabric lined one corner. Opposite were rows of horseshoes, brushes, and crops. Jars of candy sat on the front counter. Behind the register a glass-fronted cabinet held bottles of tonic and jars of liniment. Above the cabinet a poster proclaimed the corrective and invigorating powers of Hostetter's Celebrated Stomach Bitters. A woman was purchasing a length of cloth and sewing notions. A small boy pushed a toy truck back and forth on the floor behind her. A white-haired man and a taller one with almost no hair stood near the stove warming their hands and talking in low voices.

I waved to Catherine Toomey, the owner, where she stood behind the counter. She was a good-natured woman I had assisted in the birth of her twin daughters a few years earlier. I moved to the stove. Drawing off my gloves, I joined the men appreciating the slow steady warmth.

"Terrible news this morning, wasn't it?" I said, not looking directly at either of them. I wagered these two would be a rich lode of gossip to mine.

"Oh, certainly, miss," the taller one said. "May Thomas Parry rest in peace."

"It's a sad morning for his family," I murmured. "Have you heard who found him, and where?"

The slighter of the two men pursed his lips. "I won't want to be spreading gossip around, but I have heard you're a trustworthy type. Miss Carroll, the midwife, isn't it?"

I nodded and smiled with what I hoped was a trustworthy look.

"Well, it was O'Toole who reported it. Said he was on his way home from the pub when he stumbled across the body down near the lower falls, by where Wing Supply overlooks the river."

"Jotham O'Toole?" I asked.

"That's the one," the taller man said. "He ran up the hill to Market Square here yelling his fool head off. 'A body! A body!' he

173

was shouting. 'A man is dead!' " The man acted it out with great enthusiasm. "My son was on his own way home and he caught up O'Toole and asked him who the body was. 'Parry. Thomas Parry. He's been stabbed,' O'Toole told my boy. Then my son saw young Officer Gilbert driving by on the night patrol and hailed him. He sounded the alarm. And here we are. No more the wiser."

The other man shook his head. "Haven't caught the killer yet, not that I know of."

"I'm sure they will soon," I said.

"Parry had been taking a goodly amount of drink at the pub earlier on, I did hear," the tall one remarked. "And had himself some words with that Pickard fellow, the one what's always got his nose in a book."

Ephraim was involved, then.

"They had a drunken brawl outside, was what I was told," said the white-haired man.

"Have you heard what Thomas was stabbed with?" I asked, lowering my voice. "The murder weapon, so to speak?"

The slighter man gazed around, and then back at us. "They said 'twas a needle. A knittin' needle. One of them sharp ones." He pantomimed sliding a slender object up and under his own ribs.

"No," scoffed the taller one. "It was a cotter pin. See that one there?" He pointed at the wall of tools, fasteners, and the like. Several long pins with rings at one end and a sharp pointed end at the other hung from a hook. "That was the weapon. That would do the trick right nice." He narrowed his eyes at me. "What's your interest in all this, then, Miss Carroll? Don't let that detective know you've been asking so many questions, he'll say you've a been meddling."

"I'm a curious person, I suppose," I said with a little laugh as I pulled my gloves back on. "I must go," I said to the men. Each touched his forehead as if tipping his hat, if he had been wearing one instead of holding it in his hand. At the counter, I selected a piece of candy for each Bailey child, and then added several more, thinking of Orpha's great-granddaughters. Sometimes it was handy to have a few spares tucked away, just in case, a practice I had learned from Harriet. I paid at the register, exchanging a few words with Catherine. Crossing the intersection again, I headed down Water Street toward Genevieve LaChance's home in the Flats.

According to the gossip of the men in the store, who probably had no real information and were only conjecturing, the murder weapon wasn't a knife. They'd guessed a knitting needle, or perhaps a cotter pin. Either would do the job for someone who knew where to strike. How to avoid the ribs. Where the vital blood vessels lay. Or maybe the man's miming of a stab up into the heart was wrong. Perhaps Thomas's neck was fatally pierced and his life seeped out where he lay. Jotham O'Toole reported finding the body on his way home from the pub. After last call at the drinking establishment, I assumed, which set the time at about midnight. Thomas Parry, by all reports a difficult man, might easily have gotten into a brawl at the pub. But if the weapon was a knitting needle, that could mean the killer was a woman.

What would my sister think of this whole affair? She had been unfailingly loving to all she met and would have been horrified at the thought of murder right here in our town. But she also would have tried to understand the motivation of the killer, and would have been ready with as much forgiveness as possible. I missed her with a sharp dart to my heart.

I surely hadn't learned anything Kevin Donovan didn't already know, but I had expanded my own set of facts, including that it was Minnie O'Toole's brother who had found Thomas's body. After I checked in on Genevieve LaChance and her baby, I might detour over to Fruit Street and pay Minnie and her baby boy their own postpartum visit.

As I walked near the lower falls, I glanced to my right where the water rushed over sharp crags of boulders. I imagined what Thomas's death must have looked like: the dead man lying perhaps at an odd angle on the rocks, nearly tumbled into the rushing Powow itself, blood soaking his white collar like he'd dyed it red. I shuddered.

I climbed the outside steps to the LaChance flat to ascertain whether Genevieve and the baby were both healthy and thriving. I found the newly delivered mother scrubbing clothes out on the laundry porch only three days after the birth, the babe tied to her back with a wide strip of cloth. Genevieve's cheeks showed color and she moved with vigor. She slid the baby girl around to the front and invited me to sit.

I took the tiny girl onto my lap. After checking her, I asked, "And thee is recovering well?" I held the infant to my shoulder and patted her back. My Quaker sense of simplicity was nourished by this straightforward new being, who needed only her mother's milk and care to thrive.

"I am, of course. This body is made to grow and birth babies, isn't it? And that daughter of mine is a lusty nurser," she said, rising and pinning a small shirt to a clothesline.

"I'm glad to hear it. Thee holds a good attitude about thy body. I sometimes muse on women giving birth around the world and throughout all time. In darkest Africa, in the far East, in Europe — women are all alike. They carry their young, give birth to them, and then care for them. Speaking of young, how about thy boys?" I asked.

"My sons are adjusting to being big brothers. Although this one" — she gestured to the shirt — "can't quite understand he's no longer the baby." She laughed.

"And is thy husband getting used to the idea of a fourth child?"

She nodded with a quiet smile. "He realized he's going to have a little girl to dote on."

Half an hour later I was in Minnie's tiny flat. Minnie, five days postpartum, presented a picture in sharp contrast to Genevieve. Minnie wore nightclothes and her hair lay loose on her shoulder, although she was out of bed and sitting in a chair filing her nails in the dim light of curtained windows. The baby slept on a blanket in a bureau drawer resting on the bed. A glass of ale sat by Minnie's side, but neither Jotham nor the sister were in evidence. The air in the room smelled stale, like it hadn't been freshened in a long time.

I greeted her and pulled open the curtains on both windows. "How is thee?" I cracked open one window at the top.

She squinted at the light as she waved a lazy hand. "All right, I suppose. The baby doesn't let me sleep at night. I'm tired all the time."

"I recommend some fresh air. Take the babe for a walk outdoors. Thee needs to be up and around, Minnie, to restore thy health and to be able to produce plentiful milk for thy son."

"Oh, I suppose. But it takes so much energy to get up. And when little Billy wants to eat, well, he's very insistent."

"So thee has named him, then?" I stroked the baby's cheek. He opened his little mouth and turned it toward my fingers in the feeding reflex.

She gave me a sharp glance. "Yes. His name's Billy O'Toole. At least for now." She gave her head a defiant shake, as if to say, *And if you don't like it, too bad.*

"Has thy brother been by this morning?"

"Why do you ask?" Minnie's voice took

on a cagey tone.

"I've heard he had a very upsetting experience last night. Well, in the wee hours of this morning, to be accurate." I watched her.

"Oh, that. Yes, he came by and said he'd found Will — I mean, Mr. Parry's son Thomas dead by the river. It quite upset Jotham, it did."

"I should think so. Where is he now?"

"He has his own place." She furrowed her brow. "But I expect he's down at the police being questioned. He said they wanted to talk to him more. I hope they didn't think he killed poor Thomas. Jotham's got a hot head, but he always means well."

Little Billy began to stir. He whimpered several times and, when he was ignored, let out a cry surprisingly loud for such a newly minted person.

"Oh, hush, child." Minnie sounded impatient. She hoisted herself out of her chair and sank onto the bed. She drew him out of his makeshift cot and held him in the air in front of her. She cooed and murmured, but that only worked for a few moments before he commenced to howl again. She held him closer and sniffed.

"Oh, mother of God, would you smell that?" She laid him on the bed and unwrapped the cloth fastened around him, revealing a fine mess. She gazed up at me. "My sister Ida's been helping me. There's a basin of water in the kitchen and dry diapers on the line. I hope. Do you mind?"

I fetched the basin and a washing cloth, as well as two dry diapers. "Make sure thee dries him off well after thee cleans him," I said, handing her the cloths. "So he doesn't get a rash."

Minnie made an unpleasant face, but she managed to get her baby clean, dry, and wrapped up again, and her own hands cleaned, even as he continued to yell.

"He's got a good set of lungs," I said. "Give him the breast and he'll quiet soon enough." I carried the soiled items out and dumped them in a bucket of water and soap that sat at the ready, surely of the sister's doing. Minnie didn't seem like the practical sort, but she'd learn. She'd have to.

I returned to the bedroom. She sat propped up by pillows with her left breast exposed and a hungry baby latched onto it. She glanced up and sighed.

"Motherhood. It's not all nature and instinct, is it?" Her tone was resigned.

"Not entirely, no. But thee is doing a good job of it." I brought her the glass of ale. "The two of you will learn together. Keep listening to little Billy there, and to thy own heart."

The outer door slammed and shattered our domestic calm.

"That bloody copper. Can't stop asking me questions!" Jotham stormed into the bedroom.

Minnie grabbed her shawl and drew it hurriedly over the baby and her exposed breast.

Jotham stopped short when he saw me. "Oh, Miss Carroll. I didn't know you were here." He took a deep breath and the red ire in his face began to drain away.

"Is thee speaking of the detective?" I asked.

"That's him. Donovan," Jotham spat. "Bloody hell."

"Brother, I'll ask you to watch your language," Minnie said. "There's a lady and a baby in the room."

Jotham glared at his sister for a moment as if he longed to refute what she said, but he kept his mouth shut.

"Has thy sister gone home, Minnie?" I asked.

Jotham muttered something under his breath and turned away, fidgeting with his hat.

"Yes," Minnie said. "She has her own

babes to look after. But she'll be bringing dinner by."

"Excellent. I'll take my leave, then. Bring Billy by for a checkup in two weeks' time. And get thyself up and out of the house. It will do you both good." I faced Jotham. "Might I have a word with thee?"

He raised his eyebrows but followed me out of the room.

"I understand thee found Thomas Parry dead. That must have been a terrible shock."

He pulled his brows together and pursed his lips, nodding. "Yes, yes. A terrible shock." He shook his head. "Never found a dead man before. Stabbed to death."

"That was what I heard. Was the weapon at hand?"

"I didn't see it about."

"Where was he attacked?"

"Down beyond Wing's Carriage Supplies. By the lower falls. The water makes such a noise, I expect no one heard him cry out."

"I actually meant to ask where on his body was he stabbed? Thee must have seen a great deal of blood."

"What, now you're interrogating me, too? You in cahoots with Detective Donovan or something?" His face began to redden again.

"Calm thyself. Thee needn't answer if thee doesn't care to. And no, I'm simply curious.

I'm a midwife. I don't work for the police." My curiosity about the murder had nothing to do with Kevin's investigation, since he had explicitly instructed me to keep out of it. Although if I learned something, I would share it with Kevin immediately, of course.

"All right, then. It was in his neck where he was killed. But the blood wasn't fresh when I found him. Sort of dried up." His tone was matter of fact.

"I wonder who had cause to murder Thomas." I busied myself with the handle of my bag.

He shrugged. "Not my job to find out."

"Oh, Jotham," Minnie called, "can you take your nephew for a minute?"

"Nice talking with you, Miss Carroll." He rolled his eyes. "Now I'm the nanny-uncle." I spied a smile before he turned back to the bedroom.

I let myself out and walked the few blocks home under a leaden sky. So Thomas was stabbed in the neck. Jotham said he hadn't seen the murder weapon. Perhaps the killer tossed it into the falls, or carried it away to bury or hide. How would Kevin solve the case? I found the idea of accumulating evidence and solving clues intriguing. But that was his job, not mine. I had a full practice and there was no shortage of new pregnancies in town. Unless I did something egregiously wrong, I was assured of steady employment for as long as I wanted it. And if I didn't pick up my step, I'd be late for my next client, who was due at my office any minute now.

After my last client left at two o'clock, I drew several jars of dried herbs off the high shelf in my office and brought them to the kitchen table. Carefully spreading out a clean white tea towel, I measured out portions of Saint John's wort and chamomile, with smaller parts of peppermint and licorice, according to Orpha's directions. I didn't have any star anise, unfortunately. I rubbed the dried leaves together between my palms, crumbling them to make an even-textured tea, then poured it all into a clean Ball jar. I hoped it would help to stabilize Nell Gilbert's mood and lighten her spirits. I'd ask Josephine to make sure Nell drank a cup of it several times a day.

After I stowed the herbs back in the parlor and tucked the jar into my bag, I opened the side door to set out for the Gilbert house. Instead I spied Kevin Donovan walking up the path as the church bells in town tolled three times. Why was he here again?

To ask for my help with the murder, after all?

I beckoned to him. "Kevin, I am at the side here."

He glanced up with a start then made his way toward me. He stood at the bottom of the stairs, tapping his hand on his leg, squinting at the afternoon sunlight reflecting off a window across the road.

"Has there been a development in the case?" I asked. I walked down to stand next to him.

"Indeed, Miss Carroll, there has." He removed his hat and clutched it in both hands.

I clasped my hands in front of me and waited.

"I'm holding Ephraim Pickard on suspicion for Thomas Parry's murder and for the factory arson, as well. I thought you might want to know." He tucked his hat under his arm and rubbed his hands together. "We've got our man."

"Oh, gracious." Sadness crept through me. "Is thee sure? What is the evidence against him?"

"A witness came forward and placed him at the site of the murder at the correct time."

"Who is the witness?"

Kevin frowned. "That's for the police to

know. I had a thought the killer might have been someone else, but the witness account changed that. We have also learned that earlier in the evening Pickard argued in the tavern with the victim. And you, as well, said you saw someone limping right before the fire was set on Carriage Hill. Pickard limps from an old injury."

"I told thee I didn't see the person clearly." I shook my head. "It was only a shape, nothing more. And doesn't thee need evidence?"

He cleared his throat. "We're still searching for the Parry murder weapon. But I have no doubt it will be found. No doubt at all."

"I heard conflicting stories at the mercantile about the stabbing. Can thee now share with me the method of death?"

"I guess it won't hurt to tell you. The news will be about town before long, anyway. It was some thin, sharp object to the neck. That's all we know." He threw his hands open.

"Was Thomas drunk? The gossips at the mercantile said he was, and had been brawling outside."

"The autopsy hasn't been completed yet, but my officers did detect quite the smell of alcohol on him, it's true. Still isn't cause for someone to kill him."

"That isn't what I meant. I simply wondered how the killer got close enough to stab a grown man in the neck. Ephraim sheds no light on the subject?"

"He claims he's innocent, of course. Don't they all?"

Sixteen

After I delivered the herbal mixture to Nell's mother-in-law, I spent the end of the day worrying about Ephraim, to no avail. The Bailey family and I had just finished eating supper when a driver arrived in the Parry carriage. I answered the door and the driver handed me a note. I opened it to read that Lillian Parry was experiencing pains and asked that I come right away. I grabbed my satchel and cloak and ran to the conveyance. The murder must have affected Lillian more than she had let on in the morning. I closed my eyes and held her in the Light of God as we drove. A baby exiting the womb so early would likely not survive. I prayed the pains were only false labor brought on by the terrible news.

For the second time that day, I trudged up the steps of the Parry home. The maid opened the door before I could knock, her eyes wide.

"It must be the shock. She says she's having pains. Please go up, Miss Carroll."

With the doors to the library and parlor still closed, I put away my thoughts of greeting William and hurried up the stairs. I composed myself in the hall for a moment before walking quietly into her bedroom.

William sat in a chair by Lillian's side holding her hand in both of his. She moaned once and then was quiet, her eyes shut. When I cleared my throat, William turned his head and rose.

"Miss Carroll, thank you for coming. Is she having the baby?" His eyes were anguished. "It's too soon, isn't it?"

I touched his arm. "Let me examine her, William. It's common to have a semblance of labor pains at this stage. Don't worry yet," I said. I didn't need him more upset than he already was.

"If I were to lose her, too, I don't know what I'd do." He wrung his hands over and over. "Should we call Mr. Douglass? Or don't you have a doctor friend we can consult with?"

"I'm sure that won't be necessary, but, yes, my friend David Dodge will consult with me if I ask him to. Please leave us for a few minutes. I'll call thee as soon as I finish checking her." I'd welcome a chance to see

David, since it had been two days since the tea with his parents, but under happy social circumstances, of course, rather than with a difficult client.

William cast a glance at Lillian but she kept her eyes closed, and he left the room. I shut the door after him, then I drew out my listening tube and moved to her side.

"Lillian, it's Rose. Can thee open thine eyes and tell me what thee is feeling?" I took William's place in the chair, pulling it closer to the bed. "Lillian?"

She peered under heavy lids at me and then pulled herself up to sitting. "Oh, Rose. My back hurts. And I feel a pressure down there."

"How often are the pains?"

"They're not regular. It feels like a big cramp, you know, like when I used to have my monthly. Except worse."

"If they're not regular, that's good. The labor of childbirth comes along like clock-work. I'll take a listen." I pulled down the coverlet and bent over her belly. The baby's heartbeat was strong, as it had been all along.

I glanced up. "I'm going to check thee inside. I don't believe we've done this before. My hand will go inside the passage, and I'm going to feel the opening to the womb. If thee feels any discomfort, try to breathe down into my hand. It sounds odd, but it works." Despite not being taught about instructing women to breathe down into pain, I had found it helped them, and I now made counseling women in this method part of my practice.

She nodded.

"Raise thy knees up and separate them." I pushed up my sleeve and found my way to her cervical opening, the *os*. She gasped a little as I felt it, but the opening was closed nearly as tightly as a nonpregnant woman's. I drew my hand out and wiped it clean.

"I think thee is fine. Sometimes women have what we call practice pains. It's the body getting ready to give birth. But these pains aren't doing any work at all. Thy baby is safe inside to grow as big as he needs to be before entering our world."

Lillian leaned back, straightening her legs with a smile of relief. "But what can I do to stop having the pains?"

"Nothing, really. But thee will feel better by getting out of bed and moving around. Get dressed, move about. William needs thee at this time. And surely there will be callers tomorrow to express their sympathies about Thomas. Thee must be ready for them."

"William seemed like his old self just now. He was so sweet to me, and he seemed so afraid I would die, too." She bit her lip and her eyes filled. "He hasn't been that way toward me for months. Since . . . well, never mind. I should be grateful he still cares for me."

"Of course he does." It seemed to be true. The loss of someone close often made the survivor better appreciate those still living. I patted her hand. "Now, how about getting up and sitting in that chair? Put on a pretty house coat, brush thy hair, and I'll call him back up here. Perhaps the two of you can have a bite to eat. He needs thy help in his own sorrow."

"But what if I get another pain?" Lillian swung her legs over the side of the bed.

"Breathe down into it. It will pass. If thee tightens up from fear, it will be worse." I bade her farewell and made my way down the stairs. William stood in the door to the library, his face a mask of fear.

"Lillian is fine, William. She's completely well and so is the baby. Her body is simply rehearsing for the birth. It's nothing to worry about." I smiled at him.

His expression changed like a wave cresting into sunlight. "Truly? Oh, thank God."

"Go on up and sit with her. I'll have the

maid bring you both some supper."

"And thank you, Rose Carroll." He reached out and embraced me quickly, then stepped back. "Forgive me. I'm not myself. But I am grateful."

"Get thee on upstairs, now." I made a shooing motion until he trotted up the stairs. I shook my head in wonder at the complexity of humans. I had done almost nothing to cause such intense gratitude, only a simple visit and some commonsense advice. Now, where was that maid, anyway?

The Baileys departed for school and work the next morning: Frederick and Luke on Star heading to the Academy, the twins walking and Betsy skipping to the Whittier grammar school a block over, and Faith trudging down the hill to Hamilton Mill.

I had no impending births that I knew of, and no clients scheduled until the afternoon. Taking up one of the recently developed fountain pens, a gift from my father, I sat at my desk writing a letter to my parents, glad I didn't have to pause every line to re-ink the pen. I wrote of the news of the fires and of Thomas Parry's murder but told them a suspect had already been apprehended. Whether I thought Ephraim was the guilty person or not didn't belong in a letter. I paused for a moment. Maybe it had been an error for me to tell Kevin about the smudge on Ephraim's shirt. It was too late to take it back.

Returning to my letter, I included a few funny stories about their grandchildren and urged them to come for a visit before too long. It was hard for Father to find someone to mind his farm animals for a few days, and Mother was always so busy with her work for women's suffrage. Still, the children were growing up fast. The four youngest ones had been invited to the farm for the summer months, though, and that season wasn't so far off now. I was sure Faith would like to leave the city, too, but she had already said she wouldn't quit her position at the mill. She'd had to grow up fast after her mother's death. While I pined for Harriet, I knew the impact of her death on her children had been far greater.

I gazed around the room and smiled at the sunlight burnishing the wide pine floorboards. It promised to be a lovely day, now that yesterday's glowering clouds had blown away overnight. When I'd seen the children out the door a few minutes earlier, the air smelled fresh and was already warming. That would certainly encourage the trees to release their tightly furled baby leaves.

A movement in the street caught my eye. The police wagon pulled up in front of the house. Did Kevin have another revelation to share with me? I hoped it was news he had found the true killer and released Ephraim. As I watched, Guy Gilbert climbed out instead and ascended the front steps. I went to the door as he began to knock.

"Guy, what brings thee here? Will thee come in?"

The young man straightened his spine and clasped his hands behind him. He didn't remove his hat. "Miss Rose Carroll, I'm to bring you in for questioning in the matter of Thomas Parry's murder. Please get your cloak and hat." A thin line ran down his left cheek, like a scratch that was healing.

"What?" I stared at him. "What might I have to add on that matter? I didn't see the poor man killed. I know nothing of his assailant."

"Miss Carroll, please get your things." He kept his head high, but wrinkled his forehead and spread his hands. "I'm not to tell you why. I'm to bring you to the station with all due dispatch."

I nodded slowly, my insides turning to ice.

This was serious. "Give me a minute. I'll be right there." I fetched my bonnet and cloak even as I puzzled at the reason for this summons. I closed the door behind me and followed him down to the wagon, my sunny mood dissipated in an instant.

"You can ride up front with me." Guy extended a hand to help me up, then went around and climbed in.

Five minutes later I sat alone in a room in the station. How long would I have to wait? I rued not bringing my knitting to both pass the time and calm my jitters. Guy hadn't said a word as we drove, despite my questions to him. A folio of paper and a pen lay on the table across from me.

A somber Kevin Donovan entered the interview room. He carried a slender packet a foot long wrapped in cloth and set it on the table between us.

"Greetings, Kevin. What is the occasion for this interview?" I tried to smile, but a tic beat in my upper lip. "Have I been murdering people in my sleep?"

He frowned at me and rapped the table with his fingers as if playing the same notes on a piano over and over. He opened his mouth and then shut it again. He did it another time. He glanced at his package on the table and back at me, then finally spoke.

"When was the last time you knitted something, Miss Carroll?"

"When I knitted something?" I stared at him as if he were speaking a foreign language. "Why is thee asking me that?"

"We've found the object used to kill young Parry." He watched me closely.

"Wonderful news. I still don't understand why I'm here, though." I raised my eyebrows.

He heaved a deep sigh, one that sounded wrenched out of him. He unwrapped his package, presenting me with a long thin knitting needle. One of my own. I stared. How could this be?

He sat back. The pointed end of the needle was tinged with rust that ran halfway up the length, and it looked sharper than was customary.

I gazed at him and then back at the needle. I took a deep breath in to calm myself. "That isn't rust, is it? That's dried blood." A shiver rippled through me.

"Correct. Is that your knitting needle, Rose Carroll?"

"Yes. It's one of a pair my mother painted for me as a birthday present." I closed my mouth and sat with my hands clenched in my lap. This was the murder weapon. My own cherished knitting needle, used as an instrument of death to end Thomas Parry's life. This was too awful to contemplate. But I had to. I forced myself to unclench my hands.

Kevin regarding me sat in silence, as well. I'd read of this tactic in a serial novel, this silent treatment that was usually effective to prod guilty parties to talk. But I was a Quaker. I'd had a lifetime of sitting in silence. And I was guilty of nothing.

With an exasperated sound, he spoke at last. "As you might surmise, this long sharp object was the weapon of death less than two days ago. We located it on the bank near the lower falls where Parry was killed."

"Does thee suspect me of murder?" I folded my arms across my chest.

"No, of course not. But how in the devil's name did this needle get from your blasted knitting bag, or wherever it resides, to Parry's neck?" His voice rose. "Did you bring your bloody knitting when you visited Ephraim Pickard at his home, as you said you did?"

"Thee need not speak of the devil, Kevin, or use offensive language." I kept my voice level.

He let out a big sigh. "I apologize, Miss Rose. I admit to much frustration with the case. Will you please answer the question?"

"I didn't carry my satchel to the Pickards. I brought only some foodstuffs to them."

"So there is no way Ephraim might have stolen the needle? Found it lying about?"

"I can't see how he could."

"A local gent reported you were asking questions about the murder weapon down at the mercantile. Didn't I tell you to keep out of this investigation?"

"Yes. I have every right to be curious about a public event, though. How did thee learn the needle was mine, anyway?"

"It was actually Gilbert who recognized it. He said he'd seen you knitting during his wife's long labor with their daughter last year, and his wife told him of your fancy painted needles. RMC are your initials, correct?"

I nodded. "I remember knitting as Nell labored. I'd been working on a scarf to keep Luke's neck warm on the ride to school." I peered more closely at the needle but didn't touch it. "It looks sharpened. Knitting needles are pointed but not sharp at all or they would split the yarn."

"I'll consider that information, thank you." Kevin cocked his head. "Tell me, what name does the M signify?"

"Margaret. Mother wanted to honor the lady authors of New England. She's very big on women's rights. So my late older sister was named Harriet —"

"Harriet Beecher Stowe?"

"Yes. And Margaret is for Margaret Fuller, who was the editor of Mr. Emerson's journal *The Dial* and also wrote for it. But Father wanted me to be called Rose, so Margaret had to take second place as my middle name." I realized I was babbling on from nerves and closed my mouth.

Kevin examined his hands. He glanced up with a wry smile. "I'll tell you, I have never before discussed literature in this room." He sighed again. "But to get back to business. I suppose you take your knitting every time you attend a birth."

"I'm afraid so. It helps to pass the time."

"When was the last time you can recall using this particular pair?"

I ticked through the last week in my head. "I don't think I have done any knitting for several days."

"When was the last time?" he repeated, sounding irritated.

"I believe it was last Sixth Day evening. Yes, I was working on Betsy's sweater."

He rolled his eyes. "What do you mean, Sixth Day?"

"What most call Friday. Friends choose not to honor ancient deities with the names of the days of the week."

He let out an exasperated breath, then leaned forward. "And where were you on Friday evening?"

"Why, I was at home. With the Bailey family."

He pressed his eyes shut for a moment and then slumped back in his chair. "So the needles have been safe at home for five days now?"

"No, of course not. I keep them with the yarn in my birthing satchel. Which I carry nearly every time I go out. Except for this morning, obviously."

That caused him to sit up straight again. "I need you to tell me every single place you've been between Friday night, or whatever you want to call it, until now. Every place you've toted your bag of tricks along to." He reached over and pulled a cord hanging out of the wall near the door.

A bell rang faintly somewhere else in the building, and a few seconds later Guy popped his head into the room.

"Need something, Detective?"

"Come in and scribe. My writing can barely be read, even by myself." Kevin glanced at me. "Thank goodness for younger officers with a legible script."

After Guy sat and lifted the pen, I relayed

my whereabouts since Seventh Day morning. I spoke slowly, to keep pace with his scribing.

"Let's see. I visited Genevieve LaChance and then Minnie O'Toole on Seventh Day morning, carrying my satchel to both homes. Seventh Day afternoon was the memorial service, where I saw thee, Kevin, and I didn't bring my satchel along to there. First Day is a day of rest, well, if surprising an arsonist can be called restful. I went to tea with David Dodge at the invitation of his mother in Newburyport. I was called to a birth in the evening and of course I went. I delivered Patience Henderson of a little boy late that night. In the early morning of Second Day, in truth."

I waited for Guy to finish noting my whereabouts so far. He bent his head low over the paper and his tongue stuck out of the corner of his mouth like a child's.

"On Second Day afternoon I visited John Whittier, came here, and then took my satchel to visit thy very wife, Guy. While I was out I paid a call on Orpha Perkins afterwards."

Guy raised his head. His eyes displayed alarm.

"Write it down, Gilbert," Kevin demanded.

Guy bent to his task again.

When he was done, I went on. "Yesterday morning I checked in on Lillian Parry, Kevin, as thee well knows"

Kevin waved his hand. "Thomas was killed Monday night. Or in the wee hours of Tuesday morning. I don't care where you carried the bag yesterday." He rapped his fingers on the table. I supposed it helped him think, but the habit irritated me.

"So you didn't cart this satchel of yours to the Pickard house?" he asked. "Ephraim himself wasn't near it?"

"No, and no."

"That doesn't rule out somebody handing him the needle, though. He'll stay behind bars until we get to the bottom of this." He nodded at Guy. "Thank you, Gilbert. You can leave the notes here. I'll make sure it gets into the Parry file. That will be all."

Guy rose. At the door, he shot me a look, eyes wide, forehead furrowed. I couldn't interpret it. Resignation? Despair? A call for help?

Kevin tapped the table again as he studied the notes. "Never heard of this LaChance woman, or Henderson, either. O'Toole I know of."

"Minnie O'Toole's a brand-new mother," I said. "She's not left the house yet since giving birth, I don't believe." He must have made the connection between Minnie and William Parry.

"It was her brother Jotham who reported the body," Kevin said. "Gilbert's wife, well, she's a bit strange in the head lately. But I know of no cause she'd have to stab a man in the neck in the middle of the night. What about Perkins? I heard she's some variety of witch."

"What? Thee must be toying with me. She's my esteemed teacher and a very dear friend." I knew of the rumors that Orpha Perkins had helped a young woman or two safely relieve themselves of an unwanted pregnancy early on in their term, and I did not find issue with it. "Besides, she's in her eighties and much too frail to be traipsing about in the dark on her own. But most important, her life's work has been in bringing forth life. She'd never kill a man."

"Well, I'm no further ahead than when you walked in that door, Rose Carroll." Frustration etched lines into his face. He stood. "There's nothing for it but to keep on looking. I probably should search this satchel of yours at some point. When the killer stole your needle, he might have dropped something in there. A button, or who knows what."

"I don't mind it being searched. I wish thee luck. I want to know who stole the needle and killed Thomas as much as thee does."

"Luck might help. More likely it'll be hard work that does it. Now, I'm sorry if I alarmed you by having Gilbert bring you in," he said. "I had to follow procedure, you understand. The chief is breathing his dragon breath down my neck. The carriage factory owners want answers. William Parry hungers to find his son's murderer."

"I understand." I also stood.

"Do you want this needle back when we're done with it?"

I set both hands on the table and stared at him. "I don't think I do. I have others, of course, but none so special as this pair my mother painted for me as a gift when I left home. But knitting with a murder weapon?" I shuddered. "No."

Kevin peered closely at the flowers and initials before wrapping the needle up in the cloth again. "That's very close work, I admit. And quite artistic. A pity what was done with it."

SEVENTEEN

When I returned home from the station, I was drained from the experience of my jailhouse interview and from learning that my mother's gift to me had become an instrument of evil. The day had become even lovelier than it was earlier, with a gentle sun and an even gentler breeze. But it brought me no joy. In the morning mail, though, was something that did bring a smile to my lips: a letter in David's nearly illegible script. At least the post office had been able to decipher my address. That we still had a morning post after the fire was also an occasion for gratitude. Bertie and the Salisbury postmaster must have worked out a deal. I settled into the rocking chair with the missive and slit it open.

Dearest Rosie,
It was a delight to spend time with you this past weekend. It makes me greedy

for even more of your hours and sweet attention. May I have the pleasure of your company at a dinner dance this Saturday? Mother desperately wants me to attend and I can think of no one I want to escort except you. Please respond at your earliest convenience.

Your faithful admirer,
David

My joy at hearing from David in such a sweet manner was tempered by the actual invitation. A dinner dance? My heart sank. Sooner or later David would have to face the fact that he and I were simply not of the same social class. I had no frock suitable for such an occasion, and no real desire to acquire one, not to mention that party frocks weren't exactly in line with the manner of Friends. But as much as I cared for David, I had no doubt my good dress wouldn't be good enough for a society soirée. Beyond my attire, there was also the question of dancing, which was generally frowned upon among Friends.

I walked with a firm stride up the steps to Friend Whittier's home an hour later, letter in hand, hoping I was early enough not to interrupt John's midday dinner. I needed to get back for my one o'clock client, but I also wished for his counsel. I vowed to ask our elder which path he thought I should choose. I knocked and was grateful John answered it himself instead of Mrs. Cate.

"Friend Rose. Do come in."

"Does thee have a free moment?"

"Of course." He stepped aside and ushered me into his study. Sitting, he tented his hands. "Something bothers thee."

I nodded, taking a chair. "Indeed. I'm presented with a conundrum and wonder how to follow both my heart and my faith."

"Ah. Shall we hold this puzzle, whatever it might be, in the Light of God for a few minutes?" He closed his eyes.

I followed suit. I attempted to wait with a listening spirit, but my mind refused to quiet itself. Dinner dances, knitting needles, fatherless babies, smoking ruins, melancholy mothers, grieving fathers — all vied with each other for my attention. A deep sigh escaped me.

John opened his eyes. "Tell me about this conundrum."

I explained about the invitation. "I'm growing fond of David Dodge, as I had mentioned, and he of me. But his mother . . . well, I think this is some kind of test. She would rather he marry his distant cousin, who certainly owns any number of party frocks and knows how to behave at dinner dances, as well. I possess no such knowledge. And according to our views on simplicity, I should not be wearing a fancy dress, anyway."

"Does thee want to attend this affair?"

I sighed again. "David wants me to. And I want to be part of his life. So in that sense, yes, I do."

"And then there is the dance portion of the problem. Thee knows many Friends regard it as vain amusement. In the past it has been seen as frivolous, dissipated, even immoral."

"I know." I kneaded my fingers in my lap.

"But if thee is able to conduct thyself in a modest manner with regard to dance, I believe God would not judge it wrong for a beautiful young woman to wear a beautiful dress. Thee must follow thy heart in this matter, of course, but I shall not allow our Meeting to chastise thee if thee chooses to dress somewhat less plainly for this event."

"Which leads to the problem of my not owning a suitable dress." I stared at my hands. "But this isn't thy concern, of course."

He gazed out the window before returning his intense eyes to me. "I fear I do not have a solution to this part of the problem, although the concern is there." He smiled. "Thee will discern which way to turn. I counsel thee, however, to also consider the long view. What would life with this man be like, should thee marry him? Would he be able to forgo many of these social occasions out of consideration for thee? Would he be willing to study the ways of Friends and join us in silent worship? Would thee be able to keep company with his family while still honoring thy own faith? Will he honor the Friends' views on equality, giving thee equal say in the decisions of thy life together? These are weighty questions."

"They are, indeed. He has not proposed marriage." *Yet,* I added to myself. "And at this moment I am not sure of the answers to any of thy queries. But I will think on them."

I stood, thanking him, and let him show me out. I stood on the walk, unsure of where to turn. I had his blessing for wearing a fancy dress, but where to find one? Could I afford the cost of cloth and a dressmaker? Would there even be time to complete such a dress by Seventh Day, it now being already Fourth Day? And then there were the weighty questions John had left me with. I pictured the tea, with the uniformed maid waiting on us. How many other servants did Clarinda Dodge employ? I doubted she would take kindly to her son marrying a woman who cooked her own dinners, cleaned her own parlor, and mended her own stockings. I sighed again, supposing I should sit and discern in silent prayer, after the manner of Friends. One more custom of my faith that did not come easily to my impatient soul. I took a deep breath in, and with it caught an idea. I turned to my left and hurried to Orchard Street, where I had been only two days earlier.

"Thee has a dress thee can loan me? In my size?" I couldn't believe my luck. I had come to ask Orpha's granddaughter how fast she could make me a dress and what the cost would be. Instead she had offered to lend me one. Way had opened, after all.

Alma, a plump woman of about thirty, smiled. "I think it will be perfect. She's slim and tall, like you. What are you, about five feet eight inches?"

I nodded.

"A lady had me make it for some society affair, and then she said the color was all wrong for her. She didn't want it back, and she's in such comfortable circumstances she paid for an entire new dress. Let me fetch it."

Orpha sat in her rocker tatting a piece of lace. "Life brings us what we deserve; that is what I have always said."

"I hope this turns out to be something good, otherwise I'll be getting what I deserve straying from plain dress." I glanced down at my gray everyday frock, which up to now had sufficed for attending Meeting, attending births, and nearly everything in between.

"Tell me again where you will be wearing this frock that is not plain?" Orpha asked.

"David Dodge wants my company at a society affair on Seventh Day. He very much wants to escort me. Orpha, what if I don't know how to behave? What if they have a myriad of forks and knives and finger bowls? What if I address someone the wrong way, or step on David's feet as we dance?"

"Do not concern yourself with that, my dear. You will sit up straight and be your usual intelligent forthright self. You have never before given much care to what society thinks of you, have you?"

"Well, no. One can't, really, being a Friend. I'm used to being different."

"Then you will watch how your friend uses all those forks and follow suit. And if you use the wrong one, does it matter? He will not love you any less, I dare say." She rocked gently, watching me.

"Thee is right. As always."

"Do you know how to dance?"

"A bit. Harriet and I used to practice. I'm not the most clumsy person around, but not the most graceful, either." I smiled at the memory of Father playing his violin as Harriet and I pretended to be a couple at a dance. I had grown taller than her by the time I was ten, so I'd insisted on taking the male part.

"You will follow his lead," Orpha said. "You will do well."

Alma returned to the parlor. Over her arm was the prettiest dress I had ever set eyes on. It was of a shimmering rose-colored silk. She held it up. The puffy cap sleeves were edged with lace and the flounces had a deeper rose taffeta edging them, and yet the style was simple, which pleased me. The neckline was low and the waist narrow, with a bit of a bustle in back.

"See, its color even matches your name," Alma declared with a wide smile. "Come on now, try it on. I'll have time to tailor it if need be."

As we were all women in the room, I removed my dress and stood in my camisole and petticoat.

Alma laughed. "You're going to have to wear a corset with this dress."

I grimaced. "If I must. Although my own mother is always promoting what she calls healthy dressing." I was slender enough I usually got away without the fiendish device that caused so many women pain and even health problems from being so constrained. "I guess I'll need to purchase one."

"Yes, you must. It also gives a more modest, fastened-in profile. They'll expect it at such an affair. Now this." Alma fastened a simple bustle around my waist. It was like a half apron tied on backward, with rows of puffy fabric curls sewed onto it. "I'll lend you the bustle, too."

"I thank thee, but what a silly-looking thing it is." I stepped into the dress and Alma helped me arrange it half off my shoulders and then fastened up the back.

"Turn around." She motioned. "What do you think?"

I turned to gaze in a long mirror behind me, and blushed at the sight. I barely recognized myself. The dress was nearly a perfect fit, or would be when my waist was cinched in a few more inches by the corset. The color set off my nearly black hair and deep brown eyes and it made my pale skin glow. I turned away, embarrassed to be so vain. Even so, as I smoothed down the skirt, I wished Harriet could see me in it.

"Will it do, Orpha?" I asked.

"It will more than do. You will put those society girls to shame."

Alma frowned. "You'll need slippers. And evening gloves. And fine stockings."

"I can purchase those. Especially since I didn't need to buy the dress, thanks to thee."

Orpha rummaged in a small enameled box on the table next to her. She held something out. "Here. Wear this around your neck."

I took the necklace and held it up to the light from the window. It was an ivory cameo of a woman in an oval of gold. A rose-colored ribbon ran through a slot on the back.

"It is of my mother," the old woman said. "It will be perfect."

"Oh, Orpha, thee is too kind." I leaned down and kissed her soft, papery-thin cheek. "And thee, Alma, as well. How can I thank thee both?"

The five-year-old girl ran into the room. "Mama —" She stopped short and held her hands to her cheeks regarding me with awe. "You look like a real princess!"

I laughed. "I'm not even close to being one, but thee is dear to say so."

Alma hurried the girl out of the room as I glanced at the clock. It was twelve forty-five. "Oh, no, I have to rush home! I have a client coming at one." I turned my back to Orpha. "Unfasten me, please?"

Her arthritic fingers took what seemed like an hour, but soon I was back in my decidedly unprincess-like gray dress. I went flying out the door, clutching the pink frock Alma had wrapped in tissue and then canvas as I dressed.

"I am grateful for this loan," I called back to Alma, who stood with Orpha in the doorway watching.

"You take care you do not trip and fall!" I heard Orpha laugh as I hurried toward home.

Eighteen

I waited fifteen minutes, then half an hour for my one o'clock client to appear. I had arrived right when the clock struck one. I'd laid the dress across Faith's bed upstairs to keep it clean and out of the way and then rushed back downstairs.

The client was a lady whose husband owned a profitable mill in Newburyport. Another client had recommended me to her. We had a good rapport and she thought it worth the trip across the river to attend appointments. She'd never been late before, and I hoped she was well.

As I rose to fetch something to eat from the kitchen, I still puzzled at my client's tardiness. Through the front window I saw a boy run up and slip a note through the mail slot in the door. Could it be another letter from David so soon? I eagerly picked it up off the hall floor and opened it.

Miss Carroll,
My wife is withdrawing from your practice. I cannot have her care be with a midwife who provides murder weapons to criminals. I regret to inform you of this decision but I feel I have no choice.

I remain,
Yours respectfully,

And he had signed his name. What? I read the note again and stood staring at it, stunned. *Provides murder weapons to criminals?* The couple couldn't really think I had knowingly given away my knitting needle to be employed in a crime. Could they? I should write a response. As I sat, I read the note one more time and shook my head. I doubted a written explanation from me would change this husband's mind. He seemed to be making the decision for his wife, as many husbands did, so it wouldn't matter if she thought I was guilty or not.

I paced to the rear of the house and back to the front. And again. And again. Who would have talked about the knitting needle in public? Surely not Kevin. Most surely not Guy, since his house was one of the places I'd brought the needle to in the days leading up to the murder.

And the news had already traveled across

219

the river. Others right here in Amesbury might fear I was a risk, as well. My busy practice could shrink to nothing in a week if this murderer weren't found, this killer who used my own precious hand-painted implement to stab a man. I wished I could talk the matter over with David, but I had another client coming soon and was sure he was busy with his own work.

I sat at my desk once more, astonished to see the unfinished letter I had been writing to my parents that very morning, when the sun shone and spring seemed on its way, when I had felt a world better than I did right now. I hurried to sign it and prepare it for the afternoon post. Except there was no afternoon post at the moment. I set it to the side so I could put it out in the morning. I searched for the list I had drawn up of suspects and motives. Where was it? Ah, there, sitting under my client notes.

The columns and rows told me nothing. I had begun this task before Thomas was killed. It had been all about the fire, not the murder. I added what new information I had, including my knitting needle becoming an instrument of death. I sat back, staring at the paper. How had my needle gotten into the hands of a killer? Perhaps I had forgotten a place I'd stopped with my satchel, or had neglected to remember a visitor to this parlor where I keep the satchel when I was at home. Scrolling back through my memory, though, I came up with nothing other than what I had told Kevin.

I glanced up only when there was a rap on the front door. I glanced at the clock. It had to be my two o'clock client, Isabel. I shoved the papers out of the way, ran a hand over my hair, pushed up my spectacles, and prayed I wouldn't be fired by this lady, as well.

I welcomed her in. It was her fourth pregnancy and she'd put on a good deal of weight, so she waddled into the parlor with her hands on her lower back. She sank onto the chaise with a sigh.

After I examined her and listened to her concerns — which, being the mother of three, included a measure of fatigue in keeping up with the little ones — she cocked her head and gazed at me.

I smiled and waited for what I knew was coming.

"I hear young Parry was killed with your knitting needle. Can that be true?" She cocked her head.

"It's true, I'm afraid."

"How did it come to happen?"

"Either I lost it somewhere or the murderer stole it out of my bag."

"You carry that satchel about everywhere, don't you?"

I nodded. "Believe me, I've been thinking hard about where those knitting needles have traveled to."

"Well, I also hear talk you have some fault in the matter, and I want you to know I don't believe a word of it." She reached over her belly and patted my hand. She smiled the full-faced, high-color smile of a woman close to term. "You're a fine midwife and an honest woman. Don't pay them any mind."

"I thank thee, Isabel." I helped her up and saw her to the door. "Earlier today a client's husband removed her from my care, so I appreciate thy faith in me, truly."

Her mouth turned down and her eyes widened. "I'll spread the word around my friends that no one is to do any such thing. In fact, there's a newly pregnant young wife who lives in the house next door to me. I'll recommend you and your practice."

I thanked Isabel again and watched her make her way carefully down the stairs and into a waiting buggy. At least one person didn't think I was an accomplice to murder. Gossip among women could be a powerful force for good as well as bad. Having a client who was an ally, a supporter who trusted me, could go a long way toward keeping my practice intact.

I walked into Samuel J. Brown's an hour later. Machinery clacked and whirred from the back room, as shoes were no longer made purely by hand. I picked up one pair of fancy slippers after another but I barely saw them. My cheeks still burned from the stares and muttered comments I'd gotten on my way to this shoe and boot establishment on Elm Street a little beyond Market Square. I'd first stopped in at Collins' and found the corset, long gloves, and fine stockings I needed, but even there the girl behind the counter had looked wary of helping me.

Samuel himself now appeared. "What may I help you with?" The diminutive proprietor gave a little bow and smiled at me. "It's Miss Carroll, isn't it?"

I had delivered his wife of a baby boy only a few months earlier. The baby had arrived early and was born quite small, but he had survived and thrived.

"Indeed it is. How is thy son?" I asked. "And thy wife?"

He beamed. "So very well, both of them. All thanks to your expertise."

"I'm glad to hear it. But now I need a nice pair of slippers. It's for a dinner dance, and my frock is rose colored." I picked up a black pair with a fairly high heel and a huge bow at the ankle. I put it down again. "But I'd prefer something more simple than these, and in a lighter color."

The proprietor gazed down at my feet. "That'll be a size eight or so, I wager." He opened a box from the top shelf of the rack. "How do these look?"

He proffered a pair of simple low heels. I took one in my hand. It was covered in a cream-colored silk, and the inside was as soft as a baby's cheek.

"How lovely. If I purchase these, I should hope I encounter no muddy puddles on my way to the party or they would be ruined in an instant."

"Please sit, Miss Carroll, and we'll make sure they're a good fit. They're made of a high-quality kid leather."

I sat and unlaced my shoes. He perched on a stool in front of me and daintily slid a slipper onto my right foot and then onto my left. He stood and offered his hand to help me up.

"A mirror is there." He pointed. "Walk around a bit on this runner and see how they feel. If you're going to be dancing, they must be comfortable." He pointed to a narrow Oriental rug that ended at a mirror leaning against the wall.

I did as he said. The slippers pinched my toes a little on my right foot, but otherwise were soft and felt like they would soon mold to my feet. And when I glanced in the mirror I saw how pretty they were. My feet were larger than many women's, but these made them appear nearly petite, not an adjective anyone had ever applied to me. I wasn't accustomed to this focus on fashion and an ostentatious display. But if I was going to the dance with David, I'd better make a good show of it.

"What is their cost, please?" I asked him, sitting and removing the slippers.

"They're very reasonably priced at one dollar and ten cents."

I could afford them at that price, since my practice up to now had been thriving. "I'd like to take them, but can thee possibly stretch the right one a bit? It pinches on my small toe."

"Certainly." He bustled the shoe behind a curtain at the back of the room. "I'll just be a moment."

While he was out of the room, I donned my plain shoes again and idly browsed through more pairs of fancy shoes. I supposed women of great means owned more than one pair of dancing slippers, and fancy going-out shoes, and who knew what else. I had always been satisfied with my single pair of serviceable lace-up shoes, which I replaced when necessary with another pair exactly like the first.

Two women in dark work dresses emerged from the back. One tugged on gloves, while the other pinned her hat firmly to her hair. They were nearly at the door to the street when the first one glanced over and saw me. The look on her face changed in an instant from a pleasant "my shift is over and I'm going out with my girlfriend" to one of horror. She pulled her friend's arm, who also turned her eyes to me. She whispered something, then they both rushed out the door.

"Don't you worry, now." Samuel's voice came from behind me. "I know you weren't involved in that terrible affair. And the whole town will, too, when the authorities find the killer." He extended a package wrapped in paper and string to me. "You have a good time at your party and ignore those gossips."

"I thank thee, Samuel." I paid him what was due and pulled on my cloak. I wished it would wrap me in invisibility and shield me from a town's worth of accusing eyes on my way home.

NINETEEN

The three youngest Baileys burst ruddy-
cheeked through the back door a few moments after I arrived home from my shopping. I had been forced to endure a few
more comments and stares as I walked and
was glad to be in the privacy of home again.

"Rose, a p'liceman's here!" Betsy exclaimed, pushing her bonnet off her head so
it hung down her back by its ties. She ran
to the window of the sitting room and
pointed.

"Good heavens, are they visiting me on a
daily schedule now?" I set my hands on my
hips.

"But it's not the detective," Matthew
added. "The one who gave me his hat to
wear."

I joined them and checked the street. A
uniformed Guy Gilbert stood with hat in
hand. He shifted from one foot to the other,
as if uncertain whether he wanted to be

there or not. I went to the front door and opened it. The children crowded behind me.

"Guy Gilbert," I called. "Is thee coming in or am I wanted for more questioning?"

He gazed down the street and back at me. "I'll come in." He walked up the front steps.

"Children, back up and let the policeman in."

They obliged, but barely. Three pairs of eyes were bright at the prospect of speaking with yet another man in uniform. Perhaps First Day School would need another lesson on the peaceable ways soon.

"Hello, Miss Carroll. Hello, you young ones." Guy smiled at them, but his mouth twitched and his eyes sported dark shadows under them.

"Please come in and sit down," I said. "Betsy, Mark, Matthew, run along and wash up. We'll have our tea in a bit." Mark lingered, his eyes fixed with fascination on the billy club affixed to Guy's belt, but he ran after the others when I gave him my stern auntie look.

I ushered Guy into the parlor and shut the door firmly. "Thee looks uncertain, Guy. What can I help thee with? Is this an official call?"

"Oh, no, not at all." He remained standing, rotating his hat around and around in his hands. "I need to speak with you. On a personal matter."

I waited, certain it would be about Nell's health.

"It's my wife. You saw how sad she seems. It's like a darkness took her over. Sometimes she simply sits and weeps. She seems not to care about Lizzy. Or me, for that matter."

"It's the postpartum melancholia. Some new mothers experience it lightly and some not at all. But Nell seems to have a bad case."

"Is there nothing that can be done?" He spread one hand open. "No medicine that can fix it?"

"I prescribed her a tonic that is high in iron and I took her some calming tea. But I don't believe that will be enough." I rued the lack of medical help available. "The depressive state should pass with time, do know that."

He opened his mouth as if about to speak, and then shook his head.

"What is it?" I asked, wearing my imaginary pastor's hat. "Something else troubles thee." I clasped my hands in front of me.

"The thing is, she went out the other night. Alone, at night! I tried to stop her, but she turned on me and then ran out."

"Is that when thee got this?" I reached up

and gently touched the scratch on his face.

He nodded. "She was like an animal with claws."

"What night was this?"

His face twisted with anguish. "The night Thomas Parry was killed."

Oh, my. This wasn't welcome news. I thought for a moment. "Surely thee doesn't think Nell would kill Thomas," I said. "Would she have a reason to do so?"

He paced a few steps away and turned back, like an animal yearning to escape a cage. "Parry had courted her before she married me. She rebuffed him and he was mean to her, called her some right unpleasant names." He kept rotating his hat. "I tried to make her happy. And she was, all throughout the time she was carrying Lizzy."

"Yes, she seemed well." I had seen her throughout her pregnancy and had detected no problems, had heard no complaints from her. And Guy had been the picture of a doting husband and father-to-be. "Had she seen Thomas Parry recently?"

"I don't know, you see." He ran a hand over his brow. "I'm at the station every day doing my job. She could have encountered him somewhere in town, I'm sure."

As I had seen her encountering Jotham in town — the same Jotham who found the

231

body. I did not raise this with Guy, however. It might upset him even more.

"I expect thee came here because thee does not want to relate this story of Nell's going out that night to thy superior." I raised my eyebrows.

"Oh, Miss Carroll, what am I to do? I need to tell Detective Donovan. But what if he arrests my Nellie? How will I live?" He swallowed hard, seeming to fight back tears. He shook his head and straightened his back.

"Does thee think her capable of murder?"

"Not the Nell I married, no. But she's someone different now. When she rouses herself out of that sad dark place, she can act cruel. Or insane, more like."

"But how would she have gotten her hands on my knitting needle?" I took in a sharp breath and clapped my hand to my mouth. I knew well the answer to my own question.

"What is it?" Guy's eyebrows shot up.

"When I visited your home on Second Day, I carried my satchel with me. As is my habit. And those long needles often poke out of the top. Nell was alone with the bag once when I carried Lizzy into the other room." My heart was a cold stone in my chest. This was information we were obliged to share with Kevin. And if Nell Gilbert had killed Thomas, then Lizzy faced an existence without a mother and Guy would lose his dear wife.

I had dispatched an anguished Guy with firm instructions to go at once and tell Kevin Donovan what he knew about poor Nell. I hoped he would oblige, because if he didn't, I would have to and it would go all the worse for the young officer.

As soon as I began to fire up the stove for supper, Hiram Henderson appeared again, looking nearly as upset as he had when he'd fetched me on First Day evening to attend his wife's labor.

"The baby is ailing. Can you come right away?" He stood twisting his hands, his eyes full of anguish. "He's very sick."

"Of course."

Faith arrived home as I came out of the parlor after fetching my bag.

"I'm sorry, Faith," I said. "I was going to help thee with supper, but now I'm called away."

"Not to worry, Rose." Fatigue lined Faith's forehead over reddened eyes, and it was only Fourth Day. "We will do it, right, Betsy?" She put an arm around her little sister's shoulders.

Betsy nodded, and I hurried away with Patience's husband, a chilly rain now wetting our heads. My stomach complained of emptiness, but a meal would have to wait. My advice to Faith about keeping herself strong first was becoming a case of, Do as I say, not as I do.

Once in the Henderson flat, with all thoughts of a bloody knitting needle vanished from my brain, I held a critically ill four-day-old baby. He slept, but his breaths were rasping and fast, and his skin burned.

"He's so hot, and he won't take the breast," Patience whispered, her face etched with fear. "What's wrong with him?" She wore a wrapper over her nightgown and her flaming hair hung down in a braid, as if she'd never gotten properly dressed that day.

"When did this come on?" I asked.

"He was fussy yesterday, but I thought it was a touch of the colic. Last night he began to scream and was hot."

"Did thee try to cool him?" I unwrapped him down to his diaper, which I was glad to see was fastened with one of the new safety pins, much better than the straight pins that sometimes pierced a baby's skin.

"I took him outside into the cold air, but it didn't help. And then today he became listless. He's not screaming anymore, but he hasn't nursed since yesterday."

"Bring me a basin of cool water and a towel, perhaps a piece of flannel." His diaper was dry, always an alarming sign in an infant. He needed fluids badly. I wished she'd sent for me earlier, but there was no reversing the past, and it would help not at all to lay guilt upon her at a time like this.

With shaking hands, she set a basin and a towel on the table. I laid him down, removed the diaper, and began to swab him all over with cool water. His little arms and legs moved, and he let out a soft cry. I wet his head. When I wiped his neck and chest, the cool cloth warmed too fast. I wet it and wiped him again, leaving the water on his skin. After he was wet all over, I picked him up.

"Try to nurse him now." I handed him to his mother.

Patience sank into a chair and exposed her left breast. "Come on, Timmy. Please drink for Mama," she urged. She coaxed his cheek with her nipple. Her husband hovered behind her, wringing his hands. He raised a handkerchief to his mouth and coughed.

I laid a freshly cool cloth on the baby's forehead. When he turned toward the breast and opened his little mouth, Patience pressed the nipple into it. He sucked once but then flopped back into the crook of her arm.

Patience looked up at me, tears in her eyes. "See, Rose? It's like our first Timmy, except he was already six months old when we lost him."

I tried to help her express some milk into his mouth but it only dribbled out the side, a tiny trail of fluid crying down his burning cheek.

"I think it's time to take him to the hospital," I said. "Do you have a convey-ance?" I gazed from one parent to the other.

Hiram shook his head, hard. "But I can pay for one. I'll fetch a hansom cab." He coughed again.

I stood and laid an arm on his at the door. "Hurry."

He threw me a look, his eyes full, and rushed down the steps. I brought a new cool cloth to Patience and knelt to wipe baby Timmy's head and face. She stroked his cheek.

"Come on, sweetie. Drink for me." A tear dropped on his face and mixed with drops of milk leaking from her full breast. "He was so well the first couple of days. I don't understand what happened." She looked at me.

"He was a healthy newborn," I agreed.

"But their little systems are fragile at first. I'm afraid babies sicken in their first months far more often than anyone wishes." I dared not try to raise her hopes. Even if Timmy made it to the hospital, his chances were slim. And what more would they do there than we were doing here? We had to try to lower his temperature so he would feel strong enough to drink. It was simple and, at this point, seemed unlikely to happen. I held him in the Light as I wiped his hot head again.

"What do you think ails him?" she asked.

"Some kind of infection. I know not what. Unfortunately there are sicknesses that abound. Consumption, scarlet fever, influenza, even typhoid. And pneumonia, as thee knows." I thought her husband's cough might be the culprit, no matter what its cause. He'd probably had a high temperature earlier, too.

The baby's arms and legs began to shake.

"He's convulsing. Turn him on his side and hold him," I told Patience as her eyes widened. "It's from the fever."

The shaking continued. His eyes flew open but they were unseeing. His breathing grew noisier. His mouth hung open. He exhaled with a rattle and didn't inhale for a long moment. He took a labored breath in and out, and did not breathe again.

"No, Timmy!" Patience clutched him to her. "Breathe, my son. You can't leave us." She sobbed over his tiny body. "No, no, no."

As she rocked back and forth with him, the pinkness of his skin grew pale. The change traveled up from his hands and feet. The color faded out of his face. Finally his torso lost its rosy hue. I had seen this moment before, when the soul takes its leave and the body becomes a waxen shell. But it always brought tears to my own eyes and a great lump to my throat, especially in a person so new to this world.

Hiram burst into the room. "I've got a cab! He's waiting —" He caught sight of Patience rocking, weeping. He stared at me.

I nodded with sorrow.

"We've lost our boy." He let out a great cry of anguish and rushed to his wife's side. He wrapped his arms around both of them.

Leaving them to grieve together, I went to tell the hansom he was no longer needed. Instead I asked him to return in an hour to pick me up. I didn't care to walk the streets of our town alone at night, and darkness was falling.

I trudged back up the stairs. I now had to guide this devastated couple through summoning the undertaker and burying their second Timmy. Not to mention helping Patience to bind her breasts and cope with a body still producing ample sustenance for an infant who was no longer of this world.

TWENTY

The hansom, at my direction, left me at the
Meetinghouse. The lamps in the tall windows pushed a comforting yellow glow out
into the dark night. I'd felt the need to join
other Friends in midweek worship, and I
knew I wouldn't be alone walking toward
home when the hour was up, as many
Friends lived in the same direction. I didn't
always attend the Fourth Day worship but
tried to when my schedule permitted, when
I wasn't called to a birth or was too fatigued
from being up all night at one. The evening
gatherings tended to be primarily adults and
often included those seeking respite from
the cares and business of everyday life. Harriet had been a regular attender at midweek
Meeting when she was alive, taking it as an
island of calm in her life as mother of five
active children as well as a worker in the
noise and bustle of the mill.

I had arrived at least ten minutes late and

quietly took a seat on one of the benches near the door. The air wasn't overly cool, although I kept my cloak on, as had the others in attendance. The room smelled of lamp oil, weathered floorboards, and simple wooden pews. John Whittier had been a member of the building committee when this meetinghouse was constructed after the previous one became insufficient for our burgeoning membership numbers. The woodwork carried straight, elegant lines, and the high ceiling invited the spirit to soar. The undecorated but beautiful design reflected the Friends' emphasis on simplicity and lent the space a spiritual air.

My hands clasped in my lap, I tried to calm my mind and my heart. The death of a baby always sat heavy with me, even though I knew it was part of this life we lead. The thought of Nell's illness and her nighttime wanderings disturbed me, too, as did knowing Thomas's killer walked freely about the town. Picturing Ephraim sitting in a jail cell wasn't a happy thought, either.

After some minutes, the silence of gathered Friends began to soothe me, as it usually did. We waited on the Light together, with closed eyes and quiet tongues. Someone across the room snored softly. A woman cleared her throat. I pictured the room encircled with Light, and I mentally moved from person to person, holding up their concerns and joys, whatever they might be, to God's care. I also pictured my dear David's face surrounded by the Light, a thought that brought a small smile to my face.

From the facing bench, John's deep voice dropped into the pool of stillness. I kept my eyes closed as I listened, then smiled as I recognized the familiar words of his own poem, written about this very place of worship.

> And so, I find it well to come
> For deeper rest to this still room,
> For here the habit of the soul
> Feels less the outer world's control;
> The strength of mutual purpose pleads
> More earnestly our common needs;
> And from the silence multiplied
> By these still forms on either side,
> The world that time and sense have known
> Falls off and leaves us God alone.

Hearing this brought me back to the outer world for a moment, but I had to trust that way would open. That poor Patience and Hiram would somehow also be soothed. That the murderer would kill no more and

242

would soon be brought to a safe and just place. That Ephraim wouldn't only be freed but would find employment suitable to his intelligence. That Nell's troubled mind would heal. That William would now devote his care to his marriage and his baby with Lillian, while also supporting Billy. And that I'd survive the party with David's mother.

The next morning, after the family left, I checked my schedule. I had clients coming in the afternoon, but the flour bin in the kitchen was running toward empty, so I thought I'd pay a visit to the mercantile and order some to be delivered, along with several other food supplies the household needed. It was the additional money Faith and I contributed to the household that enabled us to purchase food whenever we needed it. Feeding, housing, and clothing six people on a teacher's salary alone would make things much tighter, which was why Harriet had been working outside the home before her death. I supposed Frederick was correct in abstaining from hiring household help, given our combined finances, but it would certainly make Faith's life easier, and mine, too.

After the mercantile, I decided I would check in on Patience, and on Lillian, as well.

The night's rain was gone and the air was mild for my walk into town. In the mercantile, the same two men I'd spoken with yesterday warmed their hands at the stove and conversed in quiet voices. I wondered which one had squealed on me to the police. I greeted Catherine behind the counter and we exchanged pleasantries.

"I'd like to order some foodstuffs, Catherine. Can thy brother deliver them?"

"Certainly." She took a stubby pencil from behind her ear and pulled out a pad of paper.

I asked for twenty pounds of flour, ten of porridge oats, and five of sugar. I added three bars of washing soap, a block of butter, a tin of cooking oil, and a bit of chocolate as a treat. I'd get along to the butcher, the fishmonger, and the produce market after I left here.

"Oh, and some pea seeds," I said. "It's time to get planting, I think."

Catherine nodded in approval. "We're all a little starved for something green to eat by this time of year, aren't we?" She leaned over the counter and lowered her voice. "I hear tell a baby under your care died last night. Is it true?"

It appeared there was no news that didn't travel faster than fire on a windy night. "The

Henderson infant." I nodded. "They're sorely grieving."

Catherine glanced around the store and then back at me. "A lady was in here a little bit ago calling you a baby killer. Said you had finished the babe off with your knittin' needle."

I couldn't speak for a moment. Catherine might as well have dropped an anvil on my head. "Gracious sakes. What a horrible thing to say. And besides —" I stopped as I heard my voice shake. What was the point? I shook my head. I'd surely be out of work soon if this kept up.

"I told her you weren't. That Friends don't kill anything, won't even go to war. She wouldn't listen."

"If some deranged townsperson thinks I'd kill a baby, or anyone, by any method, she needs more help than my protestations can offer." My upset had turned to anger. I knew it wasn't a peaceful reaction, but I couldn't help myself. I glanced over at the men, who were both watching my conversation with Catherine. I turned my back. I should never have spoken with them yesterday.

"Of course I told her that was a crazy notion," Catherine said. "But some people get crazy notions in their heads."

■ ■ ■ ■

As I made my way up Main Street with a goal of arriving at the Parry home, I considered taking a detour to the police station. I was curious what Kevin had made of Guy's news about both Nell's outing and her access to my needles. But I didn't want to know, at the same time. I decided to continue on my way to see Lillian. I'd hear around town of any new developments in the case. Whether the news would be accurate or not was anybody's guess.

A familiar-looking buggy clattered up next to me and pulled to a halt. David leaned his head out the side nearest me.

"Hello, Miss Carroll." He winked and doffed his hat. "Might I offer you a lift?"

"I'd be delighted, David. I thank thee." I gathered my skirts and climbed in, smiling at him as I settled myself. "I'm off to pay Lillian Parry a visit. She had some premature labor pains two days ago and I want to see if they've subsided."

"You're looking like a spring flower, as always." He clucked to the horse, who walked at a steady pace. "There is no hurry to arrive there, I hope?"

I shook my head. I straightened my back,

thinking of the deceased baby as well as my knitting needle problem. I filled him in on the latter.

"They were in this very satchel." I gestured to the bag on my lap. "And the needle that was stolen, the one that killed Thomas Parry, had been sharpened. I saw the dried blood on it." I shuddered. I was no stranger to blood, but that of a murder victim was something else entirely.

"That's awful," David exclaimed. "I hate to think of someone trying to frame you for a crime. I hope this detective gets to the bottom of the murder soon. Very soon."

"As do we all. I know it's no excuse to not have replied to thy invitation, but it's been a difficult week. I lost an infant last night, too. He was only four days old and was burning with fever. He died in his mother's arms."

"Why didn't you bring him into the hospital? Or send word to me personally?"

"By the time they called me, he was very sick with dehydration and a high temperature. I sent the husband to fetch a hansom and tried to cool Timmy down, but he died before the cab even arrived." My throat thickened again. I blinked away a looming tear.

David patted my hand. "You have a large

heart, my Rose."

"Would thee in the hospital have any other means to save him, besides cooling him?" I asked.

"Not really, no. We have no miracle medicines. Perhaps in the future one will be developed. There are so many diseases that take babies."

"I couldn't tell if he had pneumonia or if the fever was from another illness, but his father does have a bad cough." It was comforting to be able to speak of medical issues with this man, colleague to colleague.

"That could be related."

"And apparently I am now regarded not only as the local supplier of murder weapons but also as a baby killer." I sighed.

"Outrageous! Who uttered that?" He frowned at me.

"Catherine in the mercantile told me a customer had said that is what I am," I said.

"Ignorant people will say ignorant things. Don't worry. The police are bound to crack the case soon enough," he said as we passed Huntington Square. A stone pedestal was under construction. "What's going to be erected there?"

"It's to be a statue of Josiah Bartlett donated by Jacob Huntington."

"Ah, Bartlett, the famous local signatory

of the Declaration of Independence?"

"The very one. They plan to dedicate the statue on Independence Day, I have read." I glanced at him. "By the way, what is thee doing on this side of the river?"

"I have a patient to see, and I hoped to see you, too. Did you decide to allow me to escort you to the dinner on Saturday?"

"Yes, I'll come," I fell silent for a few moments, and then laughed.

"What is funny?"

"I have a real frock to wear to thy fancy party. Me, in a fancy dress. And it's quite lovely." I caught David's smile before he tried to straighten his face.

"Are you allowed to wear a party dress?"

"John Whittier, as one of our elders, gave me his blessing to slip away from plain dress for the evening." I glanced at a house we passed. "David, look!" I pulled at his sleeve.

"Whoa," he instructed the mare. "What alarms you, Rose?" He sounded worried.

"I'm not alarmed. But look there." I pointed. "Narcissus blooming. The first I have seen this spring." The home faced in a southward direction and the sun shone directly on its front garden.

David threw back his head and laughed. "You're a treat, Rose. We had been speaking of death and murder, so naturally I thought you had spied some new victim or piece of evidence. And it's only spring flowers."

"Well, they're lovely and a welcome sight. Harriet used to plant bulbs every year around the house. I should check to see if any are blooming when I return home."

"Indeed they are lovely." He clucked to the horse to move again and a minute later pulled up in front of Lillian and William's home.

I sat for a minute.

"Something still troubles you." David leaned around and peered at my face.

"I'm worried I'll embarrass thee at the party, David, or do something to turn thy mother against me. I'm not a society girl, thee knows that." All of John's questions also rolled around like so many bowling balls in my head, setting up a racket as they clanked against each other and demanded my attention.

"I don't care about any of that," he said with force. "And you should know as much."

"But what will thy mother say when word reaches Newburyport of my involvement in the murder?"

"No buts. You're intelligent and beautiful and independent and caring. And I love you for all of those traits." He smiled at me.

"Now get *thee* to work. I must be off, myself."

I squeezed his hand with a smile at his use of the Quaker pronoun, then climbed down and waved as he drove away. How did I deserve such a man? The degradation I had suffered now nearly ten years earlier raised its head once again, bringing with it the insecure feeling that had blighted my happiness ever since. I had been attracted to David from the first moment I set eyes on him a year earlier. We'd both attended a lecture at the hospital about complications with twin births, and a friend had introduced us afterward. David and I had talked about parturition, and I'd been impressed by how seriously he took my practice of midwifery, especially since some women were beginning to prefer the care of a doctor for their pregnancies. He'd offered to lend a hand when I needed it, and after we'd worked together on several difficult situations, I'd noticed his attention becoming more than professional. He joked with me, and several times I caught him casting adoring looks my way. We'd finally taken to spending delightful time together outside of work.

But this blight of mine was standing in my way. Was I afraid I would be hurt again?

251

Abused and left? By David, never; I knew that in my head. Still, returning his love was not as easy as I wanted it to be. And even if I did, I wasn't sure if he could overcome his mother's own resistance to him descending into what some considered the wild cult of Quakerism to find a bride. Not that he had proposed, I reminded myself.

TWENTY-ONE

I finished examining Lillian. "All is well. It's fine that the practice pains have subsided, but don't worry if they return."

"I'm glad not to have them. Especially today. You're coming to Thomas's funeral, aren't you?" She sat up in the bed and swung her legs over the side.

"It's today? I hadn't learned of it."

She narrowed her eyes. "The notice has been in the papers."

"I'm afraid I have been too busy to spend much time reading as of late. But yes, I'll attend, if thee wishes me to." I stood and put the listening tube into my bag.

"Yes, we'd both like you to, William and I. It's scheduled for one o'clock at St. John's. We'll be having some light refreshments here after poor Thomas is laid to rest. We'd appreciate your company then, as well."

"I hope the service won't be too upsetting

to thee."

"I'll try to remain calm." Her voice took on a somber tone and she pulled her brows together. "For William, of course. He's still quite distraught."

"And for the baby," I added. "It's important not to suffer extremes of mood in these last weeks. Thee wouldn't want those practice pains to become real before thy time."

"And for the baby, of course." She lay one hand on top of her belly and cradled it underneath with the other. She glanced up. "What's this I hear about your very own knitting needle being the weapon that killed poor Thomas?"

Not this again. "That is what the police have said. I don't understand it, and I don't know when it went missing."

Lillian stared at her hands. "It's a terrible thought, that a tool used to create garments could be wielded to take a man's life."

I bade her farewell and made my way down the stairs. I mused on the look I thought I had caught on her face as I left the room. It seemed to be one of satisfaction. But why? I sniffed as I reached the ground floor. Delicious smells wafted down the hall from the back of the house. The cook must be preparing the food for this afternoon, and I hoped she had help. The funeral was likely to be well attended, and who in town would pass up the opportunity to see the inside of this fine mansion and have something to eat and drink on Parry's nickel?

William hailed me from the library as I passed. "Miss Carroll, come and speak to me a moment, will you?"

I turned left and stood in the doorway. "How fares thee, William?"

He sat in a leather armchair and didn't appear to be faring too well at all. His eyes were dark and a tic pulled at the edge of his lip. He gestured with two open hands.

"Did you tell her?" he asked.

"I told Lillian she was well, blessedly," I said, but I suspected that was not what he was asking about. "She then spoke to me of the funeral," I said. "I will attend."

"Oh, good. You've been such a help to us in these painful days." He patted the cassock next to him. "Will you sit?"

I remained on my feet. "I thank thee, but I have clients to notify of my absence from my office this afternoon."

He stood, as well. "It's, ah, a matter of some discretion I must bring up with you." He put his hands in his pockets and then took them out, clasping them behind his back.

I waited, knowing full well what this matter was.

"The other day, last week, oh, it might have been Saturday, I saw you coming out of Minnie O'Toole's home." He didn't meet my eyes.

"And I saw thee going in."

He cleared his throat. "Precisely. I wondered if I might request of you to keep that visit to yourself. If my dear wife discovered it, why, she would be most unhappy. We don't want to imperil the baby's health now, do we?"

"I make no promise to maintain thy deception, William." When I saw his nostrils flare and his face darken, I held up my hand. "But I also want Lillian to avoid extreme upsets, and I'll not divulge your visit unless I find it necessary to do so."

"How dare you not promise this?" He clenched his fists at his sides.

"I dare because it is my right." I stood straight and still in front of this seething man.

"That will have to do, I suppose," he said, folding his arms.

"Yes, it will. Now, I bid thee good day. I'll see thee this afternoon."

I stomped down the front steps. He had the nerve to ask me to keep his dirty secret.

And now Lillian was his *dear* wife. How dear was she to him when he was consorting with Minnie O'Toole?

TWENTY-TWO

At home, I found the delivery from the mercantile on the back stoop. I'd forgotten all about it. Where had my brain gone to? I was glad the day was fine and not drenching the packages with rain. I bundled them inside and stored the staples in their appropriate bins.

I had to get notes out to my afternoon clients and I'd missed the morning post. I sat at my desk and scribbled them, even as the picture of Patience Henderson's haggard face and swollen breasts filled my mind. I'd stopped in to see her on my way home from the Parrys. I was grateful to see that her mother had arrived to help. Patience wouldn't speak to me, and her full breasts were leaking and a bit hot, but I didn't think infection had set in. Her milk would dry up in another day or two if she kept them bound. It was the most bitter of reminders of the dead baby. When Hiram had continued coughing, I took him aside and urged him to see a doctor in town before he made anyone else sick.

I'd had a client the year before who lost a baby at the tender age of one month, and a client who had died in childbirth in the same week. The bereft mother agreed to nurse the motherless infant. I saw how difficult it was for her, but she had three older, healthy children, so she was an old hand at nursing and insisted she wanted to help. A pity I could think of no infant who needed similar help, although surely not a pity that a new mother hadn't recently met her demise.

Now, who could I get to deliver these notes? If I went traipsing around town, it would take me an hour or two, and then I'd be heated and tired and late for the funeral. It was times like this I wished for a horse of my own, or even one of the new safety bicycles with their wheels of equal sizes. I glanced out the window. Speaking of bicycles, a man was cycling down the road at that very moment on an ordinary bicycle, sitting up high over its enormous front wheel.

I ran to the front door and hailed him. "Might thee deliver a few letters for me? I have some urgency for them to arrive to their destinations, all here in Amesbury."

He hopped off and touched his green tweed cap. "I'd be glad to, miss." He was younger than I and had a pleasant toothy smile.

"Just one moment." I hurried back inside and addressed the three envelopes. I grabbed a coin, too, and brought it all back out to him. "I thank thee very kindly for this favor. Here is something for your trouble." I handed him the coin.

He checked the addresses and slipped the notes into his pocket. "I'll be off. Much obliged for the payment, miss." He smiled again and mounted his iron steed.

One problem solved. Now I needed to eat, wash up, and make my way to St. John's Episcopal Church before one o'clock struck.

I approached a pew toward the back of St. John's minutes before the service began. The woman at the end edged away from the aisle closer to her husband to make room for me and I nodded my thanks. I slid in and smoothed down my good dress with my gloves as I caught sight of the casket at the front of the sanctuary, covered with a white cloth trimmed in gold. I closed my eyes, holding Thomas Parry in the Light.

My moment of silence was short-lived,

however. The organ sprang to life and the priest began to speak. The ceremony seemed to go on forever. I was so accustomed to the quiet way of Friends that it struck me as impossibly busy. The townspeople who packed the church stood and knelt and spoke in response. Hymns were sung. Biblical passages were read. I spied John Whittier across the church, and each time I checked, he remained sitting with hands on his knees, eyes closed in Quaker prayer, despite the lack of silence all around.

I glanced at a movement in the side aisle at the end of my pew. Kevin Donovan stood in a dark suit, holding his hat, his eyes roving over the attendees. Exactly as he had done after Isaiah's memorial meeting. Our glances met and he gave a tiny nod acknowledging me.

A man in a black suit made his way to the priest's podium from the front row. He bore a resemblance to William, although he was younger and with a less robust figure. When he identified himself as Thomas's uncle, my guess was confirmed. He delivered a eulogy touching only on Thomas's good points, as was appropriate, and didn't mention his violent death, saying only that he was taken into the Lord's hands "suddenly and far too early." He ended by inviting all present to the Parry home for drink and sustenance after the burial.

Finally the service ended with the priest and his white-clad acolytes walking down the center aisle, the priest swinging an exotically scented ball. Following were eight men carrying the casket, including William Parry and his brother, as well as Robert Clarke, our distant cousin Ned Bailey, the mill owner Cyrus Hamilton, and two other men I'd seen about town. The last on my side was a tall young man. I took a second look. It was Zebulon Weed. A pallbearer? Friends didn't normally participate in such ritual, but he had every right to do as he wished for his employer. He gave me a little smile as he passed. Lillian and several other women, all dressed in mourning attire, black lace veiling their faces, followed the casket.

By the time the attendees had filed out, the casket sat on a hearse hitched to four elegant black horses ready to convey it to the Union Cemetery. The burying yard sat on Haverhill Street half a mile down Main Street toward the Merrimack River. The pallbearers lined up behind the wagon, and the entire population of the church set out behind. I was pleased to see Lillian climb into a carriage for the short trip. She should not be walking even that far at such a stressful time. A light-haired young man handed her up, the same one I had seen in her carriage and at the Parry home last week.

Bertie fell in at my side. As usual, she tucked her arm through mine as we walked.

"Does thee know who that fellow is?" I pointed to the carriage where the slender blond man now climbed in beside Lillian. "I saw him at the Parry home."

"Lillian's ne'er-do-well brother, Alexander Locke."

"What has he never done well?"

"Gambling, for one. He's lost great amounts of money. I hear he's trying to straighten out. Don't know how he will with that father of theirs always paying off his debts."

"Was thee in the church?" I asked.

She nodded. "And what is a humble midwife doing at the funeral for a murdered man?"

"I'm watching over his stepmother's pregnancy."

"The child bride."

"Not exactly, though her and William's ages are quite disparate. They both seemed keen on my attending, so here I am. I hadn't even known of the service before this morning."

"I'll bet you're also hoping to learn more

about exactly who murdered Thomas with your evil implement of death." She grinned up at me.

"Thee heard. Thee and all the rest of this town. I still find it hard to believe someone would do such a thing. I suppose for a person already resolved to kill, stealing a knitting needle would be a trifle. But thee, Bertie — what brings thee to this somber event?"

"Curiosity. Do you have any idea how much about the town's underbelly I overhear in the post office? I know Thomas wasn't universally liked. Hardly liked at all would be more accurate. And, with no current workplace, I actually have time to do this."

We strolled along in step, her forthright short-legged stride keeping up with the reach of my longer legs. As the trolley passed us going toward town, the conductor slowed the team of horses, doffed his hat, and rang the bell slowly ten times.

"Maybe the murderer was sitting right there in the church with all of us. Think of that." Bertie sounded delighted at the idea as we walked on.

"Kevin Donovan had the same idea. I spied him focusing all his attention on the mourners and none on the service." I now saw him walking ahead of us but at the edge of the crowd, his eyes still roaming. "See, there he is." I pointed. Guy Gilbert was keeping pace with the crowd on the other side. I hoped I'd get a chance to ask him how it went when he told Kevin about Nell being out the night of the murder.

"Ah, the infamous detective," she said.

"Infamous for what?"

Instead of speaking, she only waggled her eyebrows.

The graveside service was short and somber. When they lowered the casket into the grave and the time had come for William to throw a handful of dirt onto the elaborate box, tears broke through the stoic manner he'd maintained until then. He sank to his knees sobbing Thomas's name. William's brother needed to help him away from the gravesite. Lillian, on the other hand, sat composed throughout, her head bowed. I guessed I needn't have worried that the funeral and burial would upset her enough to endanger her pregnancy. After William's demonstration, she stroked his back in a comforting move. I found it reassuring to see her showing care for him.

I felt an upswelling of tears myself at one point, remembering Harriet's burial a year ago, but I shook my head and swallowed the sorrow away.

After the burial, most present continued on up Haverhill Street to where it curved into Highland. We walked past the windmill, which always made me feel like I should be in Holland, and from there it was only a few blocks to the Parry mansion. I stood in the parlor and accepted a glass of punch from a maid who circulated holding a tray of drinks. Bertie, on the other hand, helped herself to a glass of claret.

"You ought to let your hair down and have a drink one of these days," she told me. She took a sip and sighed. "That's more like it."

"Thee knows Friends don't imbibe. Thee shouldn't even suggest it. Although —"

"Although what?"

I told her about the invitation and my party frock. "I hope I won't be pressured to drink alcohol at the affair."

"Ooh, joining high society, are we? I don't envy you. I've had a run-in with your Clarinda Dodge," Bertie said. "She's a woman to be reckoned with, that one."

I grimaced. "What kind of run-in?" Hearing that certainly did not set my mind at ease. I had only two more days until the dinner.

Before Bertie could answer, Zeb appeared

at my elbow also holding a cup of punch. He greeted me and I introduced him to Bertie.

"Bertie Winslow, I'm pleased to meet thee." Zeb smiled.

"Ah, another Quaker." Bertie smiled back and shook his hand. "Nice to meet you, as well, Zebulon. I'm so sorry about the loss of your brother in the fire."

"I thank thee." Zeb's smile was gone. "I miss him terribly."

"I'll let you two talk," Bertie said. "I'm off to sample the best mourning food Amesbury has to offer, and see what gossip I can pick up." She headed for the dining room, where we'd been invited to partake of non-liquid refreshment.

"Zeb, I was surprised to see thee as a pallbearer," I said.

"Not as surprised as I when William asked me." He shook his head.

"How did that come about?"

"I had worked for Thomas and not complained too much. Perhaps William thought we were friends, since Thomas was about the same age as I am. I didn't mind. I'm tall, young, strong. Some of those other gentlemen, the factory owners, they were struggling a bit to keep their hold on the coffin."

"Was it not difficult for thy heart, so soon after losing thy brother?" He had certainly also carried Isaiah's casket, although his simple burial had taken place in the Quaker section of the Union Cemetery late on the day after the fire. Only the family and a few close friends had been present, Faith had told me.

He swallowed. "Yes. But it was a way to pass on all the comfort I have received."

I sipped my punch, which tasted of strawberry and mint. Its cool temperature and sweetness was most welcome to my throat after all our walking. The day had become almost warm, at least for Fourth Month. I imagined how miserable it would have been for all if the chilly rain from the night before had persisted.

"I think I'll find a bite to eat, then go through and pay my respects now the line is dwindling." I patted his arm.

"Be well, Rose."

"And thee, Zeb. Come visit Faith soon. She misses thee."

He nodded. On my way toward the food, Ned Bailey suddenly blocked my way. His hair was slightly tamed compared to how it usually sprang out in all directions, but he exuded nervous energy as always.

"Miss Carroll! What a delight to see you."

Beaming, he reached for my hand and held it in his sweaty one.

"Greetings, Ned." I pulled my hand back with some difficulty and surreptitiously wiped it on my skirt.

He lowered his voice. "When can I take you out on the town? I want to show you a fine time. Get to know you better and all that." He glanced around. "I hope you don't mind me asking at such a solemn occasion."

I swallowed. "That is a kind offer. I'll have to check my calendar and get back to thee." Perhaps never, I added silently.

"Excellent, excellent." He patted his stomach with satisfaction. A man across the room waved him over. "I'll talk to you soon, then," he said before leaving me.

I escaped with relief at last into the dining room. Dozens of delicacies filled the long table. I spied chicken salad, lobster salad, turkey and jelly, ham and dressing, and a cold beef pyramid. The sideboard held assorted cakes: jelly cake, coffee cake, sponge cake, Washington pie, and other pastries I couldn't even name but that tempted my empty belly mightily. I filled a small plate with both kinds of salads, a small roll, and a sliver of sponge cake.

A man I knew only by sight from around town took one look at me and, with a grim set to his face, whispered to his wife. Her eyes flew open in alarm as he took her arm and steered her in the opposite direction from where I stood. How would I ever overcome my new reputation as Supplier of Murder Weapon? I picked at the food on my plate. My appetite had vanished, though, and as I could barely taste even the lobster salad, I set the plate on a tray in the corner with other abandoned dishes.

I moved through to the library, where William and his brother stood. Blessedly Lillian wasn't standing but sat in a comfortable chair next to her husband. I noticed her brother wasn't at her side. Well, he wasn't related to Thomas except through his sister's marriage. And Lillian didn't seem to need comfort from anyone.

A dozen townspeople preceded me in the line. I was surprised to see the round head of Jotham O'Toole. Hat in hand, he moved restlessly several places ahead of where I stood. His social class was far from that of the Parrys, if one attended to such things. I imagined William and Lillian paid close attention to class, along with all the other factory owners and their wives. This reception had been opened to the public, though. Certainly no one would try to oust Minnie's brother, although I didn't remember seeing him at the church or at the burial ground.

Jotham glanced at the line behind him. I caught his eye and had started to nod when he turned back. His face was ruddier than usual, likely from helping himself to more than one glass of claret. I remembered his anger in Minnie's rooms and hoped he wasn't about to confront William about her. He had every right to, but not here. Not now. The line inched forward. Cyrus Hamilton leaned over, paying his respects to Lillian. He was a trim man of average height with a neat dark mustache and a hairline halfway toward the crown of his head. Another man with a difficult son; if Stephen were convicted for the Meetinghouse fire, the sentence for arson was severe. Which would be worse, to lose your son to death or to years in either prison or the Danvers Hospital for the Criminally Insane, both places nearly as bad as death?

The line moved again. Jotham reached William where he stood turned away and still speaking to the lady in line ahead of Jotham. William turned back and his eyes widened as if he'd seen a specter. Jotham stuck out his hand and grinned. William shook it but drew his hand back as soon as he could. Jotham leaned in so his mouth was near William's left ear and he spoke so softly I couldn't catch it.

"No!" William cried out, shrinking back. "Leave! Get this man out of here!" His face became the color of bleached linen.

The room quieted. Cyrus, now on his way out of the room, whirled and took a step. Lillian glanced up at the commotion.

Jotham returned her gaze. "Howdy, Mrs. Parry. How's that baby of yours doing? My sister's got one just born, did you know? Named him Billy, she did."

Lillian gasped and crossed her hands over her belly.

"How dare you?" Cyrus arrived at Jotham's side and grasped his arm. "You, who plied my son with matches at every turn."

Jotham twisted out of Cyrus's hold and sauntered to the doorway. He glanced around the room. Laughing, he left the house as the mourners watched, shocked and aghast.

TWENTY-THREE

After I made sure Lillian was stable, I left the library. Jotham O'Toole was up to no good, that was clear.

"Miss Carroll," a man's voice said from behind me. I turned to see Cyrus Hamilton. "Miss Carroll, I want to apologize to you and to your congregation for my son's actions on Sunday. It was inexcusable."

I gazed into his distraught eyes, his somber face. "I thank thee, Cyrus. Stephen doesn't seem well."

He shook his head. "He's not. I've tried to get help for him, but nothing has succeeded. And now . . ." He spread his hands as if in entreaty. To whom I wasn't sure.

I reached out and patted his arm. "Thee is in a difficult situation."

"I would ask for your prayers for him, if that is possible."

"We shall hold him in the Light of God."

"I thank you." He straightened his back.

"I would like to make a monetary contribution to your church — that is, your, uh, Meeting — for any repairs due to the fire."

"I believe that would be most generous, and most welcome." I gave him the name of our treasurer. "I'll tell him to expect it. Friends thank thee and wish thee well with thy son. We harbor no anger toward him."

He bowed his head in acknowledgment then returned to the library. I stood in the foyer, uncertain about my continued purpose here. Perhaps Bertie would provide guidance. I went in search of her.

She stood in the dining room holding forth on the novels of George Eliot to a small group. I stood nearby until she spied me.

"Excuse me," she said to her listeners, then turned toward me.

Beckoning her away from the group, in a quiet voice I told her about the altercation with Jotham.

She let out a whistle. "I didn't hear a thing. What do you think he said to Parry?"

"I wasn't able to discern. But I'd wager it was about Minnie O'Toole's baby. If I were the wagering type."

"Want to bet?" Bertie laughed. "I'll corrupt you yet, Quaker Carroll."

I laughed in return. "I sincerely doubt

that. Is thee ready to leave? I have had enough polite company for one day."

"Likewise for me. Let's go. Did you pay your respects?"

"After a fashion," I said. "I was in line behind Jotham, so I made sure Lillian didn't suffer from his outburst. And I was already here this morning tending to both Lillian and William. And thee?"

"I don't believe in standing in line to tell somebody I'm sorry their son died. I'll do it in person next time I see each of them." She glanced around. "Didn't see your David here. He's not interested in funerals?"

I laughed. "He doesn't know the Parrys. It's a bit of a different world across the river in Newburyport. Besides, he's at work. I didn't expect to see him here."

We fetched our wraps from the foyer and made our way onto the veranda, where we encountered a frowning Kevin Donovan.

"Ah, Miss Carroll. And Bertie Winslow in the bargain. Did either of you happen to be in the room when O'Toole made his move?" He gazed at me, then at Bertie.

"I was," I said. "But I couldn't hear what Jotham said to William Parry."

"No one but Parry did, apparently. And he's not talking." Kevin removed his hat and rubbed his head until his carrot-colored hair

275

stood straight up. "I suppose I'll have to go track down this Jotham character. We can't have ruffians like him being rude to upstanding citizens like Mr. Parry."

"I can tell thee where Jotham's sister lives," I volunteered. "I delivered her of a baby only one week ago." I described how to find Minnie's place on Pearl Street.

"And why did this Jotham feel the need to bring up that baby with William Parry?" Kevin shook his head.

I glanced at a bright-eyed Bertie. I lowered my voice, even though the porch was empty but for we three. Bertie edged closer to me and Kevin leaned in to hear.

"I might as well tell thee. Minnie's was the flat I saw William Parry enter. She seems to be of little evident means of income, yet wears fine clothing and paid me in full for my services on the day of her son's birth."

"Ah, so the plot thickens, as they say in those books of yours." Kevin spread his feet and clasped his hands behind him.

"In fact, William Parry asked me directly not to mention to his wife that he had paid a visit to Minnie." I held up a hand when I saw Kevin about to speak. "I didn't promise to support his subterfuge, but I also don't want to upset a client getting close to term."

"So Parry has been running around and

he now has a bastard child to show for it." Kevin rocked on his heels. "The secret of the harlot's identity comes out at last."

"I told thee she isn't a harlot. A young woman who was taken advantage of, certainly. But remember I said I wondered if somehow Minnie's baby might be at the root of the recent troubles? The fire and Thomas's stabbing, that is."

"Your theories again." Kevin snorted. "Well, when you figure out more details of that fantasy of yours, Miss Carroll, do stop by the station and let me know." He walked into the house.

I stared as he disappeared through the doorway into the house. Wasn't he the one who'd asked me to keep my eyes and my brain working for him?

Bertie tucked her hand through my elbow. "Doesn't sound so fantastical to me. Come on, let's talk it through as we walk. I did hear a rumor in the post office about Parry being a little too friendly with dear Minnie since before his marriage to Lillian. But how does that get Thomas killed?"

I sighed as we made our way down the steps of the veranda toward the road. "Suppose . . . no, that doesn't work."

Bertie glanced at me.

"I thought perhaps Minnie would want to

get back at Lillian, but why? Anyway, Lillian didn't even like Thomas. Maybe she hired someone to kill him."

Bertie grimaced. "Talk about a wicked stepmother. It sounds like something out of *Grimms' Fairy Tales.*"

"I could see Jotham setting the fire, though, to punish William for impregnating Minnie. I surely hope the arsonist wasn't Ephraim Pickard."

"Ephraim's wife is my second cousin," Bertie said.

"Did thee know Kevin has arrested him for both the mill fire arson and the murder?"

Bertie nodded, her eyebrows nearly touching. "Ephraim is always trying to get ahead but hasn't had much luck yet. I'll take his wife some food. Poor thing. I'll take some to Ephraim himself, too. I can only imagine what slop they serve in the jail."

"Maybe Jotham killed Thomas to punish William further. I wonder if Kevin has thought of that." We crossed over Sparhawk and made our way along Whittier Street.

"Not if he's focused on Ephraim, he hasn't."

"I am resolved to find a solution to these mysteries. The mill arson and the murder. I no longer have much faith that Kevin will."

We reached the small house Bertie shared

with Sophie, tucked behind a larger home. Her cottage garden in front was already sprouting bright-colored tulips and jonquils, and I knew the rambling rose that decorated the low fence would be a riot of pink come June.

"Come in while I put together a couple of meals?" Bertie cocked her head, one hand on the gate. "Sophie's at work and I can use your help. Then we can visit Ephraim together."

I hesitated. "I'm tired from all my walking to and fro this day, and I need to get back."

"You need a horse," Bertie said. "Or a bicycle."

"I had that same thought this morning. One of those new safety bicycles."

"I saw them for sale at Clark's. Do you know how to ride, though?"

"I do, in fact," I said. "My wild cousin Sephronia taught me one summer when I was still in school. The balance takes a bit of learning, but I think the wheels of equal size should prove much easier."

"I can lend you some riding bloomers." She opened the front door. "Are you coming in, then?"

"Oh, why not?" Two sleuthing heads should be more effective than one and perhaps we could learn something from the poor jailed man.

Bertie and I stood in the police office anteroom a couple of hours later. She held a basket covered by a checked napkin.

"We simply want to have a word with Ephraim Pickard after we bring him his supper," Bertie said, gesturing to the packet wrapped in paper and string I held and raising her basket.

The young officer at the desk pursed his lips. "That's not common," he said.

Bertie flashed him a brilliant smile. "We'll only be a minute."

"We feed the prisoners, you know." He lifted his chin.

"I'm afraid the fare from Mrs. Colby's boarding house scarcely provides a nutritious meal. Let us pass now, if you will."

The poor fellow was no match for Bertie. I found it curious she knew so much about what prisoners were fed, though. He stood.

"Let me inspect the basket, then."

Bertie pulled the covering cloth aside and the officer poked about in it.

"Looks like food, all right," he said. "And smells mighty enticing, I must say." Fetching a ring of keys from the drawer, he led us back to the cells. Two men faced each other on a cot in one cell, playing cards in the space between them. In another enclosure a grizzled man flashed us a toothless smile. The air smelled of men crowded too close: old sweat and a hint of urine, seasoned by fear, anger, and hopelessness.

The guard pointed to the far set of bars, where Ephraim sat bent over on the edge of a cot, his head in his hands. "Visitors, Pickard — ladies," the guard barked out. "Sit up, now, and mind you behave." The guard reached forward and unlocked the door, then stepped back to wait several cells away.

Ephraim raised his head. When he saw Bertie, a weak smile broke open his misery, but then he turned his eyes to me. The brief moment of sunshine became a scowl.

"What's she doing here? She's the one what put me in here." He rose and shook a finger in my direction.

"Calm yourself, cousin, calm yourself," Bertie said. "Rose and I brought you some supper we cooked up ourselves."

"I believe in thy innocence, Ephraim." I tried to keep my own countenance calm, clasping my hands in front of me.

"You told that detective you saw me at the fire," he said. "I never set it, and I didn't kill nobody, neither."

"I'm sure the detective will discover the

true arsonist and murderer soon and thee will be freed," I said.

Bertie sat on the cot. "Let us show you the victuals we brought."

"You shouldn't be bringing me food. I get fed here, after a fashion."

"I know Mrs. Colby's cooking." Bertie snorted. "She skimps on every dish, plus she's half blind. It can't taste like anything."

"I'm not complaining. It's my wife and children, now, they're being the ones who need —"

"We dropped off a full basket for them, as well," Bertie said. She patted him on the arm. "Don't you worry."

Ephraim sank down next to Bertie, his elbows resting on his thighs.

I remained standing near the door. "Can thee tell us why the detective thinks thee killed Thomas Parry?" I asked.

"Because Thomas fired me. But if every man he'd fired came after him with a weapon, he'd a been dead long ago." He folded his hands and stared at them.

"Does thee not have anyone to vouch for thy presence during the hours before Thomas's body was discovered?"

He gazed up at me. "Detective asked me the same question. It's called an alibi. After supper I was so distraught at being out of work I went walking. I made it all the way up to Powow Hill and just sat there, looking at the stars. It's one of my interests, see, the study of astronomy. The constellations and the planets." He shook his head. "I was alone and didn't come back home until near dawn."

"And Donovan doesn't believe you." Bertie narrowed her eyes.

"No, he does not."

"He can't have any real evidence," I said.

The guard approached us. "Time's up, ladies." He jingled the ring of keys.

Bertie stretched her arm around Ephraim's back and squeezed him in for a sideways embrace, then stood. "You'll be out in two shakes of a lamb's tail, cousin. Not to fear. I will watch out for your family, too."

"I wish thee well and hold thee in the Light, Ephraim."

He gazed at me for a moment. "Thank you, Miss Carroll. I suppose that's your Quaker way of prayer, and I can use all the prayers I can get."

Bertie and I watched as the officer locked the cell door and then we followed him back to the office. Before the door clanged shut, I glanced back. Ephraim sat with head in hands just as we had found him.

Twenty-Four

Bertie and I stood on the front steps of the police station.

"How remarkable, he studies astronomy," I said.

"Ephraim has great depth. It simply isn't reflected in his income," Bertie said.

"Yet he has no alibi for the murder."

"They'll find the real killer, Rosetta. Ephraim isn't the one. And it's wrong of them to hold him without yet charging him with a crime." She pulled her coat closer about her. "I'm off. You'll get home all right?"

"Surely. Thee knows my house is only three blocks distant." Evening had fallen while we were inside but the street lamps were lit and I didn't have to pass through any unsavory areas between here and home.

"I still say you ought to get yourself a bicycle." Bertie grinned as only she can.

"I might. Thank thee for thinking to bring

Ephraim food. I'm sure he'll appreciate it."

"He's family. And it was a chance to spend time with you, too." She squeezed my hand.

I watched her stride away. I turned in the opposite direction only to see a uniformed Guy Gilbert running toward the station. He pulled up short in front of me, panting. "Miss Carroll, we have dreadful news."

"What is it, Guy?"

"There's been another murder."

"That's terrible. Who was killed?" Was I in a nightmare? Another murder in our peaceful town, another death? A cold breeze ruffled my bonnet, echoing the chill in my heart.

"Miss O'Toole. Her with the new babe and all." His jaw worked and his hands clenched and unclenched, over and over.

I stared at him. "Minnie O'Toole?" I pictured the round-faced young woman, whom I'd last seen suckling her . . . *Oh, no.* "What about tiny Billy?"

"He's alive and well."

I let a breath out. "That is a blessing, at least. How was Minnie killed?"

"I must raise the alarm." He hurried through the front door.

My head roiled with questions. Who was with the baby? Who would have killed poor Minnie? How was she killed? I followed Guy into the station as the alarm bell near the roof tolled. Guy was conferring with Kevin Donovan at the desk. Kevin looked up with a quick move.

"What are you doing here?" Kevin didn't quite glare, but he didn't smile, either.

"Minnie O'Toole was my client. I delivered her son only a week ago. Is someone with the baby now, Guy?"

He nodded. "A neighbor woman came and took him."

"Miss Carroll, you may go check on the infant," Kevin said. "But we need you out of the way of our investigation."

I opened my mouth to ask how Minnie was killed. Before I could speak, Kevin said, "Now. Go." He pointed to the door. "And we're still inspecting her flat, so don't think of going in there."

I set out for Minnie's flat in the gloaming, my mind filled with images of a week-old baby boy with no mother. And of his mother lying dead. Billy would need to feed, and likely soon. Newborns didn't thrive well on cow's milk. Perhaps the farm on Lions Mouth Road would have a nanny goat that had recently given birth. Goat's milk tended to sit better in a baby's stomach. The new infant formulas like Mellin's Food were available for a price, as were tins of condensed milk, but they weren't healthy substitutes for the breast. And then I stopped in the middle of High Street. Billy didn't need the milk of an animal or sustenance from a can, either.

Taking a detour of several blocks, I rapped on the Hendersons' door. When I received no answer, I called out.

"It's Rose Carroll. The midwife," I added, in case a family member who didn't know me was caring for Patience.

Patience herself opened the door. Her eyes were haunted and her face drawn. She wore a wrapper over her house dress but I could see the stains of a leaking bosom.

"May I come in?" I rued that I hadn't visited her earlier in the day. It had been a full one, though. And wasn't yet over.

She turned without speaking and I followed her into the flat. She sank into a chair.

"I'd like to see how thee is faring," I said.

When she nodded, I knelt next to her. Taking her wrist in my hand, I monitored her pulse.

"I can see thy milk is flowing. How is thee physically in other respects?"

She didn't speak for a moment, and then said, "I am empty. I can't stop weeping."

"Is thee able to eat and drink?"

"Not particularly."

"I'm so sorry for thy loss, Patience." I moved to the chair next to her. "Thee has been through this before. The pain will lessen with time, and I know thee will never forget thy son. Either son."

She swallowed and dabbed at her eyes with a handkerchief. A shred of lace trailed across her cheek.

"There is something thee can do for another baby, though. May I tell thee?"

"What could I possibly do?" Her voice was plaintive.

"I have just learned a newly delivered mother in town has been killed. I'm on my way to check on the infant, a week-old boy. He'll need to be nursed."

Her eyes widened. "You want me to feed a motherless boy."

"It would greatly increase his chances of survival."

"What does his father say?"

I cleared my throat. I hadn't had much time to think on how to tell Billy's story. "His father isn't present. Minnie, the deceased mother, has a sister and a brother, but I'm certain they would approve."

She sat with her hands folded, gazing at me. She turned her head to look out the window, then back at me.

"He's a healthy child so far? Of a good weight? If I do this, I wouldn't want to be accused of not nourishing him enough."

"Billy seems quite healthy," I said. "He wasn't too small or prematurely born, and he has a good cry. I wouldn't worry about being accused of anything. The family will be grateful."

"Then I agree." She sat up a little straighter. "Do I go to him or bring him here?"

"Babies so young need to eat around the clock, as thee knows. It might be best to keep him here. Will thy husband agree to this plan?" I hoped Hiram's cough wasn't contagious.

"I'm sure he will."

"I'll go there now and make sure the family is in agreement. I'll then bring little Billy to thee."

"I'd better straighten up while I have the chance." Patience looked around at the disarray her sorrow had caused. Dirty plates sat abandoned on the table, a cushion from the settee lay on the floor, and a stack of books had slid sideways on an end table. She stood and rubbed her hands together as if preparing to work. "You've given me purpose, Rose. Thank you."

I also stood and made my way to the door

but encountered Hiram coming in. After I explained the plan and he agreed, I said, "Thy cough concerns me. Has thee seen a doctor?"

"Thank you, Miss Carroll, I did." His face lightened. "I'm not sick. It's a cough from the coal dust I breathe on the railroad, see? So it wasn't me who killed my Timmy."

"I'm very glad to hear that. And this news rests my heart at bringing the orphaned newborn into the house. It's still prudent to be as well as possible. And I've heard of late that frequent hand washing can help to keep a family healthy, especially after coughing. Thy lungs might be more susceptible to illness than others."

He stared at me. I couldn't read his expression. I didn't know if he was about to throw me out of the house or agree.

"All right. I'll do anything to make sure another baby doesn't die." He turned toward the kitchen.

"I'll return within the hour, I expect," I said to Patience. Now all I had to do was convince Minnie's siblings of the wisdom of my plan. And pray a man like William Parry, accustomed to controlling his world, wouldn't become a problem.

TWENTY-FIVE

A uniformed officer stood with hands clasped behind his back at the bottom of the steps to Minnie's flat. A lamp in every window pushed light out into the evening. A clump of people, mostly men, stood on the opposite side of the street, smoking and talking in low voices as they gazed at the building.

I approached the officer and introduced myself.

"No one goes in, miss."

"I don't wish to enter," I said, even though I wanted to. "I'm looking for the infant. I was Minnie O'Toole's midwife and I delivered her baby only a week ago."

"He's just there with the neighbor woman." The officer pointed to the next house. A window on the side looked directly onto Minnie's porch.

A hearty woman in her fifties answered my knock, with tendrils of salt-and-pepper

291

hair escaping her puffy white mob cap. Her eyes were kindly and her flour-streaked apron confirmed a delicious aroma of fresh bread that flowed out from the open door.

I repeated my introduction, adding that I wanted to check on Billy's well-being.

"I'm Therese Stevens. Come in, then, and sit. We'll get out of sight of that clutch of vultures." She pointed to the group of curious onlookers, then ushered me into a modest sitting room whose surfaces gleamed from polish. Not a thing was out of place, except baby Billy nestled into a blanket on a big stuffed chair.

"He's just gone to sleep at last, poor tyke." She snugged the blanket up closer under his chin. "Will you take a cup of tea?"

"I thank thee kindly. It has been a long day for me, and it's not over yet."

She bustled out and I bent over to check on Billy. His brow was warm but not hot. Recent tears still dampened his cheeks. My hostess returned in no time bearing a tray with a cup of tea and a plate of warm buttered bread that she set on a low table near me. A small pot of purple preserves sat open with a knife at the ready.

"Has thee spoken with Minnie's brother or sister?" I took a sip of the tea, grateful she had sweetened it, and spread preserves on a slice of bread.

"The sister was the one who found her, bless her soul. She's still next door being questioned, I believe."

"Such sadness for her. How was Minnie killed?" I felt compelled to ask.

Even though no one was nearby to listen, Therese leaned toward me and lowered her voice. "She was stabbed in the neck."

A chill rippled through me. The same method of murder as with Thomas. By the same person? At least this time it hadn't been done with my knitting needle.

"With a letter opener, they said," Therese added.

"How awful." I imagined Minnie's fear when she saw her killer coming for her. "Did thee see anyone acting oddly come to call?"

Therese nodded. "I saw only a woman wearing a long cape and a large bonnet visit Minnie late this afternoon. Never seen the likes of her before. Couldn't get much of a glimpse of the face, the bonnet came that far forward."

"That might have been Minnie's killer. Did thee see the hair color or any other identifying features?" I took a bite of the bread, which tasted as good as it smelled.

"You're sounding like the police there. Or

those vultures out there. Why are you asking so many questions?" Therese cocked her head as she gazed at me.

I swallowed before I spoke. "I am only curious, but strongly curious, I admit. Whoever killed Minnie must be brought to justice."

She nodded. "I think I spied a wisp of light-colored hair. And the woman was thin-like. A bit taller than you, even."

The mention of a cape stirred the memory of the shadowy figure I'd seen before the fire. I shivered.

Billy stirred in his makeshift bed. "How will we feed this child?" Therese asked. "He'll need to eat soon. I don't know the sister's plans for him. I might have a can of condensed milk in the kitchen."

"Thee won't need that." I told her of Patience's recent loss and her willingness to nurse Billy.

"That's splendid, then. I heard the father isn't known. Although" — Therese watched me as she spoke — "I've seen a certain gentleman come to call several times. A gentleman well-known in Amesbury." She raised her eyebrows.

I nodded. "I saw him once, as well. I believe he's the baby's father. His own wife is also with child, though. I don't know if he'll acknowledge Billy or not."

"The poor innocent infant who did nothing to deserve his fate." Therese made a tsking sound. "At least he'll be able to eat." At a knock on the door, Therese rose and disappeared into the hall.

She returned with a round-faced woman in her forties. A spot of pink was the only color in her otherwise pale cheeks and her dark hair bore a few streaks of silver. "Rose Carroll, this is Ida. Minnie's sister."

I rose. "I can see the resemblance. I'm so sorry for the loss of thy sister, Ida." I held out my hand.

Ida clasped it, then knelt next to Billy. "Them police kept asking me questions, and all I wanted was to come see the wee one." She stroked his cheek. "They finally let me go."

"You found Minnie?" I refrained just in time from saying *Minnie's body*.

She glanced up, tears overflowing eyes as blue as cornflowers. "I was coming to check on her and Billy. She didn't answer my knock but I could hear him crying. I pushed the door open and there she lay in the hall. Dead." Ida sank back on the floor and clasped her knees in her arms, rocking as she hugged herself. "My little sister, with that, that *thing* sticking right out of her

295

neck. Who would do such a terrible deed?"

"Come now." Therese helped Ida up off the floor and into a chair. She pulled a bottle out of a high cupboard set into the wall near the hall. "You need a spot of spirits," Therese said, pouring the brandy into a small glass and handing it to Ida. She poured a spot for herself, as well, but I shook my head when she glanced at me holding a third glass.

Ida sipped the spirits and grew less agitated. "What will I do with my nephew? I have six of my own children at home. And the youngest is five. I don't have a drop of milk left in me."

I leaned toward Ida, my elbows on my knees. "I have a client who lost her own newborn son this week. She's agreed to feed and care for Billy for the time being. With thy permission, clearly."

"Who is this woman? And what happened to her poor son?"

I told her about Patience and Timmy. She nodded slowly.

"That poor woman. If she takes Billy in, I can go and see him when I want, surely?"

"Of course," I said, sitting back.

"That's fine, then."

"Will this plan meet thy brother's approval, too?" I asked. "Or that of other family members?"

"It's only me and Jotham. He and I don't see eye to eye, you might say. But he can't argue with making sure Billy is fed the right way."

"Can thee think of anyone at all who might have held a grudge against your sister?" I watched her.

"Now there you go badgering her with these same inquiries," Therese said to me. "That's not rightly your business, Miss Carroll."

Ida shook her head. "It's all right, though the detective asked me the same question. I don't know of anyone who disliked Minnie. She was just a sweet girl who went a little wrong. That Mr. Parry took advantage of her, he did. But he at least did the right thing by supporting her."

"Thee is confident that he's Billy's father, then," I said.

"Oh, indeed he is, wrong that it is." Ida's voice of misery changed to an angry tone. She tossed back the rest of her drink and gazed at the baby. "He'd better keep on paying, too. For his son."

TWENTY-SIX

Billy suckled at Patience's breast thirty minutes later as if he always had, his head nestled in the crook of her arm.

"He's not my Timmy, but I'm glad I'm good for something." She glanced up with luminous eyes.

With me by her side, Ida had carried Billy to Patience's. I was pleased to see Patience's home was now tidy and she had tidied herself up, as well. She'd pulled her hair back and donned a clean dress, and her face appeared freshly washed.

"You're good for a great deal," Ida said.

"I agree," I said. "He could be fed one of the new infant formulas, but I've seen several babies sicken from that method."

"And we have small clothing and diapers. I'm happy they have a use," Patience said, stroking Billy's head. Hiram stood behind her, his hands on her shoulders.

When Billy was finished eating, Ida laid

him on her shoulder, patting his back to induce a burp. She was clearly an experienced mother. When he'd let go of the gas bubble, she handed him back to Patience and we said our farewells.

"I need to get back to my own babies, large though they may be," Ida said. "I'll come to check on this precious nephew soon." She put a hand to her mouth, her eyes welling over.

"You will be welcomed," Patience said with a sad smile. She reached out and squeezed Ida's hand.

"My sister was a sweet girl. She didn't deserve to die."

I said good-bye to Patience and Hiram. "I'll return to check on the baby, too." Ida and I made our way out. "For now, with Patience as wet nurse, there is nothing to pay," I said to her as we strolled back the way we had come. "But certainly as Billy grows, he'll need food, clothes, schooling. Perhaps I can try to speak to William Parry on Billy's behalf."

"I'd send my brother, but he's a bit of a hothead."

"Jotham? Yes, I've seen as much."

Ida's mouth pulled down. "When do you think they'll find Minnie's killer?"

"I don't know. The detective and his team

will do their best, I'm sure." I said good-bye when I reached the path leading to my house, glad of a chance to gather my thoughts alone as I walked in the dark. My feet felt as leaden as an anchor now that this latest murder truly had time to sink in.

The killer must be the mysterious woman Therese saw. She had said she'd relayed that information to the police. I hoped to God the "thin-like" woman in the long cape wasn't Nell. I couldn't imagine why she would kill Minnie, but she was acting crazy lately, so there was no telling what she might or might not do. It was the job of the police to untangle this mystery, not mine, but the puzzle nagged at me. The arson. Thomas's murder with my knitting needle. Minnie's by a similar method. William Parry was the hub connecting these spokes. The way through to the answers, though, was still as dark as the night.

I left Allen's Hardware the next morning on a brand-new safety bicycle, a White Star Number Two. I'd resolved upon wakening to purchase transportation. I couldn't keep traipsing all about town on foot, and Bertie had planted the seed. The thirty-eight dollars almost exhausted my funds, but I would be paid soon enough for assisting at more births. The bicycle even came with fenders on the back sides of the wheels, a wicker basket strapped to the front, perfect for my birthing bag, and a little brass bell I could ring with one thumb without taking my hand off the shiny nickled handlebars. I couldn't wait to show David. I knew he sometimes cycled for recreation and wanted to see the surprised pleased look on his face when I told him I could now accompany him on a ride along the banks of the Merrimack some sunny Seventh Day.

I wobbled a bit as I headed up High Street toward Orpha's on a morning promising a warm day and one with enough sun to melt the rest of the snow. My ankles were well-exposed, however, and I was glad for the pair of bloomers Bertie had convinced me to take on loan the day before. I was also grateful for the fenders on the wheels, otherwise my back would be spattered with mud. Two boys ran alongside watching me remember my balance.

"What kind of funny contraption is that?" one called.

"Did you shrink the wheel in the wash?" the other said, then guffawed.

I gave them a wave and pedaled on. It took the inventors awfully long to realize that one huge wheel and one tiny one

301

weren't a good idea. With this lady's bicycle, I could easily put my foot on the pavement when I needed to stop. I was navigating a corner when a red-faced man stepped in front of me. I managed to brake in time to avoid running into Jotham O'Toole. His brows pulled together and the corners of his mouth turned down like an angry bull's.

"My sister's dead," he spat. "And you stole her baby." His ire seemed to vie with despair in his eyes, but the anger won.

I lowered one foot to the ground but kept my hands on the handlebars. Anger like this might need escaping from.

"I'm so sorry for thy loss, Jotham. It's a terrible thing to lose Minnie." I reached one hand out to touch his arm but he shrank back from it. "But little Billy is in good hands. He's being fed by a wet nurse who lost her own infant son this week. The arrangement has your sister Ida's blessing, of course. Thee can visit him at Patience Henderson's whenever thee likes."

"Good." His nostrils widened as he glowered. "That Parry killed my Minnie. I know it. Him or his stupid child bride."

"Does thee know this for a fact?" I cocked my head. Perhaps I could pass information on to Kevin. "Does thee have evidence?"

"Who else would want to get rid of her?

Probably tried to kill my nephew, too. I told my Minnie she never should have taken up with that pompous ass." He swallowed hard, the sadness taking over for a moment. "She was my little sis. I always said I'd take care of her. And I failed."

"Thee didn't fail thy sister. It's not thy fault some evil person ended her life. I wonder if thee has evidence of William's guilt in the matter? Perhaps it was someone else."

He looked at me as if I were a fool. "He'll confess to it when I show him my brass knuckles. He's guilty, no question." The old brash Jotham was back. He rushed off muttering to himself.

I remounted and bumped away slowly over the paving stones, thinking I should detour past the police station and warn Kevin that Jotham was on the rampage in his grief. I doubted Jotham could get close enough to William to harm, him, though, especially after Jotham's behavior at the reception yesterday. I saw the sadness Jotham was experiencing, but his anger left me less sympathetic than I might have been otherwise.

I was nearby Orpha's home on my way to the police. A large wagon passed me too closely on my left. I veered onto the muddy dirt track, but the front wheel encountered a rock and the bicycle stopped with a jerk. I managed to fall sideways away from the wagon but crashed my knee onto a root of a large elm tree that bulged up above the ground. I pulled myself up to a side sitting position, my left foot weighted down by the bicycle's heavy metal frame.

A woman rushed toward me. "Rose!" Orpha's granddaughter Alma set down her marketing basket and picked up the bicycle so I could free my foot. "Are you all right?" With her other hand she pulled me to standing.

"I hope so. I thank thee for coming to my rescue." I tried to wipe the mud from my hands, then rubbed my knee. It felt strained but when I gingerly put weight on it, the leg held. "I feel rather foolish just now. I hit my knee on that root."

"Come along home with me. We can apply a cold compress."

"I was planning to visit Orpha, anyway." I straightened my spectacles, then took over the bicycle as Alma picked up her basket. We walked slowly along to the house, where she left me knocking at the door. At Orpha's appearance, I leaned the bicycle against the house and limped in after her. A few minutes later my leg rested on a hassock with a cold cloth draped on my knee.

Orpha gave me an inquiring glance. "You did not come over only to show me your new transport, I dare say."

I smiled, then frowned. "No. There have been several disturbing events of late I wanted to discuss with thee."

She nodded gravely. "I have heard some news, but you tell me what you find most unsettling."

I proceeded to lay out my thoughts about the arson, Thomas's murder, and Minnie's death. My encounter with Jotham this morning. What the police had found. My concerns about Nell, about Jotham, about baby Billy. Jotham's comment at the funeral reception, and Cyrus's accusing Jotham of plying Stephen with matches.

"I wonder what Cyrus meant by that," I said. "Perhaps he thought Jotham was responsible for Stephen Hamilton's attempts at arson. I still cannot believe Ephraim Pickard started the mill fire. Could Jotham have been encouraging Stephen to burn down the factory?"

"But why? And anyway, young Hamilton didn't. You said he was at a pub when the mill fire was set. And he's been in jail for several days now."

"But he did try to burn the Meeting-house."

"True. The neighbor did not recognize the woman who came to Minnie's home?" Orpha asked.

"She said she didn't, only that the woman was thin and a bit taller than I. Perhaps she told Kevin more."

Orpha sat silent for a moment, then said, "I am concerned for Nell, poor thing. It sounds like a classic case of postpartum blues."

"I hope she wasn't out wandering around with my knitting needle and then went crazy on Thomas. But why?" I frowned. "When will we find an effective treatment for the sadness that arises after childbirth?"

"Time. Time heals it. But the mother and children must all be kept safe until that happens. It is not easy."

"Well, at least Billy is cared for," I said. I fell silent. I gazed at my hands folded in my lap but instead imagined Minnie's fear and desperation when she saw her death approaching.

Orpha cleared her throat. "I am not surprised to see you sorting through these questions, Rose. You have a gift."

I glanced up, confused. "What kind of gift?"

"Did you know you were born in the caul?"

"I was?" Babies sometimes emerged with all of the amniotic sac unbroken, in a beautiful translucent bubble, or with a piece of the caul stretched like a thin mask over the face. I'd never known my birth was one of those.

"The caul was intact," she went on. "I was the midwife at your birth, you know."

I nodded. "My mother told me."

"But she did not tell you about being born in the caul, did she?"

"No, never. You didn't, either, even while I trained with you."

"After your niece's birth, when you came to me asking for an apprenticeship, I wanted our relationship to be professional, without a special privilege. I needed to see how you would do. If it turned out you were not well suited for your calling, I didn't want anything to stand in the way of my letting you know that."

"But —"

Orpha held up a hand. "I suspected you would be a talented midwife, caring and skilled at once, and you indeed are."

"I hope to improve."

"And you will, with experience. I would never have let you out on your own if I did not think you were ready, though."

"But why would being born in the caul give me any special privilege?"

She smiled. "Babies born in the caul often have the gift of sight. Of seeing their way through whatever confronts them. Some become actual seers, some use their gift in the ministry, some become great leaders."

"So why didn't Mother tell me about being born in the caul?"

"She thought any talk of a gift was silly superstition. Your mother is a very modern woman."

I had heard this superstition and hadn't given it much credence. But I now knew that sometimes superstitions are based in fact of one kind or another, couched in the language of myth to make them easier to understand. Perhaps if a baby's first view of the world was through a translucent membrane, he or she would try harder throughout life to see the truth.

I wrinkled my nose. "I'm no great leader, Orpha."

"But you do see things, and you have a strong sense of justice."

"John Whittier said the same thing, that I have the gift of seeing. I didn't know what he meant, but I'm sure he doesn't know about my being born in the caul."

"It does not matter," she said. "You will see your way to solving these puzzles. I am confident of it."

"I hope so. It's terrible that a murderer continues to walk free in our town. That it might be two different killers plus a dangerous arsonist is worse."

"I have no answer for you, except that you must trust your own sense of right."

"I'll try." I removed the compress and palpated my knee. It didn't feel as if I had seriously harmed it. I certainly hoped not, since it would be hard to dance with an injured leg. And I very much wanted to dance with my dear David.

Orpha sighed. "Now I am tired." She waved a hand. "Be off on your fancy bicycle, my dear, and let me rest."

After I'd taken my leave of Orpha, I walked the bicycle slowly. This news of my being born in the caul had struck a curious nerve in me and made me think back on my life. I wasn't sure I felt that I had a gift of seeing, but a consistent thread in my experience had certainly been persistence and solving problems. I'd been good with arithmetic in school and now found satisfaction in solving the problem of a slow labor or a stuck baby. With the first I found that making the laboring mother feel safe was a great assist, and with the second it was often a question of the mother assuming the right position to free up the infant so it could continue its passage into the world. Perhaps understanding how to fix those problems was a kind of seeing.

Or perhaps it was my need to see right done in the world. My parents, especially my mother, had often spoken of the role of Friends in achieving equality in our society. Mother had been adamant that I should make seeking truth and justice my life's work no matter what profession I pursued.

After some minutes of walking, my knee felt strong enough to ride again. I re-mounted my steel steed and resolved to go directly to William Parry. He had to acknowledge Billy, and I wanted to warn him about Jotham's threat, as well. William had buried his first son only yesterday, though. I didn't know if he'd still be at home or out seeking to reestablish his business. As it was ten o'clock, I decided to search for him on Carriage Hill. Sure enough, after I cycled up the slope, I spied him striding away from the ruins of his factory toward a waiting carriage, a liveried driver standing at attention.

"Oh, William," I called. I didn't dare lift a

hand from the handlebars in case I lost my still precarious balance. "Hello?" I tried out the bell and was pleased when it dinged twice, once as I pressed the thumb handle, once when it released.

William turned his head and slowed to a stop as I rolled up. "Yes, Miss Carroll? My, that is some kind of transport."

I nodded as I swung my leg through the vee of the cycle to dismount and tried to regain my breath from pedaling up the steep incline.

"You were looking for me?" His eyes carried sadness and something more, but he squared his shoulders.

"I was." I swallowed. "Pardon me while I catch my breath. I'm recalling my bicycle skills from long ago." I smiled, then inhaled deeply.

"It's a new model, that," he observed. "I'd read about the safety bicycle. Appears much more sensible than what is in common use."

"It is." I became more somber. "William, has thee heard the awful news?"

He narrowed his eyes. "Awful news?"

"Yes. Minnie O'Toole, newly delivered of a son only days ago, was murdered last evening." I watched him. "It's terribly sad."

"What? How can that be? How do you know?" William stared at me for a moment, then turned away, sinking his brow into his hand. With a shake of his head, he faced me again, his nostrils flared, his hand dropping helplessly to his side. "What happened to her?"

"I'm afraid she was stabbed. I heard of it from the police. They are investigating, of course."

"Of course." He paused, his eyes downcast, before saying, "So much death. Too much death."

"William, I believe Minnie's infant son, Billy, is thy child. In fact, she named him for thee. Is this true?"

He stared at me again. He blinked hard, then pressed his lips together.

"Thee does not wish to acknowledge thy offspring, but many have linked thy name with Minnie's. Including thee, to me, only last week. Or does thee not wish to remember our conversation?" I knew I was being bold, but I didn't care. The baby needed his father, now more than ever. I had to seek justice.

His face reddening, he took a step toward me. I took my own step, placing the bicycle between us. He glared but still didn't speak.

"The baby is in the care of a wet nurse for now. But he'll need thy support as he grows." I mounted my cycle but kept my feet on the ground. "Please take the moral high ground and acknowledge thy son. It is only just."

"My wife wouldn't stand for it. Don't you see?" His face changed from angry to stricken, and the words sounded ripped out of him. "She thinks our baby is the only one in the universe. She'd kill me."

"She might not be the only one. I should warn thee I encountered Jotham O'Toole earlier this morning. He's dreadfully angry with thee."

"That hothead." His tone dismissed Jotham. "He had the nerve to come into my home, with my Thomas barely buried."

"He said to me he believes thee killed his sister." I watched William's face change again, this time to incredulity.

"Why would I kill Minnie? She was a sweet girl." He spread his hands wide, his eyes still sad.

"Or that thy wife did."

"Lillian?" He laughed. "She wouldn't hurt a fly. And couldn't, either. She's a hothouse flower at any time, and now, in her condition? This man must be some kind of lunatic."

"I'm only conveying what I heard. He also threatened thee. I might advise traveling with a bodyguard of some kind."

His eyes narrowed as he turned on his heel and strode for his carriage. He called over his shoulder, "Nobody threatens William Parry."

Twenty-Seven

I rolled down the hill, William's words echoing in my ears as the cobblestones rattled my teeth. A client would visit my parlor clinic at one o'clock. Before then I needed to visit Billy and Patience, and perhaps check on Nell, as well. I braked and then put both feet on the ground as I reached Market Square, waiting for an open spot in the traffic before I attempted to cross and head up Main Street. When I felt a hand on my shoulder, I whirled, only to laugh.

"John Whittier! You startled me." I patted my heart.

"Thee has acquired a conveyance. An excellent choice for thy profession, I dare say." His eyes twinkled.

"Well, it will be once I find my balance again." As always, I was pleased to see him. "I learned to ride a bicycle on a packed dirt road at my parents' farm. It's not as easy on these paving stones."

"And did thee find the fancy dress of which we spoke?"

"I did. It's actually a simple fancy dress, which suits me. It's even the color of my name." I smiled, thinking of the little girl calling me a princess.

"I would be lost in that regard. My mother discovered, after she sent the six-year-old me out to harvest strawberries, that I do not see colors. Or at least not the difference between red and green." He laughed. "She was well displeased when I proudly carried in a basket of hard unripe berries."

"Gracious, that is a funny story," I said, then sobered. "I'm not as certain about my comportment at the event itself, but David Dodge assures me I'll do fine."

"Good. There will be that of God in all who attend. Thee needs only to search for that sameness we all share."

I nodded. "True." It would be a challenge, but I'd attempt to meet it for David's sake.

"And what about my visit with David's mother that we discussed?"

"So much has been happening I forgot all about it." I cringed a little at my absent-mindedness. "When is thee free?"

"I could see her this afternoon. Not this Seventh or First Day, as I'm off to visit Hampton Falls, where my friend Celia

Thaxter will join me. Or I could receive David's mother early in the next week. Whenever she likes, if it helps thee."

I snorted. "I'm not certain anything will help me with that society matron who wants to see her son marry a young lady of his own class. But I'll write her a note as soon as I arrive home from my visits."

"It sounds to me as if David has a mind of his own. Thee should not worry." He patted my shoulder. "Where is thee off to now?"

My smile disappeared. "To see a baby without his mother and a mother without her son."

"Minnie O'Toole's child." His twinkle also vanished. "Another murder in our fair town."

I nodded. "And Patience Henderson, whose infant son died only days ago. She agreed last evening to nurse tiny Billy, and I must check on them."

"I'll accompany thee partway."

"I'd be pleased." I dismounted my bike and we made our way across the busy intersection.

John strolled at my side wearing a somber expression, his cane appearing more for show than for support. "Our Kevin Donovan must be feeling less than effective," he said. "To have a suspect in jail and yet another killing occur. There are either two murderers or the wrong one has been arrested."

"I'm convinced of Ephraim's innocence." I steered my cycle around a pile of manure.

"Does thee have evidence?"

"I'm afraid not. I simply don't believe he would kill someone."

"The court of the land will need more than that, Rose."

I sighed. "I know. If I could find the real killer, I wouldn't need evidence of Ephraim's innocence. And yet . . ."

John watched me for a moment. "And yet, what?"

"I fear Nell Gilbert might have acted insanely."

"Young Guy's wife?"

"Exactly. She's suffering from an acute depressive state and also had access to the murder weapon." I winced at the thought of my mother's lovely painted tool plunging into Thomas's vein, bringing his life to a sudden close.

"Thy knitting needle. But why would Nell kill Thomas Parry? She is a young mother and wife. Did Thomas wrong her in some way?"

"It's possible at some time in the past.

Now she hasn't a reason in the world to harm him. But insanity doesn't consort with reason much, I think."

Kevin strode out of George Wendall's barber shop directly in front of us, rubbing his newly smooth cheek with one hand as he placed his uniform hat on his head with the other. "What's this about insanity?" A trace of shaving lotion trailed along his right jowl and lines were etched on his face despite smelling of a bracing tonic.

"Good morning, Kevin," John said with a smile. "Thee appears freshly shorn."

"I've been keeping some long hours and have an appointment with the judge before noon. Wouldn't do to look a mess. And my long-suffering wife appreciates a smooth cheek, as well." He grinned. "Now, what are the town's most important Quakers discussing?"

"What will thee talk with the judge about?" I asked. "Is it to free Ephraim Pickard?" I hoped so, and also hoped to avoid telling him my fears about Nell. If they were groundless, there was no point in her being accused of something she didn't do. If she was guilty, it was a thought too hard to bear. For now. I wasn't concerned about being thought too curious, as Kevin was accustomed by now to my questioning him.

"He's concerned about the safety of our town. But, no, Mr. Pickard remains safely locked up where he'll not harm anyone else." Kevin patted his robust stomach in satisfaction.

"What about Minnie's killer? Has thy investigation led thee anywhere yet?" I watched him. "At least thee knows it wasn't Ephraim this time."

He met my eyes. "We're following up every lead, Miss Carroll."

"Minnie's neighbor Therese said a woman came to call that afternoon," I said. "Has thee discovered her identity? She could be the killer."

"You leave the detecting to us, now." Kevin's voice was stern. He set his fists on his hips, regarding me. "I'm serious. I don't want you putting yourself in danger's way. A killer runs loose in our town and my department has its hands full. The last thing we need is common citizens trying to help and getting hurt, instead."

"No one wants that, Kevin," John chimed in, glancing from Kevin to me and back.

I raised my chin. "Thee did ask me to keep my eyes and ears open, Kevin. I can't help my inquisitive personality."

Kevin rolled his eyes as the bell on the Congregational Church next to us tolled eleven times. "Try," he called over his shoulder, hurrying down the street.

Having parted ways with John, I parked my cycle outside Patience Henderson's home ten minutes later, my mind awhirl. I longed to return to a life consisting of the simple interactions of midwife and client. Explaining the age-old process of gestation, labor, and birth. Helping babies into the world. Assisting the natural union of mother and child at the breast. All this commotion and mystery surrounding violent death wasn't to my liking, despite my strong Quaker need to see justice done, which led to my curiosity about who had killed and why.

I set my foot on the first sun-splashed step of the outside staircase and rubbed my still-sore knee. I paused and smiled at the distinctive whistled notes of the cardinal — *wheet, wheet, due-due-due-due-due-due* — its song such a treat for the ears in early spring. Over it I heard a door slapping open. Jotham stood on the landing outside Patience's flat with a blanket-wrapped Billy in his arms. All his attention on the baby, he rocked Billy and cooed at him. I watched in silence.

"Bye-bye baby Billy, father's gone a-hunting, mother's gone a-milking . . ." He broke off his version of the familiar nursery rhyme, his voice quavering. He took a deep breath, then started anew, stroking the baby's cheek with each rhythmic phrase.

"Bye-bye baby Billy, father's gone a killing, mother's gone a-dying, uncle's gone-a hunting, to find some true justice, to wrap the baby Billy in."

Billy let out a soft cry, and Jotham shifted him to rest on his shoulder, patting the baby's back. As he did, he caught sight of me. The tender smile vanished. He opened his mouth as if to shout at me, glanced at his nephew, and shut it again.

"I've come to check on Billy's health." I smiled, hoping to hide my nerves. Would he use his brass knuckles on me? No time like the present to find out. I continued up the steps until I shared the landing with them.

Jotham held Billy tight against his chest. "You're not taking him from me." He took a step toward the stairs.

I moved to block him. "Of course not. Thee is his uncle, his blood relative." I stood in place. He'd have to push me down the flight of stairs before he'd get by. "But thee isn't able to provide him the nourishment he needs. Only Patience can." I saw movement behind Jotham. Patience appeared in the open doorway, alarm painted on her face.

"I told him not to take the baby outside," Patience said, her voice trembling. "I went into the kitchen for a moment and when I came back, he was gone." She stretched her arms toward Billy. When Jotham turned his back, she dropped them and stared at me. "Rose, do something."

"Jotham, Billy needs Patience's milk." I kept my tone low and calm despite the agitation I felt. "If thee takes him, he'll sicken and likely die. Thee can visit him here whenever thee likes. Isn't that right, Patience?"

Eyes wide, she nodded. She swallowed. "Of course." The tone of her voice now matched mine.

Jotham faced us again as Billy set to wailing. Jotham kept patting his back, but the baby was inconsolable. I had seen this effect before. Billy already recognized the smell of Patience's milk, and possibly also the sound of her voice, even though he'd been with her less than a day. She was the only person he wanted.

Jotham, with his brow drawn in and his eyes dragged down, relinquished the baby to Patience. Patience drew Billy into her arms and hurried back into the house, with a worried glance behind her before she shut the door. The lock clicked.

"Let me pass now, will you?" Jotham's sad expression changed to a scowl, like a thunderstorm overtaking a gentle rain.

"Thee will be Billy's uncle his whole life," I ventured. "Please let him thrive now under Patience's care so thee can throw a ball with him in a few years' time."

He stomped down the stairs. "I will. For now."

I watched him go. The cardinal began his song again, but all I heard was *father's gone a-killing, uncle's gone a-hunting, to find some true justice.* I shuddered at the meaning of those words.

TWENTY-EIGHT

I left Patience a few minutes before noon, satisfied Billy was nursing well. I assured her she was doing the right thing, and that I thought I had convinced Jotham, as well. I didn't speak of the foreboding nursery rhyme version he had sung. At a pang from my stomach, I decided to head for home and have a bite to eat before my first client arrived. I really needed to carry some kind of sustenance in my satchel to tide me over. A whole-meal biscuit, perhaps, and a bit of cheese. I decided I didn't have it in me to visit Nell at this time. I must see her, but I could pay her a visit later this afternoon.

I cycled slowly up Highland to Hillside, turning right. The clatter of horseshoes swiftly became louder behind me, followed by a stream-lined black gig passing so close by I could have touched its shiny metalwork. Two men occupied the two-wheeled vehicle. The passenger threw back his blond head and roared with laughter, his hat flying off into the street. A moment later, he tumbled out of the gig and fell on the ground. I dismounted, letting my bike fall to the side, and rushed to him. The driver pulled the horse up a few yards away.

"Young man," I said as I knelt by the man's supine form. He was indeed young, barely out of his teenage years. He wore a fine gray suit in the latest style, although his tie was askew and there was a wine-colored stain on his collar. I patted his cheek and took a closer look at his face. His eyes were closed, but I recognized him as Lillian's brother Alexander.

"Alexander Locke? Can thee hear me?" I laid my fingers on his neck to take his pulse. I let out a breath when I felt a slow but regular beat, although his skin was cool and clammy.

His eyes popped open. "Hello, beautiful. Are you an angel?" His words came slowly. "I must be in heaven." His smile was lopsided.

"My name is Rose Carroll. I'm going to examine thy head. Please don't move."

He winced slightly as I lifted his head from the ground, bracing it with one hand, and felt his crown with my other hand. I let his head down gently. My hand showed no blood and I had felt no lumps. I stretched open his eyelids one by one, then sat back on my heels. I rested my hands on my knees.

"Does anything hurt? Thy arms or legs?"

Stretching, he tested his limbs. "All as usual. Why d'you talk like that?"

"I'm a member of the Society of Friends."

"So I've been rescued by a Quaker angel, it seems." He smiled in a lazy fashion.

"How did thee come to fall out of the carriage?" I asked as his dark-haired friend strolled up, a friend of about the same age who seemed not at all concerned about Alexander's fall.

Alexander extended a hand to the other man. "Lend me a lift, old bean." The man helped him to sitting before acknowledging me.

"I'm Alex's classmate." He suppressed what sounded like a giggle. "He's always falling out of things. And into things."

They both burst into laughter.

I stood, brushing off my knees. "Thee seems to be well enough, Alexander. Do see thy doctor if a severe headache comes on."

"Aren't you a doctor, Miss Angel? You know everything and came out of nowhere." Alexander's lazy smile was back as he also stood. "You should call me Alex, you know."

"I'm a midwife, not a doctor. Thy sister's

midwife, in fact. And since neither of you appears to be carrying a baby, I'll be on my way."

"Ooh, Lillian. Naughty, naughty Lillian." Alexander shook his head slowly. "Good luck with her."

I mounted my bicycle and headed away.

"Ride safely," he called after me. "And don't run into any more crazy boys."

"I'll do my best," I replied, glad to get away from the two. From his constricted pupils as well as his behavior, I could tell Alexander was clearly drugged with something, perhaps morphine. Probably his friend was, too. No wonder Alexander fell out of the gig. But what had he meant by "naughty" Lillian?

Josephine Gilbert opened the door as the nearby church bell rang four times, Lizzy on her hip. "Rose, come in."

"Is Nell here?" I asked, stepping in. I gave Lizzy's round belly a little squeeze, making her laugh.

Guy's mother nodded, then pointed her chin toward the sitting room.

"She's still in a bad way," she whispered, shaking her head.

"The tea isn't helping?"

"It is not, more's the pity. She's been

drinking it. At least I think so. Maybe she's dumping it out the window when I'm not watching." Her dark eyebrows were drawn together and she pressed her mouth into a flat line.

"Mo!" Lizzy exclaimed, leaning toward me. "Mo."

Her grandmother's face lightened and she chuckled. "She's saying *more* — more tickling."

Lizzy nodded, repeating her request, so I tickled her behind her ear. After it produced more giggles, I gave her belly one more gentle squeeze.

"Nothing like a baby to cheer the spirits," Josephine said.

I smiled in return. As I opened the door to the sitting room, I heard the demand for "mo" turn into a wail disappearing in the opposite direction.

Nell sat in a rocking chair by the front window, gazing out. Her chair creaked with every forward rock and *thadumped* with every return. The room smelled stale, even sour.

"Hello, Nell." I pulled up a stool next to her, but she kept her eyes on the window. The stale scent came from her. "How is thee faring?" I patted her hand and kept smiling. "How do you like the tea I sent over?"

She tore her eyes away from the view of the street and stared at me. Her eyes looked like they had seen a great darkness — or were still seeing it.

"How should I fare?" She cocked her head. "I, who have brought death." She stopped rocking.

My heart sank. "What is thee talking about? Thee brought life. Lizzy is thriving."

Nell shook her head. "No, I brought death. I didn't want to." Her long fingers grabbed repeatedly at the cloth of her skirt, pleating the same piece again and again. Her unkempt nails caught at the fabric.

"Whose death?"

She gazed at me with wide eyes. "You don't know?"

I shrugged, hoping she'd explain.

"You do know. You're only pretending." She snorted. "He said people would. Anyway, the Devil made me do it."

"Do what?" I leaned toward her.

She shook her head again. She locked her gaze with mine. "You don't understand."

"I'd like to."

"You can't. He said so."

"Who, Nell? Who is he?"

She laughed, a high-pitched warble, but the corners of her mouth were turned down. It wasn't a laugh of joy. "The Devil, of course." She focused on the window again and resumed rocking. Back and forth. *Creak, thadump. Creak, thadump.*

Twenty-Nine

That evening we joined hands around the table in silence, after the manner of Friends, before we ate. The entire Bailey family, plus Zeb and Annie, were gathered. My eyes closed, I felt Faith's petite but strong hand on one side, her skin increasingly roughened by the hard work of a textile mill girl. In my other hand rested Luke's slender fingers, still young and smooth, not yet developed into the hand of a man. The air smelled of savory comfort.

"Blessings on this food, this family, and our friends," Frederick said.

In near unison we squeezed hands, opened our eyes, and fell to eating. After my antenatal client visits and my call on Nell Gilbert, I'd put together a meal for all — a white chicken stew with the end of last year's potatoes perked up by some early ramps I'd found, plus fresh cornbread, and an apple grunt. The work of preparing supper had calmed my roiling brain, and I had tried to put thoughts of murder away for later. I'd laid the table with a cheery cloth and cut a few forsythia branches, which now sat in a vase broadcasting their happy yellow sunshine around the room. The only thing that would improve the scene would be David at the table again, but I knew I would see him tomorrow night.

Now we passed dishes, ate, and conversed. The twins vied with each other to tell the story of a fight they'd seen at school, while Faith and Zeb seemed content to eat quietly next to each other.

"Elihu even got sent to the woodshed," Mark announced, wiggling in his chair.

"He hauled off and slugged Otis," Matthew added, with excitement warming his voice.

"Now boys, that doesn't sound very peaceable, does it?" I said.

"Rose, when can we try out thy new bicycle?" Mark asked.

I laughed. "It's too big for thee. And I need it for work. Luke or Faith can go for a ride on First Day if I'm not out at a birth, and they can teach thee when thee grows."

"Me, too," Betsy said, bouncing in place. "Thee, too."

Frederick frowned at me. "How much did

that cycle cost thee? Perhaps if thee can afford such a luxury, thee might want to start paying a monthly rent."

I held my tongue. He'd offered me the use of the parlor free of charge, for which I was grateful, but his recent moodiness seemed to be taking a miserly turn.

"Father, she needs it for work, just as thee needs thy horse," Faith said in a quiet voice.

Frederick grunted out a low "hmph" but said no more.

I'd had enough of his dark mood. "Annie, how are thy reading lessons coming along?" I asked.

Annie sat across from me, between Frederick and Betsy, who glanced up and smiled at Annie.

"I finished Betsy's first reader," Annie said with pride in her voice. "I'm on to the second one."

"You'll be reading Alcott before you know it," Faith said.

"My friend Annie Webster at school says she's going to be a policewoman when she grows up," Betsy piped up. "Can she do that, Father?"

I laughed, and Frederick gazed at his youngest without smiling. "Of course she can," he said. "Thee has learned of the importance of equality, both here at home and in First Day School."

"But she's not a Friend." Betsy shook her head.

"One doesn't have to attend Meeting to practice equality," Faith said. "As long as there isn't a law against women in the police, your friend should follow her dream. And if there were a law, perhaps she can find a way to change it."

Betsy nodded. "I'll tell her. And Father, may I invite John Whittier to my tea party next week on First Day?"

"I don't see why not. I imagine he's quite fond of tea." Frederick's serious tone was accompanied by crinkling around his eyes.

I smiled at Betsy, glad to see Frederick's caring side. I'd read my niece the poem John's friend Lucy Larcom had written, "At Queen Maude's Banquet," which described a tea party the two had shared with a young friend of John's, Carrie "Maude" Cammet. Betsy had been quite taken with the idea of tea with John.

After the four younger children finished eating and were excused from the table, Frederick turned to me.

"Is there any news about these killings in town?" He frowned, folding his hands on the table. "I know thy knitting needle was the instrument of death. Thee shouldn't

335

have been so careless."

"I wasn't careless, Frederick." How dare he accuse me of perhaps aiding a murder, even if inadvertently? I swallowed down my own temper. "I wish it hadn't been so," I said. "But I have heard no news." I had been so enjoying a family evening of respite from worry and fear, I didn't much want to begin hashing through my ideas about the crimes and their perpetrators.

"What a week it has been," Zeb said, his thin face suddenly drawn and pale.

"Ephraim Pickard is in jail for the arson, isn't he?" Faith asked.

"Yes, and Thomas Parry's murder, although I don't believe he's guilty. Kevin Donovan does, I'm afraid." I sighed. "William Parry seems to be the hub of it all, but I can't quite figure out how."

"Pickard is an interesting character," Frederick said. "He consulted with me last year about his interest in astronomy. I lent him a book on the subject. He certainly does not seem like a murderer, if we even know what that type is."

"And what about the new mother, Minnie?" Annie asked. "She was killed, too."

I nodded, my heart heavy. "Yes. Fortunately, her baby is being well cared for by a mother in town whose baby also died this week." As Annie's eyes widened, I hurried on, "Of natural causes. He had a high fever and succumbed, but now his mother has plentiful milk for Minnie's son." I didn't add, *if Billy's uncle doesn't try to steal him away.*

"What are things coming to in this town?" Faith asked. "It used to be quiet and ordered. Didn't it, Father?"

"In a way, although when one is a child, life appears simpler. In a town bustling with commerce as is ours, intrigue and disorder abound. I think, my dear, it feels more disordered to thee now thee is an adult." Frederick smiled at Faith.

"Speaking of disorder," I said, remembering my encounter of the afternoon, "Frederick, or even thee, Zeb, do you know of Alexander Locke? He's Lillian Parry's younger brother. About thy age Zeb, I'd say."

"I know of him." Frederick pursed his lips. "He was at the Academy. And was in trouble constantly. He has a bent toward addictions."

"Gambling is one, I've heard," Zeb said.

"We finally had to expel him." Frederick pulled his heavy brows together. "Why does thee ask about Alexander?"

"He and a friend nearly ran me down today," I said. "Their gig almost knocked me off my bicycle. It brushed by me so out of control that Alexander fell out onto the ground. When I rushed to help him, I noticed he was under the influence of some kind of drug. His pupils were contracted, and his manner was both lethargic and gay, as was his friend's. Perhaps they take morphine."

"I wouldn't be surprised," Frederick said. "Although their father, Henry Locke of Newburyport, is of substantial means, I think Alexander's impecunious and frivolous ways might be eating into the family wealth."

Faith rose and began to clear the table. When Zeb stood to help, Faith gave him the sweetest of smiles. "Thee is a different sort of man. I like that." Her face glowed and her eyes crinkled at their edges.

"And why should men not help in the work of the household? Do we not live by the principles of equality?" Zeb took the stack of plates from her hands and carried them to the sink.

Frederick snorted but blessedly kept quiet. Sometimes I wondered why he even claimed to be a Friend, since he acted in decidedly unFriendly ways when his temper flared and he became the opposite of peace-loving and charitable. But because his mood swung so unpredictably and almost violently from one extreme to the other, I suspected he suffered from a kind of mental unbalance. Not like Nell's, but some other sort of disorder, although I knew many would say it was a weakness of character, not an illness. Whatever its cause, his swings of temperament had worsened since Harriet's death, but his family had certainly experienced it before, Harriet most particularly. I'd asked her several times about her husband's rages, but she'd only said she loved him, warts and all.

I watched Faith and Zeb's simple affection, suddenly dreading tomorrow night's affair. Why couldn't my feelings for David, so strong and sweet a man, take a simple form, too? Why did I have to wrestle with his mother and dress up to share a part of his life? I rubbed my brow and then leaned my head onto my hand, suddenly tired. I longed to be with David, but what would that life be like without a common faith? Would I always feel out of place and unacceptable to his mother? Or was I putting the cart before the horse and worrying before I needed to?

"Is thee well, Rose?" Frederick asked.

I glanced up to make sure he wasn't harboring storm clouds in his question. His face was still, so I responded. "It has been quite the week." I thought for a moment. "Does thee know anything of Guy Gilbert or his wife, Nell? She is quite unwell at the moment. Unwell in her head, I should say."

"He's the young police officer."

I nodded.

"He didn't attend the Academy, so he must have gone to Amesbury High School. Why does the name Nell ring a bell?" Frederick stroked his trim beard. "It's possible her maiden name was O'Toole. I believe Harriet knew her mother."

I opened my mouth and then shut it again. If Nell was related to Minnie and Jotham and Ida, then the light on this case might be brightening. Or darkening.

The next morning's post brought a note from David saying he would pick me up at seven, and that he was looking forward to seeing me. I sighed and checked my outfit once again. The pink dress hung in the wardrobe, the new shoes sat underneath. The stockings and gloves still lay in their paper and Orpha's cameo rested on my desk.

"But what will I do for a bag?" I said aloud to my armoire. I'd forgotten about acquiring one, and I owned no small fancy bag to carry. I didn't think Faith did, either. But maybe Bertie possessed such a thing. I donned my cloak and set out on my bicycle for Bertie's house. I was glad for the cloak, as it was a cloudy, chilly morning. Five minutes later I knocked on her door.

Bertie peeked through the window, then opened the door with a smile followed by a yawn. Her curly hair danced on her shoulders and she wore a flowered wrapper over her nightdress.

"A pleasure as always to see you, Rosetta. But the hour is early yet. What brings you out and about?"

"I'm going to a fancy dinner dance tonight and —"

"That's right, I had forgotten. Come in and remind me of the details." She led the way into her compact kitchen, where lamplight streamed onto a buttery yellow tablecloth, the air warm and redolent with the rich smell of coffee and the allure of something with cinnamon baking.

"Sit." Bertie pointed to a chair and plopped herself down into the one across the round table. She drew both knees up and wrapped her arms around them.

I sat. "It's David Dodge's mother's party. She insisted David attend, and he very much wanted me to accompany him. I mentioned to thee that I have a party dress. I obtained new shoes, stockings, gloves. But I have no bag to carry. Does thee have such an object?"

"What color is the dress?"

"Rose," I said with a smile. "What other color could it be?"

Bertie jumped up and held a finger in the air. "I've just the thing." She hurried out and was back in a flash.

She laid a small reticule on the table. I picked it up and examined it. Yellow, purple, and rose-colored flowers were worked in petit point into a cream brocade fabric. Green leaves peeked out from behind the blooms in the design, and a honeybee rested on a stem. Two small beads shaped and colored like roses decorated the slender chain the bag hung from, and the clasp was a tiny crown. I opened it and found it lined in rose silk.

"Oh, it's lovely. And the colors are perfect." I put my hand to my mouth. "I don't sound much like a Quaker, do I?"

"Folderol. Aren't you always talking about 'that of God' in everyone? What about that of God in things of beauty? You should be able to appreciate beauty, too."

I nodded. "Tell me where thee purchased the bag."

"I like doing petit point in the evenings," Bertie said with a grin.

"Thee didn't make this thyself." I stared at her.

"I certainly did. Well, I bought the bag itself but it was plain. I simply added the decoration. I like pretty things."

"Thy talents are endless. I'd love to borrow this pretty thing, if thee can part with it."

"You can have it. I'll make another for the next fancy dinner party I go to." She laughed, ending with a snort. "As if I went to fancy dinner parties."

"Thee is wonderful. I must confess I'm uneasy about going to this event. David's mother — well, she's not an easy woman." I smiled. "But his father, Herbert — what a delight."

"Oh? The shoe magnate?"

"Yes. He's a successful businessman, but quite direct, with a simple manner full of joy. Much as is his son. I liked Herbert greatly when I met him at tea last First Day."

"I've met your young doctor and I agree. He takes after his father."

"I'm grateful for that. The affair tonight will provide a welcome respite from a week full of murder and lies. At least I hope it will."

Bertie sobered. "I've heard no news, or no good news, that is, about them letting Ephraim go."

"Perhaps thee has the answer to a question that arose at supper last evening. Thee seems to know everything and everyone in town. Does thee know Nell Gilbert's maiden name?"

Bertie tapped her fingers on the table as she stared out the window. "Irish, I think, even though Guy's family is French-Canadian. O'Grady, maybe? O'Neil? No."

"How about O'Toole?"

"That's it." She stared at me. "Same as dead Minnie."

I nodded.

"Now I remember," Bertie said. "I think Minnie and Nell's grandfathers were cousins."

"Which makes Nell, what, Minnie's third cousin? And that of her sister and Jotham, the unpleasant brother." Perhaps that was why Nell and Jotham were speaking that day. "They both lied to me, Nell saying she didn't know Jotham, and he the same about her." I narrowed my eyes, thinking.

"I wouldn't want to be related to that scoundrel Jotham." Bertie frowned, too.

"What has he done?"

"He always seems to be in the middle of trouble. He gets in fights, he picks fights, and he doesn't stay employed long because he's so difficult to get along with."

I told her about my encounter with him and the baby the day before. "You should have heard him singing to little Billy. He seems to want to hold tight to him, but I think I convinced him to let Patience nurse Billy."

"Of course she should," she scoffed. "What's Jotham going to do, pour a tin of milk down the infant's throat?"

"Let's hope not."

Thirty

As I bicycled homeward, the bag tucked into a pocket in my cloak, a large open-sided carriage pulled up slowly across from me.

"Hallo, Rose Carroll!"

I inwardly groaned but managed to smile back at Ned Bailey, who reined his pair of horses to a stop and leaned into the unoccupied passenger seat.

"Good morning, Ned." I also stopped and set a foot on the ground. I rubbed my already chilled hands together, wishing I had remembered my everyday gloves. The sun peeked out from scudding clouds, but it wasn't enough to warm the air.

"I'm delighted to see you," he said. "I'd offer you a ride, but I see you have your own transport." He chuckled. "That's quite the contraption."

His gaze strayed to my exposed ankles. I

cleared my throat and he hastily looked up again.

"It helps me get to my various sites of work. It's quite useful."

"Indeed, indeed."

I cocked my head. Ned was a lifelong resident of Amesbury and was in the carriage trade. Perhaps he could shed light on the week's events. All the deaths being connected to William Parry was eating at me.

"Ned, what can thee tell me about the Parry factory? Before the fire, I mean. Is William a successful businessman? Thee must have regular dealings with him."

"Why do you ask?"

"The deaths this week, the fire last week — they all seem linked to William."

"But what affair is it of yours? That's more properly the realm of the police, I should say."

"I am called to seek justice." I waited with what I hoped was a look inviting his confidence.

He scooted all the way onto the passenger side and swung his legs out to face me. "See this carriage?" At my nod, he went on. "Bailey carriages are made with the finest workmanship. We pay top price for the best-quality wood, metal, leather. Our design is both the most durable and the most beautiful. We hire the most skilled workers and pay them accordingly."

"It's a lovely vehicle," I said. "Its lines flow and it appears sturdy and well made."

"It is. And the ride is the most comfortable you can imagine. Would you like to take a spin around the block?" His smile bordered on a leer.

"No, thanks. I've ridden in a Bailey buggy, however. It was truly a luxurious experience."

"Now, certain of our competitors cut corners. They hire workers who are less skilled and don't treat them well. They buy cheap parts. They rush to production without the care that ensures quality."

"Does thee speak of the Parry factory?" I asked.

"I might. I might, indeed. Their sales have been in slump of late. That cheap quality has caught up with them."

"Interesting." Also interesting that he seemed to be a man invested in running a high-quality business, proud of his workers and his product. A pity he wasn't more sensible when it came to trying to attract female attentions, if how he acted with me was any indication.

"And then we had the curious incident of the fire," he went on in a lower voice. "Suppose someone wanted to collect the fire insurance payout?"

My face creased into horror. "Does thee mean a factory owner would have burned his own place down to collect the money?"

He lowered his voice. "It's a possibility."

"All those men who died, all the other buildings destroyed. It would take a monster." I shivered, and not only from the cold.

"If last week's conflagration wasn't an accident, I agree. It was truly a monstrous act."

My thoughts tumbled furiously in my head. I stared at the handlebars on my bicycle. Would William have set the fire? Or arranged to have it set?

"These are purely speculative thoughts, mind you. Don't worry your lovely head about them."

I glanced up at Ned. "I'll worry about what I wish. This is very disturbing, thee must admit."

"Oh, indeed." Ned gave a little cough. "So did you check your calendar?" His tone brightened as he waved toward town with an expansive gesture. "I could take you out tonight. The Currier Hotel has a very fine dining room. The chef is up from Boston, they say."

The man's desire to court me was relentless. "I'm afraid not, Ned, but I thank thee for the invitation. I'm otherwise engaged tonight. In fact, I should have told you straight out earlier my affections lie elsewhere. I must be getting home now."

"I won't give up, you know." He grinned. Ducking his head, he climbed back into the driver's seat. He clucked at his team and shook the reins.

I shook my head and placed one foot on the pedal but waited until he drove off before beginning to ride. The police station was on my way home. Perhaps I could have a moment with Kevin.

The detective himself strode down the front stairs of the police station as I rode by minutes later. He halted as I pulled up and dismounted.

"Miss Carroll. Top of the morning to you." He tipped his hat.

"And to thee. I heard a disturbing thing a few minutes ago."

"What's that?"

"I saw Ned Bailey in the last hour. He conjectured that the arson last week could have been the doing of a factory owner."

"Like Parry himself, for example?"

I nodded. "It might be simply Ned's pride, but he mentioned some of his competitors cut corners and produce substandard wares, which eventually results in lower sales. And that they or William, specifically, might have needed the insurance money."

"Do you really think we haven't thought of that?" he asked with an air of self-satisfaction. "You're not to worry about such things."

If one more person told me what to do or not do, I mused, I might explode. I folded my own arms on my chest, letting the bicycle rest against me.

"Our investigation will be thorough and complete," he continued. "When it's complete. Now, how's that ride of yours?"

I didn't smile, but I answered him. "It makes my life easier. Most of the time." I pulled my mouth to the side. "When I don't run into an errant cobblestone and when errant vehicles don't run into me."

"What? Did a carriage knock you over?" He raised his eyebrows.

"Not quite, but I've had a couple of close calls." With that reminder, my knee twinged. I might have to take it to the doctor, a prospect that made me smile.

"And you're staying out of trouble, I suppose, since I haven't seen you in, what, an entire day?"

"I did learn something I'm much concerned with. Thee might consider it trouble."

Kevin's eyebrows shot up. "Something about Minnie O'Toole's death?"

"No."

"What, then? Is this thing news I need to hear?" His voice was impatient.

I took a deep breath. "I went to see Nell Gilbert again yesterday. Guy's wife. She's most unwell in her mind." I pictured Nell's tormented face and again smelled her stale, sour odor.

He frowned. "Yes, I know. But I try not to delve too deeply into my colleagues' personal lives."

I lowered my voice and glanced around, ascertaining no passersby were near. "She said she's brought death, even though she didn't want to."

Kevin took a step closer with his gaze focused on me.

"And that the Devil made her do it." I kept my hands firmly on the handlebars.

"So Mrs. Gilbert is still off her head. What do you think she meant by that?" He cocked his head, also using a tone only I could hear.

"She goes out wandering in the town alone." A pang of remorse struck me, talking with Kevin about poor Guy's troubled wife, but I felt obliged to do so. "And she has the kind of postpartum melancholia that can lead to acts of insanity."

Another police officer strode down the street toward Kevin. He opened his mouth to speak, but, hearing my last comment, he glanced at me with alarm.

"I've got this, Joe," Kevin said to him, holding up his hand. "I'll talk to you inside."

The officer headed for the building, glancing behind himself at us before he entered.

Kevin waited until the door closed after the man before speaking again, still in a low voice. "An insane wife and mother is sad and terrible. But how does this concern me?"

"Kevin, she could have taken my knitting needle when I paid her a call last Second Day."

"You think she killed Thomas." He watched me, hands clasped behind his back, rocking on his heels. "This is an interesting turn of events."

"I hope not. But I'm afraid it's possible." A cold gust of wind nearly blew my bonnet off. I snatched it with one hand, but in doing so knocked my glasses askew. I awkwardly straightened them with my free hand. When the bike began to slip away, Kevin reached out a hand to steady it before

I grabbed the handlebar and held on tight.

"Surely Nell wasn't out wandering around in the wee hours of the morning, though," he said, one hand firmly on his own hat.

I stared at him. "But she was. Guy was to have told thee about her going out the night of Thomas's death."

"He did not." Kevin spoke in a stern tone. "That Gilbert is going to be in hot water."

"He and I spoke of it several days ago."

"When, exactly?"

I shook my head. "This week has blurred into a kaleidoscope for me. I'm afraid I can't remember exactly."

"Nell could have stabbed Minnie, too. The neighbor reported seeing a tall woman visit that afternoon," Kevin said. "Nell's a tall woman."

"Of course. Therese told me that." I was even more afraid for Nell now.

"We haven't had any luck tracking down the mysterious visitor. I'll have to question Nell, and Guy won't be a bit happy about it."

"And there's one more thing. I'm not sure it's important —"

"Have out with it. I'll be the judge of what's important and what isn't." He tapped a hand on his leg, glancing up at the clock above the station.

"Nell's maiden name is O'Toole. She is — was — Minnie's third cousin. And so also Ida and Jotham's third cousin."

He frowned, pursing his lips. "So if her insanity drove her to murder Minnie, she'd have killed family."

"Yes. But why would Nell kill anyone? That's what I don't understand. She had no bone to pick with either Thomas or Minnie, as far as I've learned. Or at least not a current one. Guy told me Thomas was sweet on Nell before she and Guy married, and that Thomas treated her badly when she chose Guy over him."

"You yourself said Nell is bordering insane, even if temporarily. Crazy people do crazy things."

THIRTY-ONE

I spent the rest of the morning working at home in the quiet, since the children and Frederick were at school until one in the afternoon. I brought all my records up to date. I made note of who was due next and wrote a few case notes, then began to clean. As I flicked the duster over my grandmother's clock, my thoughts kept returning to all the unsolved questions.

Kevin would soon question Nell's mother-in-law, and Guy, too, on Nell's whereabouts. I so much hoped she'd been securely at home on Fifth Day afternoon and evening, even though I knew she had been out the night of Thomas's death. Nell herself would be in for an interrogation, as well. Kevin was unlikely to glean any useful information from her. If she began to speak of the Devil, he wasn't going to get a straight answer about anything. She might even be committed to the insane asylum.

I thought back on exactly what I'd heard. Nell had said she'd brought death, that she didn't want to, that the Devil made her do it. And something about the Devil telling her people would pretend not to understand, and that they couldn't understand. I hated the thought of one of my clients having the capacity to deliver a violent death, even though I knew women were as capable of terrible deeds as were men. The Friends' belief in equality held true for good and bad alike.

I rolled up the braided rug in the center of the room, then fetched the corn broom and swept out the entire space, reaching under the chaise and behind the desk. Suppose these thoughts of the Devil didn't come from Nell's addled brain? Suppose this "Devil" was a real person? Even if Nell was convinced to do the deed, the person who had directed her to kill was the true murderer. I knew it wasn't Ephraim. Then who?

After I emptied the dustpan, I carried the rug out the back door and draped it over the fence as the noon whistle sounded. The skies had cleared, finally, and while the air was still cool, at least it was sunny. A brisk breeze danced with the branches of the young white oak in the yard. I beat the dust out of the rug, asking myself who the Devil incarnate could be. Jotham didn't care for William Parry and was angry about him impregnating Minnie. He might have put Nell up to stabbing Thomas late at night. For that matter, any of the disgruntled workers Thomas had managed might have been angry enough to do away with him. But then they wouldn't have had a connection with Nell, unless it was one I had no knowledge of. Lillian hadn't seemed to like Thomas much, and hadn't been visibly upset by his death, either. Could she have ordered him killed?

I whacked the rug. What about Minnie's death? I was certain Jotham wouldn't have ordered his own sister killed, at least not Minnie, although he and Ida didn't seem to get along at all. Their past could be simply a matter of two siblings not liking each other, or something more serious might have happened where one couldn't forgive the other. Humans were a complicated lot, and for some reason forgiveness was one of the most elusive actions for many. I considered Lillian's opinion of Minnie — she'd called her a strumpet and was aware of William's dalliance. Perhaps Lillian was involved in Minnie's death. She was fairly tall for a woman. But no — her advanced state of pregnancy was unmistakable. Therese would surely have noticed her protruding midsection.

I sneezed but continued swinging the rug beater, smacking the oval green-and-rose-colored rug. And then there was Ned's idea of the arson being carried out, or at least ordered by, William himself, to collect the fire insurance money. It was a horrible thought. Kevin said the official investigation was aware of the possibility. But they clearly didn't have an answer yet, because he'd added, "When it's complete." Because of my recent dealings with both Parrys, I felt I might be able to make some headway where the officials could not if only I could organize my thoughts correctly.

But my thoughts were a pot of beans at a fast boil. They popped up and dove down, vying with each other for importance and position. I wanted to put a lid on them and shove them to the back of the stove. Instead I turned the rug and kept beating the poor thing, as if I could force answers out with the dust.

An hour later, after I'd finished my cleaning and ridden over, the house maid opened the front door of the Parry mansion. This time the maid's cap was in place and her apron, too.

"Good afternoon." I smiled at her. "I didn't catch thy name earlier in the week."

"Della, miss. Della Majowska." She curtsied.

"Is Lillian in?" I glanced into the foyer, where a grandfather clock marked one thirty with a single chime.

"No, miss. She went shopping with her sister for baby things. And Mr. Parry is out with a friend."

I hadn't noticed her accent before but now it was more pronounced. "I see. Are they expected home soon?"

Her brow furrowed. "I'm not sure, miss. They only left at noon. Mr. Parry's friend lives on the other side of Merrimack."

"Ah, the former West Parish of Amesbury."

"And Mrs. Parry went into Newburyport," Della added.

"Perhaps I can come in to await Lillian? I wanted to, uh, check on her health," I lied. "What with the death this week and all." Surely young Della here would have noticed any funny goings on. I'd simply have to figure out how to elicit information from her without her realizing what I was doing.

Della crossed herself. "It's been a terrible thing. Terrible." She shook her head, then stood back and gestured for me to enter. "You can wait for them. Come into the parlor."

She held out her arms for my cloak and bonnet, which I handed her. After she hung up my things, Della led me to the front room, which I had last seen on Fifth Day, full of mourners, both the sad and the curious types. A day that now seemed a week ago instead of only two days in the past.

"You can sit," she said. "Would you like a cup of tea?"

"I'd love some, thanks." I stayed on my feet.

As Della turned toward the hall, I followed her. She glanced back at me.

"Oh, miss, you sit in the parlor." She waved her hand toward the front of the house.

"I'll just come along and keep thee company in the kitchen. I don't mind." I laughed to soften her shock, and waved her on ahead of me. I hadn't yet set foot in the back area of the house, and I had no intention of wasting my afternoon sitting alone in an overdecorated rich person's parlor, especially when I had a household insider to question.

The expansive blue-and-white tiled kitchen was decked out with the latest gadgets. An enormous stove, wide enough to hold a half dozen full-sized pots on the top, featured three ovens below. A large icebox sat in the corner, and glass-doored cabinets on the walls held all manner of fancy goblets and fine china, with cookware hanging from hooks near the stove. On the far wall sat two deep sinks and a drain-board. Electric lights dotted the walls.

I sank into a chair at the enormous work table in the middle of the room. "This is quite the kitchen," I said.

"It's pretty, yes? Cook likes having such a modern place to make food."

"She won't mind my intrusion, I hope?" I knew some cooks in homes like this were highly proprietary of their realms.

"No, she's not like that. Anyway, she takes her afternoon rest now. Mr. Locke and his friends come for dinner tonight, and they like the fancy foods. Lots of foods, and never mind the mess they leave."

"So she'll need all her strength, is that what thee is saying?"

Della set the kettle on a burner and lit it, then turned back, smiling. "That's right, miss."

"Alexander Locke. I saw him yesterday. He seemed a bit giddy."

"Yes, he is." She bit the corner of her mouth. "He's like that some of the time, I tell you."

"Oh? It must be hard for him to hold down a job while acting like that."

She sat in a chair across a corner of the table from me. A sigh escaped her lips.

"Thee works hard for this household." I smiled.

"I'm lucky to have the job. I don't mind hard work."

"Neither do I."

She leaned toward me. "Mr. Locke, he does not work at all."

"No?"

"His papa pays his way. He goes to the gambling parlor and loses it. His papa gives him more."

"I had heard that." It was certainly wrong for Della to be gossiping like this, and probably wrong of me to encourage her, but I rationalized that if the information helped in the investigation of the town's crimes, it was worth our moral transgressions.

"After he loses, he gets very angry." She shuddered, rubbing one arm with the other hand. "And he takes, you know, the drugs."

"Have you seen him do that?"

"He left syringes in the guest suite. Needles in them." She nodded soberly. "Then, after he takes the drugs, he acts silly." She looked around quickly and leaned toward me. "He borrows my mistress's dresses, even. I've seen him sneak out wearing one more than once. Where could he possibly be going dressed up like a woman?"

I stared at her with a deep, cold sensation spreading through me. I knew one place he might have gone. Alexander was taller than the average woman. Blond. A drug addict. He needed money. What had Lillian convinced him to do? More to the point, how could I prove it to Kevin? And then I had another thought: If Alexander had killed Minnie, he could have killed Thomas, too. It had been the same means of death for both.

"Did Alexander and Thomas get along well?" I asked.

"No, not well. Thomas didn't like hardly nobody, though. But he especially looked down at Alexander because he didn't work and he spent so much money. They argued more than once."

I thought back to the afternoon of the funeral. Alexander had been at the service and at the cemetery, but I hadn't seen him here at the reception.

"Della, thee must have had thy hands full with Alexander acting silly at the funeral reception."

"Oh, no. He didn't even attend the reception. Mr. Parry, he wasn't happy about that."

"Thee is sure? Why didn't Alexander come here after the burial?"

The kettle sang out and Della jumped up. She switched off the burner and busied herself spooning tea into a china teapot she drew out of a cupboard.

"I'm sure. He came back only for a moment." She faced me. "He ran upstairs and then left through the kitchen here. Cook wasn't happy about that. Mr. Locke carried a parcel and said he had no interest in a crowd of mourners."

"I suppose he didn't say where he was going." I tapped a spoon on the table.

"No, miss. And I didn't see him again until the next day."

THIRTY-TWO

I tied my bonnet under my chin in the Parry's foyer as the clock struck twice. I'd had a quick, if distracted, cup of tea with Della, then told her I couldn't tarry any longer. My brain was filled with an imagined image of a dress-and-bonnet-clad Alexander stabbing Minnie in the neck. And my mind churned with questions, too. Why had Minnie even let him in? Had Lillian paid her brother to get rid of the competition, so to speak? It was awful to imagine a woman about to become a mother plotting the murder of another, but I knew it was possible. For Nell, for Lillian, perhaps for anyone.

Della might not be willing to tell the same story to the police as she'd recounted to me. My plans for a quiet afternoon of rest and reflection before the evening soirée were clearly in shreds. I needed to tell Kevin what I had learned, and soon.

"I must go," I said.

"You don't want to wait for Mrs. Parry?" Della stood beside me with my cloak in her arms.

As I shook my head, the front door burst open. Della gasped and drew a hand to her throat. Alexander Locke strode in with an angry air that contrasted with the freshness of the day behind him. Gone was his lethargic, giddy mood. He stopped short, narrowing his eyes.

"What are you doing here, Miss Quaker Angel?" His voice was gravelly.

"Good afternoon, Alexander. I was asking about thy sister. I wanted to check on her well-being."

"I wouldn't mind doing that myself." He glanced at Della. "Where is my sister, girl?"

"I don't know, sir. She's out shopping." Della's face had gone pale.

"Spending my money, no doubt. She owes me and she's withholding it." He nearly spat the words in a breathless way. He pushed his bowler back and rubbed his forehead.

I took a closer look. His right hand shook and tiny pearls of sweat decorated his face. His dingy collar sat askew. I suspected he was in withdrawal from the drugs.

"Is thee unwell, Alexander?" I asked.

"None of your business. Is that scoundrel

William in?" he asked Della. "The one who humiliated my sister?"

She shook her head. "Not him, neither."

His gaze strayed to the wide staircase. "I think I'll help myself to some of Lill's jewels in lieu of payment. Since she's not here." He pushed past us and set a muddy boot on the first step.

"You can't do that," Della said. "Sir," she quickly added with fear drawn on her face.

"I'll do what I want." He ran up three more steps.

"But you can't. She locks her door when she goes out." Della pleated the cloth of my cloak between her fingers, but she stood up straight.

"Give me the key then, girl." Alexander clattered back down the stairs, leaving clods of dirt in his wake.

Della shook her head fast. Alexander raised a hand, but I reached out and caught it before he hit her.

"Alexander, calm thyself," I said in my most firm tone. "Do not strike this young woman."

Glaring at me, he twisted out of my hold but let his arm fall to his side. He snarled at Della, "Give me the key."

"You don't understand, sir," she said. "I don't have it. No one does."

"Cook must." Alexander's tone grew more desperate. "There must be a master key somewhere."

She gazed in my direction as if imploring me to help. "There is no other key. Mrs. Parry locks her door and puts the key in her bag. We can only clean and freshen up the bed and such when she's in the house."

"It sounds like thee is unlucky for today, Alexander," I said.

He turned, his face red, and stormed back out the way he came. We both watched him go.

"Take a deep breath, Della. And then tell me — has he hurt thee in the past?"

She nodded slowly, rubbing her arm, not looking at me until Alexander had reached the street and disappeared out of sight. She handed me my cloak.

"When he loses money, he's mean. He hit me once when he passed by in the hall. He tried to grab me, but then Mrs. Parry called for him and he let me go. I don't like Mr. Locke."

"I don't blame thee. He seems to have little likeable about him." As my eyes roamed the foyer, I noticed a black box on the wall. "Is that one of the new telephones?" I'd seen only one or two.

She nodded. I strode to it. "Does thee

know how to work it?"

"Oh, no, miss. I don't. Only Mr. Parry is allowed to use it. He makes that very clear."

A cylindrical device about a hand's-length long was connected by wires to the box; it hung from a hook on the left side. I lifted off the device and examined it, the metal cool in my hand, then put the end to my ear.

"Hello? Hello?" I said to the round mesh-covered hole in the middle. But I heard nothing. I tried speaking into the cylindrical part with no better effect. I hung it up. How easy it would have been to ring up the police station and tell Kevin he must bring Alexander in for questioning. With a sigh I donned my cloak.

"Thank thee for the tea, Della. I'm off now. Be well. And try not to be alone where Alexander is."

She nodded with wide eyes.

THIRTY-THREE

"But I must speak with him." I stood at the front desk of the police station fifteen minutes later. The air, as usual, carried the smell of old wood, stale smoke, and the metallic tinge of gun oil.

The officer Kevin had addressed as Joe that morning shook his head. "He went out. You can't talk with him if he's not here, then, can you, miss?" A twist of curly red hair at his temple escaped the otherwise carefully plastered-down do.

Perhaps Kevin was out questioning poor Nell, following up on the news I had brought him. I tapped my fingers on the side of my leg. "May I trouble thee for paper and pencil, then?"

He rummaged in the desk until he came up with them. A man standing behind me cleared his throat, so I took the writing materials to the wide windowsill. Gazing out the window, I thought for a moment.

Would Kevin understand if I jotted down a tale of Alexander borrowing Lillian's clothes? Of Lillian putting him up to murder? His accosting Della? I shook my head. I didn't know, but I had to tell him.

I drafted my note carefully, outlining what Della had told me. I urged Kevin to find Alexander and question him, and then do the same with Lillian. Who knew what damage a drug addict would do next? Folding the paper in half, I wrote Kevin's name on the outside.

"Please see he gets this with all due haste," I said, handing it to Joe. "It could be a matter of life or death."

Joe nodded in mock seriousness. "Yes, miss. With all due haste." He patted the note, smiling at me as if I were a silly-headed girl.

"It's a serious matter relating to the recent murders in town." I stood up to my full height. "I should hope thee wouldn't impede the investigation in which Kevin Donovan asked me to assist." He had at the beginning of it, anyway.

He widened his eyes, the indulgent smile gone. "Yes, miss. I'll let him know."

I thanked him and left, making my way back to where I'd left my bicycle leaning against a lamp post in front of the station. I planned to return home and rest for the afternoon. I didn't want worry and fatigue to mar my appearance for the party. Murder really was a case for the authorities to solve, not a midwife. I'd done what I could, reported to Kevin what I discovered. He would need to take it from here.

I pedaled slowly toward the Bailey house — my house now, as well. I mused for a happy moment on where David and I might live if we joined in marriage. Perhaps a modest home on a hill overlooking the river. I would prefer to stay in Amesbury near my clients, but a house near the river would put him close to the bridge so he could easily get to work at the hospital and keep his clientele in Newburyport. I imagined having babies of my own. I pictured David and me both gazing at a sleeping infant in his arms, and smiled at the thought of a household full of bright little Dodges. I would raise them as Friends, sure he would not object. I wasn't sure why my anxiety over his mother's regard of me had lessened or what had happened to my involuntary holding back from him based on my terrible experience of long ago. I welcomed this new ease and felt confident I could meet the challenge of tonight's party.

But for now, the Bailey children and Frederick would all be home from the Seventh Day half session of school, and I hoped the household wouldn't be too noisy for me to take a bit of sleep.

As I was about to turn off High Street onto the path leading to the Bailey house, a man hailed me.

"Miss Carroll!" Jotham strode toward me.

I halted my steed and put my foot down, waiting for him to approach.

"Miss Carroll, exactly the person I wanted to see." Breathing heavily, he removed his hat, his face red. "I'd like your help. I'm sorting through the baby things Minnie got for little Billy. I wanted to take them over to Mrs. Henderson's for him. But I'm not sure, you see, what is what. Can you come and help me?"

"How can I help?" I cocked my head. "Doesn't thee simply need to place them into a satchel and carry them to Patience's?" Why did he need my help for such a simple task?

He fluttered his left hand at his side. "I'm all a-fluster going through Minnie's things. I'd like a woman's assistance in the matter."

"The police have finished their investigation of her flat, then?"

He nodded, smiling at me, a tic vibrating at the edge of his upper lip. He replaced his hat on his head.

I sighed. All I wanted to do was rest and anticipate dancing with my David. But Jotham had suffered a loss, and it was only right to help him. "I'll come. But only for a few moments. I need to be getting home soon. It's been a busy day and I'm going out tonight."

"I thank you. It won't take long." Jotham gestured down High toward the way he had come.

After Jotham ushered me into the dark hallway of Minnie's flat ten minutes later, I heard the *snick* of the key turning in the lock behind me as I made my way to the bedroom in the rear of the flat. I craned my head back.

"Why does thee lock the door, Jotham? We won't be long, I'm sure."

He took a long stride toward me. My answer was his suddenly glowering expression and his hands on my shoulders, pushing me down the hall ahead of him.

"What is thee doing? Don't push me," I cried as I extended my arms before me to avoid crashing into the closed bedroom door. A muffled sound came from behind it.

"Open the door," he growled.

Something cold the size of a thumb pressed into my back. It echoed the cold now spreading through me. This was no visit to sort baby clothes.

I felt for the handle and gasped after the door swung open into the room. Lillian sat on the bed, her back at the headboard. One foot was tied to the knob at the foot of the bed and her hands were bound in her lap with a silken cord. A kerchief encircled her head, gagging her mouth. Her unpinned hair lay in disarray about her shoulders and stuck up above the kerchief. Her eyes implored me as she worked her chin and shook her head, trying to get free of the gag. I rushed to her side.

"We must free thee at once," I said. My hand was on the kerchief when Jotham barked from behind me.

"Don't touch her." He slammed the door shut and moved to the other side of the bed. A gun in his hand pointed at me.

"She's pregnant. Thee can't have her tied like this." I reached for the kerchief again. I had a million questions for him, but now wasn't the time.

"Stop. I'll shoot you, and her, too, if I have to. She's going to start screaming like a banshee if you take that off."

Lillian moaned. She closed her eyes as a

tear escaped, rolling down her pale cheek. She moaned again and her eyes flew open. She held my gaze.

Oh, no. "Thee is having a pain."

She nodded, then grimaced.

"What kind of pain? Don't let her bamboozle you," Jotham said with a snarl.

"I believe she might be in early labor." I glanced at a small clock on the bedside table.

"Having her baby here?" The gun wavered for a second, then he held it firm again.

"It's possible," I replied. "She's less than two months from her time. Look at me," I said to Lillian, laying my hand atop her bound wrists. "Take a deep breath through your nose and let it out." She did what I said. "Now another," I coached her. "Don't hold thy breath in. That can increase the pain."

The pain seemed to pass. She slumped back on the pillows, watching me.

"Thee did well." She had to be wondering what was happening. I needed to calm her down if I could. "Thee might be starting thy labor, or it might be the false contractions we talked about. Remember?"

She nodded.

"Try to stay at ease. Have these pains just begun?"

She shook her head.

"How long has thee . . ." No, I had to ask her questions she could answer with a yes or a no. "Have the pains been going on all day long?" It was now nearly three o'clock.

She nodded.

Then this wasn't false labor. Braxton Hicks contractions happened sporadically and didn't continue for so long. I thought quickly back to our visits. She had about eight weeks before labor should have started. If the baby was born today, it would be too small and too weak. I doubted it would survive. I wasn't concerned about not having my birthing satchel. I had made do before with the simple supplies any household stocked: clean cloth, hot water, a razor. Supplies not including a loaded gun, of the kind I believed they called a revolver, one capable of several shots before reloading.

"I'll get us out of here, I promise thee." I hadn't a notion how, though.

Jotham laughed, a bitter sound. "Oh, no, you won't." He smelled of a nervous sweat.

I stared at him, my ire rising. "What is this about? How did you get her here? Why does thee hold her, and me, as well?" I set my hands on my hips. "This woman is in labor, I'm sure of it."

378

"She killed my sister. I decided it was time to take justice into my own hands." He glared at Lillian, who shook her head back and forth, her eyebrows drawn together.

I watched them both. He had discovered what I had surmised, as well. Perhaps Lillian hadn't directly killed Minnie, but if she put Alexander up to it, she might as well have.

"And you've been snooping around," he went on, keeping the gun trained on me. "I've seen you asking questions. Too many questions."

"That's because many questions about this week's events remain unanswered," I said. "For example, what makes thee think Lillian killed Minnie? Does thee really believe she, in her advanced state of pregnancy, could even come over here and stab thy sister?"

"I have my sources. She put somebody else up to it. I know she did."

"What does thee mean to do with us?"

He stared at me through narrowed eyes. "Haven't quite decided yet. Her" — he jutted his chin at Lillian — "I'll hand over to the authorities. Or maybe she'll have to die. Just like my Minnie did." He grinned at Lillian and laughed when her eyes widened and she tried to speak through the gag.

I swallowed. "And will thee kill me, as well? The police will find thee, Jotham O'Toole. Killing more people in this town solves nothing. It will only add thy own death to the tally when they convict thee." My heart beat in my throat, but I tried to take my own deep breath to relax. No one knew I was here. I couldn't depend on Kevin or anyone else to swoop in and rescue us. I needed to figure out how to get Lillian and myself out, and soon.

"I'll do what I see fit," he snarled.

"And what about thy nephew? When thee is apprehended, thee will lose the chance to see him grow up, to help care for him."

He frowned at this but went on. "I'll take him with me. You fancy people think you control the town. I plan to make my own life elsewhere, with little Billy at my side."

"I'm scarcely a fancy person, Jotham. Thee knows Friends follow simple, modest habits."

"Maybe, but you help the fancy ones. Like this one." He moved the gun to point at Lillian. "Well, it's my town, too, or has been. The likes of Parry ain't going to get the better of me. I showed him, didn't I?"

"What does thee mean?"

Jotham threw back his head and laughed, then an expression of satisfaction came over his face. "The fire? Thomas? All my doing. All of it."

I stared at him. "Thee burned down Carriage Hill."

He nodded, looking like a fox who had just finished off a hen. He licked the corners of his mustache. "Served all those fancy folks right. I even limped along for a stretch on my way there and back, hoping somebody would think it was old Ephraim who was the firebug."

"It wasn't only fancy folks who were killed in the fire. It was ordinary workers like thyself."

He glanced away. "Couldn't be helped."

"And thee stabbed Thomas?" Perhaps Alexander wasn't the murderer, nor crazy Nell.

"I tried to get that lunatic woman, my cousin, to do it. She stole your knittin' needle just like I told her to. But in the end she wouldn't stick him. I didn't mind doing it. It was my idea, my revenge. And the coppers are too stupid to figure anything out."

I'd never heard someone sound so proud of himself.

Lillian moaned again. I checked the clock again. Two minutes had passed since the start of the last pain.

"Breathe, Lillian. Slowly, calmly. Just breathe."

Thirty-Four

"I insist thee untie her," I said to Jotham as I listened to the clock tick away the minutes. The hour hand had approached four and then passed it. We'd been in the room for sixty minutes now, and Lillian's pains came closer and closer. She often cried out from the intensity, her voice as muffled as the stale air. I wiped her brow with my handkerchief and then sat again in the chair I'd dragged to her bedside. I didn't want to examine her internally in Jotham's presence, but I palpated the baby through her dress. Its head was well down into the pelvis and in the right position.

Jotham paced the small space, mopping nervous sweat from his brow. Every time he came near me, I gauged if I could wrest the gun away from him, and every time I decided there was too much risk of a shot hitting Lillian or her baby. Or both.

"Not yet. I can't have nosy neighbors

stopping in to ask what all the commotion is about."

"Why does thee keep us trapped here? What does thee stand to gain?"

"I don't need to tell you that," he said with swagger, but he glanced around as if he could find the answer in the corners of the room.

I suspected he'd gotten himself in deeper than he wanted and now didn't know what to do with us. Well, while we were trapped here, perhaps I could find out more. We'd be out soon enough, somehow. We had to be. In the meantime I could extract information to pass on to Kevin.

"Tell me how thee came up with the idea Lillian was behind thy sister's murder. And who does thee think she put up to the job?"

Lillian's eyes widened again, this time not from the pain. She shook her head back and forth violently.

"See? She's scared I'm going to tell you. Well, I am. It was her brother who killed my sister. So this is justice right from the Good Book. Biblical, I'd say. An eye for an eye. A sister for a sister."

"How did thee figure it out?" I had deduced the same, but was curious what he would say.

He snorted even as Lillian moaned with

another contraction. "I've been following that sissy Locke around, too. He's in big trouble, he is, with his gambling and his drugs. She sent that brother of hers a note after my Minnie was killed and I happened to get hold of it."

"How did you obtain her note?"

"The idiot Locke dropped it in the street when I was watching him."

"Did thee read it?"

He looked at me like I was an imbecile. "Of course I read it. She thanked him for the deed and said she'd pay off his biggest debt." His grin turned into a scowl. "Ain't that right, Mrs. Parry?" He hissed her title, making it sound like the worst of insults. He patted his pocket. "I still have it right here."

Lillian let out a whoosh of breath and collapsed back on the pillows, her eyes closing, her arms suddenly limp.

I watched her. "She's fainted. You must let me free her." I prayed he would agree and not simply shoot her instead. "Her baby will be along shortly. Please, Jotham."

He stared at Lillian. Her face had gone pale and a contraction rippled through the dress covering her belly.

"My poor Minnie," he murmured. He placed his left hand under his right and steadied the gun, aiming it at Lillian's head.

I held my breath. And I held Jotham in the Light. The seconds ticked by, sounding in the silence as loud as a baby's heartbeat through my listening tube. I watched emotion pass over his face, tiny movements of his facial muscles, and thoughts racing in his eyes. Please let him —

He lowered the revolver. "All right. Set her free." He turned his back.

My heart pounding, I untied the kerchief serving as a gag, and then fumbled with the cord around her wrists. Despite it being of a silky material, it had bruised and chafed her wrists through her struggles and had further tightened. Jotham thrust a sharp knife toward me. I gasped.

"Use this to cut it," he grumbled.

I grabbed the handle and cut through the cord, then freed her foot before laying the knife on the bedside table. My hopes of keeping the weapon were dashed when he came around, still pointing the gun at us, and snatched it up.

"Lillian, thee must awaken." I patted her cheeks and rubbed her wrists. "Lillian?" I hooked my elbows under her armpits and hoisted her back up to sitting. "I wish I had some smelling salts," I muttered to myself.

I rued ever coming over here. Well, not

that, for Lillian would surely be dead by now if I hadn't come with Jotham. So I regretted I hadn't brought my birthing satchel with me, instead. Except I hadn't thought I was going to a birth. I knew I could make do, but it would be easier with my supplies.

Lillian's eyes popped open. She drew her knees up, grabbed me by the shoulders, and began to bear down, uttering a fierce deep cry. I braced my hands on the bedstead behind her and hoped she wouldn't tear my arms from their sockets.

When she finished pushing, she flopped back and closed her eyes again. I had a flash of Minnie giving birth in this same bed a little over a week ago, but I couldn't dwell on that image.

I said, "This baby is coming out now. Jotham, I need clean cloths. Sheet, towel, whatever thee finds. Clean water, a shoelace, a razor or scissors, some alcohol. Rum, ale, anything." I glanced up at him. He'd let his gun hand drop to his side and he was sweating.

"Go," I urged. Too bad I couldn't take a chance and grab the gun out of his hand, but my priority was helping this baby out safely. It was bound to be tiny, being so early, if it was even alive, and it would need care I wasn't sure I could even provide, but I had to try. Jotham hurried to a bureau on the right side of the room and rummaged in a drawer after setting the gun on top. He tossed me a clean sheet, then disappeared out the door.

After laying the sheet on a corner of the bed, I knelt and pulled down Lillian's drawers. I slid my hand up her birth passage and didn't go far before I felt the baby's head. I brought my hand out.

"Lillian, with the next pain, I want thee to bear down with all thy strength."

She regarded me through glazed eyes, but nodded. A moment later she grabbed her raised knees and started to push, this time with a gravelly grunting sound that grew louder and louder until the baby's tiny dark-haired head slid into my waiting hands. I swept out its mouth with my pinkie and wiped its nose free of mucus.

"One more push, please."

As she bore down, one shoulder appeared and, with the other, the baby's body slid free. It — she — was one of the smaller newborns I had ever held, only a bit longer than my two outstretched hands that held her and feeling as light as a bag of feathers. I'd be surprised if she even weighed four pounds. Lillian must not have reported the date of her last monthly correctly.

"Thee has a baby girl, Lillian," I said with a smile, but I didn't feel like smiling. The baby was limp. I patted her face and, laying her on the sheet, rubbed her all over with my warm hands. She let out a weak cry and began to breathe, but her muscle tone was still lax and she wasn't pinking up well. I kept rubbing her tiny torso, her feet, her hands. Sometimes it took several minutes for a newborn's body to come alive.

"A girl?" Lillian asked. "I have a daughter?"

"Thee does." I held the baby up for her to see. "Thee will have another pain when the afterbirth comes out. Push with it, and then I'll give thee thy baby." I laid the baby on the corner of the bed well out of the way of Lillian's feet and pulled the sheet over the tiny body.

Jotham burst in carrying a bowl of water. He stopped short, making water slosh over the brim of the bowl, and gawked — at Lillian's private parts displayed, at the baby, and at Lillian's bodily fluids staining the bed cover.

"Mother of God," he blurted. He set the bowl on the floor near me and turned his back.

"I need scissors or thy knife, Jotham. A

bottle of alcohol. And one of thy bootlaces. Right now." I had to make do and was grateful at least he was cooperating for the moment. I pushed my glasses up with my arm.

He rushed out and returned almost immediately. Without looking at me or Lillian, he extended a pair of rough scissors and a bottle of rum, then knelt and removed his bootlace and handed it to me, as well. He remained bent over kneeling on his heels, facing away, head in his hands. I didn't have time or concern enough to ask him how he was.

I cut the long lace in two and tied off the baby's cord, then again an inch distant. I poured rum over the scissors — that would have to do for cleaning them — then snipped through the cord between the ties, once again marveling at the thick strength of the membrane. I poured a bit more rum over my handkerchief and daubed the cut end of the cord attached to the baby, hoping to avoid infection from the scissors that harbored rust and who knew what else. Then I swaddled the baby tightly in the sheet.

As Lillian let out another grunting cry, the afterbirth slid onto the bed. I sighed, having not even a vessel to put it in as I examined it. The last thing we needed was a hemorrhaging mother, but the membrane appeared intact. I wetted the kerchief that had served as Lillian's gag and wiped her as clean as I could. I wrapped the afterbirth in the kerchief, then washed my hands in the basin of water and stood, glad my legs held me. This had been the most tense birth I had ever attended, and under the worst conditions. I took a deep breath and let it out.

"Lillian, move to the other side of the bed." She had been mostly on the left side and the right was marginally cleaner.

After she scooted over, I pulled her dress down over her legs and leaned across to hand her the baby. I walked around the still kneeling Jotham and made sure the baby was still breathing, which she was, but the breaths were rapid and shallow. Lillian peered into her daughter's dark eyes as the baby gazed back with the calm, mystical awareness all newborns have.

"I'll name you Emma," Lillian said to the baby.

My job as midwife done, I turned and grabbed the gun off the bureau.

Pointing it at Jotham, I said, "Thee will stay there. On the floor." I steadied it with both hands.

He whipped his head toward me and

began to rise.

"No. I will shoot thee if I must." My hands began to shake, but I willed them to be still. "Thee has done enough damage, and thee is a murderer."

"So's she!" he yelled, but he plopped down on the floor.

"I believe that is true," I said, my voice calm and steady.

Jotham scooted back as far from me as he could until he leaned against the wall. He raised his knees and rested his arms on them.

Lillian glanced from Jotham to me. "I'm leaving. I don't need to listen to this." She swung her legs over the side of the bed.

I pointed the gun at her. "Back on the bed, Lillian. Thee is equally as guilty as Jotham."

"I'm not." She glared at me, then glanced at the precious bundle in her arms and sighed, swinging her legs back onto the bed.

"New mother or not, thee needs to be brought to justice, as does he," I told her.

But how?

THIRTY-FIVE

The clock kept ticking. I was astonished to see it was nearly five o'clock. Lillian cooed softly at her baby. Jotham tapped his fingers on his knees. I kept the revolver raised and pointed it at whichever of them appeared more likely to rebel. I'd never fired a gun in my life, but if I had to, I hoped the Light of God would steady my hand and guide me to wound, not kill. And would let me aim half as well as the famous Annie Oakley.

Five o'clock. David's soirée. Poor David. I had no way to get word to him that he would be without a date tonight. I needed to make a plan on how to get out of this impossible situation. But even if I did . . . well, there was no point in dwelling on the idea of completing a last-minute toilet and being ready by seven. And then the thought of coping with his mother's haughty airs —

"Rose, she's not breathing!" Lillian beckoned to me, anguish in her eyes.

This could be a ruse to wrest the gun from me. I wouldn't put it past Lillian to try such a thing even while holding her newborn child. She had ordered a woman killed, after all.

Or it could be a prematurely born baby passing away. I transferred the gun to my left hand, praying that hand was strong enough to pull the trigger if need be, and sidled to the side of the bed. Pointing the gun at Jotham, I laid two fingers of my right hand on the little girl's neck and watched her. Her eyes were open but gone was the light of life. No pulse beat in the silken skin of her neck.

"I'm afraid her spirit has been released to God, Lillian. She was born too early."

"Noooo," Lillian wailed, "No. She's my daughter. She can't die." She held the motionless bundle in front of her face and kissed the baby's cheeks, her little nose, her rosebud mouth. "Emma, come back to Mama. Please, baby, please." She gazed up at me with tears pouring down her cheeks, now clutching the baby to her chest. "Can't you do something? Can't you bring her back?"

I shook my head. "Babies born so tiny often have trouble breathing. I'm so sorry. There is nothing anyone can do."

Lillian stared at Jotham. "You killed my baby! She wouldn't have died if you hadn't abducted me." She wept as she returned her gaze to the bundle in her arms.

At a noise from my left, I glanced sharply at Jotham, who had started to rise. I switched my voice from gentle to stern and the gun back to my right hand. "Get back down. Now."

A thundering pounding came from the hallway. Lillian gasped and Jotham jerked his head up. He sprang to his feet and took a step toward the window.

"On the floor," I barked at him. He took another step. I secured the gun with both hands, took aim, and pressed the trigger.

Jotham cried out and fell with a thud even as my ears rang and Lillian screamed. My heart beat in my chest with the force of a steel driver. Had I killed him?

From a distance I heard, "Rose Carroll! Are you in there?"

"Yes," I shouted, never so glad to hear Kevin Donovan's voice. To hear anyone's voice except Jotham's and Lillian's. "Yes!"

Then came a roar of crashing and splintering. A moment later Kevin burst into the bedroom, gun in two hands. Guy Gilbert followed him, also armed. As Kevin took in the scene, a slow smile spread across his face. Me still pointing a smoking gun. Lillian cowering in the bed with the dead baby in her arms. Jotham writhing in a ball on the floor, holding his leg. What a blessing I had not ended his life.

"Well, well, Miss Carroll. It appears I'm not even needed here."

"I wouldn't say that, exactly," I said. "I'm grateful for thy arrival."

Jotham held his knee to his chest. "She shot me. She tried to kill me!"

"Quiet, O'Toole." Kevin trained his gun on Jotham.

"Jotham has said he not only set the carriage factory fire, but also killed Thomas Parry."

"I never said that. You can't prove it," Jotham protested. "And I'm hurt, I tell you."

I continued. "Jotham and I both deduced that Lillian put her brother Alexander Locke up to killing Minnie."

Kevin nodded. "We had arrived at the same conclusion."

"I didn't," Lillian cried.

"Let's get this man into custody, Guy." Kevin moved farther into the room, letting Guy deal with Jotham.

When Guy managed to haul Jotham to his feet, he pointed to a black streak on Jotham's leg. "Lucky for you Miss Carroll here's a lousy shot. Your trousers are singed and that's the extent of the harm." He cuffed Jotham's hands behind his back, none too gently, either, and marched him out, Jotham still proclaiming both his injury and his innocence.

"You can put that down now, Miss Carroll." Kevin indicated the gun, which I still held, although it now pointed at the floor.

I laid it with great relief on the bureau. "It's Jotham's. I managed to take possession of it."

"So you did, so you did. A good thing of it, too," Kevin said.

"What a blessing I did not kill him." I suddenly felt quite weak in my legs and grasped the bureau to steady myself.

"And it appears there is a new Parry in the world?" He glanced from Lillian to me and his smile faded away. "What?"

"The baby was born prematurely," I said in a soft voice. "She died only minutes ago."

Lillian began wailing anew. "My Emma. My little Emma."

"Oh, now that's a pity, it is." His tone was sincere as he removed his hat. "Didn't get Last Rites, I guess." He made a *tsk-tsk* sound as he crossed himself.

Therese Stevens now filled the doorway. "I told him. I told the detective I saw that man bring Lillian in, and then come back with you. When I reflected on what I saw, it just didn't seem right. Not at all right." She folded her arms and shook her head.

"You were correct, Mrs. Stevens." Kevin nodded approvingly. "If only all citizens were as alert and responsible as you."

"Go on with you." She batted away the thanks. "Who wouldn't report such a thing?"

"Many, I can assure you," Kevin said. "I'm only sorry it took my men so long to find me." He smiled sheepishly and lowered his voice so only Therese and I could hear. "I was out throwing a ball with my lad, who never gets enough time with his busy old da."

"I thank thee, Therese. Thee can't even imagine." I moved to her side and patted her arm. "I didn't know how I was going to get out of here. One gun, two murderers, and a newborn." When her face lit up, I lowered my voice. "Now dead, I'm afraid."

"Oh, the poor wee thing." Therese crossed herself, then moved to the bedside and stroked the baby's head.

Kevin turned his back on Lillian. "Is she strong enough to be jailed?" he asked in a low voice. "Mrs. Parry, I mean? My job is to apprehend criminals, and Lillian Parry qualifies with flying colors. Does she need medical attention first?"

"She should have some days of rest. But I don't believe she's at risk of bleeding — the birth was easy, as births go, with such a small one, and —" My eyes widened as I glanced behind him. "What is thee doing, Lillian?"

Kevin whirled to see Lillian thrusting the baby's body into Therese's arms with a quick move. Lillian looked around with the wild eyes of a rabbit caught in a trap. Without a word, she slid off the opposite side of the bed, knocking the wrapped placenta to the floor, and hurried out of the room through the open door.

"Wait," I called, starting after her. I glanced back to Kevin, who leaned against the bureau showing no sense of urgency. "Doesn't thee need to catch her?"

"I've another officer stationed outside. I cautioned him." He nodded with satisfaction. "He'll have her by now."

I sank down on the corner of the bed, fatigued beyond measure. "Kevin," I said, "how did thee learn of Jotham's guilt? And of Lillian's?" I removed my glasses and wiped them with a corner of my skirt, then rubbed the bridge of my nose before replacing them.

"After you told me of Nell, I went to talk with her. Her insanity lifted enough for her to say Jotham was the one she called the Devil." He frowned at the memory of the conversation. "She said she stole your knitting needle, but that she refused to kill Thomas. She saw Jotham do the deed, though."

I nodded. "He said as much. And he confessed to setting the fire. He must have thought I'd never survive to relay his confession." I shuddered. "But how did thee learn of Lillian's culpability in Minnie's death?"

"The note you left me. You're a fine detective, Miss Carroll."

"Please call me Rose."

"All right, Rose." He laughed.

"But I'm not a detective. I'm a midwife. An overly curious one, I suppose."

He nodded. "Because of you, we interviewed young Miss Majowska, the maid at the Parry mansion, and were able to apprehend Alexander Locke. There's a weak-spined man if I ever met one. He told the whole story, including assigning full blame to his own sister." He shook his head in disgust.

"It was a man in woman's clothing I saw, then?" Therese said. She laid the bundle of baby on the bed but continued stroking the dead girl's head.

"Indeed," Kevin said.

"I thought the person was tall," Therese said. "And I saw that light hair."

The clock dinged once, marking the half hour. My hands flew to my face. "I must get home. I have a . . . a . . . well, an engagement tonight."

"I'll take you home in the wagon," Kevin said. "You and your bicycle."

"My nephews will be delighted. I thank thee."

He offered me a hand. "It's the least I can do."

THIRTY-SIX

After I arrived home, I asked Faith and Frederick to sit at the table with me as I ate a bit of bread and cheese to tide me over. I wanted to fill them in on the day's events, at least some of them. And I'd never been so happy to be in a warm, clean, simple home with people who spoke truth and loved me.

Bertie rapped on the back door as I began my tale, pressing her face against the glass and waving. I opened the door and invited her in.

"I had a notion you were in trouble, Rosetta. Had to come and make sure you were all right." She took a seat at the table, too.

Frederick narrowed his eyes at the sight of Bertie. I knew he didn't care for her and hoped he would act in a civil fashion. I couldn't tolerate one more moment of tension in this day.

"I was in a bit of trouble, as it happens." I stared at a morsel of bread on the plate and stroked the grain of the long table, its smooth, worn lines a comfort under my fingers. How much of my grueling terrifying afternoon should I share with them?

Frederick's eyebrows went up, but he waited in silence.

The twins wandered in. "Who's in trouble?" Matthew asked.

"When's supper?" Mark chimed in.

"I'm hungry," Matthew added.

"No one is in trouble, and thee is always hungry," Frederick said in a sharp tone. "Take a couple of apples and run along, both of you."

"But we saw the police wagon bring Rose and her bicycle."

"Kevin simply gave me a ride home, boys." I waited until the boys had left the room with their fruit before I continued. I told my companions of my conversation with Della that morning, and how I'd left a note for Kevin laying out my suspicions.

"So Alexander Locke killed Minnie O'Toole," Frederick said.

"It appears so. On Lillian's orders."

"That young man has been on an unhealthy path for some years. This news does not surprise me." Frederick tented his hands on the table.

"Oh, and earlier in the day I had told Kevin about Nell's ill health, and her talk of the Devil. Well, it turns out the Devil was Jotham O'Toole all along. Nell told Kevin how Jotham pressured her to kill Thomas. It was she who stole my knitting needle."

"Does thee mean Nell killed Thomas?" Frederick asked.

"No. She was out that night, but in the end she refused, and Jotham did the deed. Except I didn't know about it when he came to fetch me."

"Why did he come for you?" Bertie asked.

I shook my head. "He said he wanted me to help him sort through little Billy's baby things. I shouldn't have agreed, but I did. And once we got to Minnie's flat, he locked the door, stuck a gun in my back, and led me in to where he had Lillian Parry tied up and gagged on the bed."

Faith gasped.

I patted her hand. "She was in labor with her baby. Many weeks before it should have been born, too." I went on to tell them about the rest of the afternoon. Untying Lillian. Helping her birth her baby. The infant's weakness and then death.

"Heavens, Rose. How ever did you master

Jotham?" Bertie sat forward with bright eyes.

"He was so overwhelmed by a woman giving birth in the room that he left his gun on the bureau when he went to fetch a few things for me." I laughed, but it was without humor. "After the baby was born and in Lillian's arms, I took the revolver and ordered Jotham to stay seated on the floor. I also made sure Lillian stayed put."

Faith's face shone in admiration. "Thee is so brave."

"I only did what I had to. What anyone would have done."

"Would thee have shot either of them?" Frederick's face was somber.

"I prayed I wouldn't have to. And then, when I was obliged to shoot at Jotham to prevent him from leaving, I prayed for guidance to be able to wound without killing. With God's help I succeeded in barely scraping his leg."

He nodded. "Tell us how thee escaped these killers."

"That was, finally, not of my doing at all. Minnie's neighbor, Therese Stevens, saw Jotham bring first Lillian and then me into the house. She was suspicious and eventually fetched Kevin Donovan. He blessedly brought other officers to back him up." I laughed, this time truly amused. "He thought it was rather entertaining to find me training a gun on two murderers."

"I wonder how Jotham convinced Lillian to come along with him." Bertie cocked her head.

"I don't know. A gun in the back can be pretty persuasive, though." I shivered remembering that feeling. "He must have abducted her when she was out shopping."

"But then who set the carriage fire?" Faith asked.

"Surely not Ephraim," Bertie said.

"Jotham told me himself he set the fire and that he faked a limp going to and from the factory. I think he also meant Stephen Hamilton to be accused of the arson, because he'd been offering Stephen matches."

"Which he used on the Meetinghouse instead." Frederick tapped the table. "This Jotham O'Toole harbored a great hatred for the Parrys, it seems."

"He was angry beyond reason with William for getting his little sister with child," I said. "But Minnie seemed happy with the arrangement. I don't believe Billy is the result of William forcing himself on her."

"Billy is now William's only child," Bertie said. "I'll wager he adopts him and dotes on him."

"And Patience will be left without a child again," I said with some sadness. I pulled my pocket watch out. "Gracious sakes alive. David will be here in forty-five minutes!"

THIRTY-SEVEN

I pulled on my gloves as the clock in my room chimed seven times. Faith sat on the chaise and Betsy bounced in my desk chair. Bertie leaned against the dresser twirling one of her curls in her finger.

"Thee looks so pretty, Rose," Betsy said. "I want a party dress, too."

"Hush, Betsy," Faith chided. "This is a special occasion for our auntie."

"I suppose I'm setting a bad example with the dress, the corset, the whole undertaking," I said. I'd had no time for a rest, but my mind was still a-roil and I knew I wouldn't have been able to sleep, anyway. I'd taken care washing up, and Faith had helped me arrange my hair after I'd dressed, with Betsy handing her hairpins. Bertie had simply looked on with folded arms and a little smile. Now I glanced in the glass above the mantel.

Reflected back was a simple upswept

hairdo framing a face with cheeks matching my rose-colored dress. I supposed my spectacles spoiled the effect, but I couldn't see without them. Orpha's cameo hung just in the hollow of my neck. The corset had further slimmed my waist, although I hadn't let Faith pull it too tight, and the dress fit like one of my gloves. The fancy shoes were surprisingly comfortable and the lovely embroidered bag was ready with my best handkerchief.

I fingered the cameo. Orpha had said I had a special talent. I had certainly seen my way through whatever confronted me today, so perhaps that was my gift, my special talent.

"I wish Mama could see thee," Faith said, dabbing at her eyes.

"I do, as well, my dear." I turned from the mirror and embraced her. "She's smiling at us from Heaven though, doesn't thee think?"

Faith nodded, smiling through her tears.

"I know she is," Betsy chimed in. "Mama's always watching us and smiling at us." She nodded with certainty.

At a knock on the front door, Bertie picked up the evening bag and handed it to me. "Off you go, Princess Rose."

"Stop it, Bertie. It's only a dinner with

dancing." My heart sank. I'd been so busy getting ready I'd had no time to worry about Clarinda Dodge. "Oh, dear, a high-society dinner dance." I felt like shedding the dress and diving back into the comfort of plain muted colors, and into the society where I belonged: the Society of Friends. What had happened to my place of optimistic confidence from the early afternoon? Perhaps being in peril for my life had shaken it out of me. "How ever am I going to get through this night?"

"Like thee always does," Faith said. "With thy strength and thy humor and thy grace." She smiled gently, wiping away a last tear.

I gazed at her. Such wisdom for a young woman. "I thank thee, dear niece. I will try." I squeezed her hand.

The knocking sounded again. Frederick strode down the hall, passing our open door with a quizzical glance, and invited David in.

"The women appear to be fussing, but I believe Rose is ready," I heard Frederick say.

I took a deep breath. My ladies in waiting smiled to a one, and a grinning Bertie made a shooing motion with her hands.

"You'll be fine," she whispered. "Just go."

I carried the reticule into the hall and paused.

David, resplendent in evening wear, his snowy white collar peeking out from under a black cashmere scarf, took in a breath when he caught sight of me. "You're lovely tonight, Miss Carroll."

That made me laugh, which burst my bubble of tension. "And you, as well, Doctor Dodge." Maybe I'd make it through. David's own strength, humor, and grace would be at my side, after all.

I selected my best cloak, the black wool one, off its hook. Frederick took it from my hands and draped it around my shoulders.

David proffered his elbow. "Shall we?"

I waved good-bye to Bertie and the Baileys, who were all crammed in the hallway together, and made my way down the front stairs, carefully holding the hem of my dress up off the ground.

As David handed me up into his carriage, he said, "Did you have an interesting day, Rose?"

That was putting it mildly. I smiled in the darkness. "Thee could say that, yes."

ACKNOWLEDGMENTS

I am delighted that *Delivering the Truth* and the Quaker Midwife Mysteries series have made their way into the hands of the reading public, as this historical setting and these characters have a special place in my heart. Many thanks to Terri Bischoff and Midnight Ink for accepting the manuscript and the series proposal, and to my agent, John Talbot, for encouraging me and facilitating the process. Joining the Midnight Ink mystery author club is a deeply satisfying prospect. Thanks, too, to Amy Glaser, Nicole Nugent, and the rest of the Midnight Ink crew, for shepherding my book through to publication.

To the Monday Night Salem Writers Group, I send my gratitude for your sharp ears and insightful critique of nearly all of this book. The Wicked Cozy Authors encouraged me through the process and held me up with support and friendship. I love you guys: Jessie Crockett/Jessica Estevao, Julie Hennrikus/Julianne Holmes, Sherry Harris, Liz Mugavero/Cate Conte, and Barbara Ross. The superb independent editor Ramona DeFelice Long gave the book a close look, and it is much improved for her insightful comments and questions — the easy ones as well as the hard ones.

As I now write four mystery series, I owe a special note of thanks to New England author Sheila Connolly, who writes four concurrent popular mystery series, plus short stories and the occasional stand-alone, all of which I've read and greatly enjoyed. I've been trying to channel Sheila's energy and discipline for a while now, and I thank her for being a role model, a friend, and a high-bar setter. I imagine she gets even less sleep than I do.

As ever, I'm also grateful for my Sisters (and Brothers) in Crime, particularly the Guppies and the New England chapter. As I always say, I would not be published if it were not for what I've learned from my fellow mystery authors.

Midwives Risa Rispoli and Debbie Becnel-Bush vetted the birthing details in the book, and Gene Declercq provided me with information about midwifery in the late 1800s. I borrowed the name of my local police consultant, Detective Kevin Donovan, for the detective in the book, which does not imply that he would have acted the way my fictional Kevin does. My friend (and Friend) Martha McManamy lent me her nineteenth-century Newburyport house for several solo writing retreats, so I wrote the house in as the Dodges'.

As always, my sons Allan and John David, my sisters Barbara and Janet, and my partner Hugh support me in my struggles and triumph. They're almost as pleased as I am with this series coming to life. And the members of Amesbury Friends Meeting, my second family — I couldn't have done it without you.

ABOUT THE AUTHOR

Edith Maxwell (Amesbury, MA) is the vice president of the New England chapter of Sisters in Crime and a longtime member of the Society of Friends. She is the author of the Local Foods Mysteries, the Lauren Rousseau Mysteries, and the Country Store Mysteries. She blogs at wickedcozyauthors .com.